RABBIT CAKE

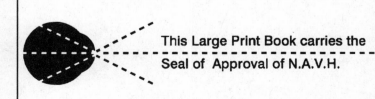

RABBIT CAKE

ANNIE HARTNETT

THORNDIKE PRESS
A part of Gale, Cengage Learning

Farmington Hills, Mich • San Francisco • New York • Waterville, Maine
Meriden, Conn • Mason, Ohio • Chicago

GALE
CENGAGE Learning®

LIBRARY OF CONGRESS CATALOGING-IN-PUBLICATION DATA

Names: Hartnett, Annie, author.
Title: Rabbit cake / by Annie Hartnett.
Description: Large print edition. | Waterville, Maine : Thorndike Press, a part of
    Gale, Cengage Learning, 2017. | Series: Thorndike Press large print peer picks
Identifiers: LCCN 2017003958| ISBN 9781432838416 (hardcover) | ISBN 1432838415
    (hardcover)
Subjects: LCSH: Sisters—Fiction. | Mothers—Death—Fiction. | Fathers and
    daughters—Fiction. | Family secrets—Fiction. | Alabama—Fiction. | Large type
    books. | Domestic fiction. | Psychological fiction.
Classification: LCC PS3608.A74936 R73 2017b | DDC 813/.6—dc23
LC record available at https://lccn.loc.gov/2017003958

Published in 2017 by arrangement with Tin House Books, LLC

Printed in the United States of America
1 2 3 4 5 6 7 21 20 19 18 17

To my parents —
you are both very good rabbits

On my tenth birthday, six months before she sleepwalked into the river, Mom burned the rabbit cake. "Ten might not be a great year for you," she said, squeezing my shoulder. I couldn't tell if she was kidding. The rabbit's face and ears were charred black.

Mom always said we needed a cake to mark every new beginning, and whether it was a birthday or a first day of school or a new moon, rabbits mean good luck to a new start. A rabbit cake is baked in a two-sided aluminum mold, producing a three-dimensional cake. That's the miracle of it: the cake stands up on its own, on its four paws. If the frosting job is done right, it looks like you are eating a real cottontail, one that hasn't even been skinned.

"Why don't you bake another?" I asked. I didn't want ten to be worse than nine.

"You like burnt toast." Mom shrugged.

I was happy that after Mom covered it

with a thick layer of white cream-cheese icing fur, I couldn't see the blackened parts. Mom let me help decorate, and we used Red Hots for the eyes. "He's a New Zealand white," I announced. A New Zealand white is a medium-sized albino rabbit. They are from Mexico, not New Zealand, and companies test makeup on them.

"My little research assistant," Mom said, when I showed her the pictures of the rabbits with sore-crusted eyes. Sometimes I wondered if Mom really liked animals, even though she had taught me a lot about them and she was the one who brought home Boomer, our border collie, from the shelter nine years ago, without asking Dad. But Mom used to test on animals in labs when she was in graduate school at Auburn University; plus she always laughed when she cut open a rabbit cake. She'd put a half jar of raspberry jam in the middle of the batter, so that the cake oozed fake bunny blood all over the plate.

"What are you going to wish for?" Mom asked, as she added licorice whiskers to the New Zealand white. Mom was big on wishing.

"Not sure," I said. I was thinking about wishing for my sister to be nicer to me, but when the time came to blow out the candles,

I forgot to wish for anything.

That same year my birthday cake came out of the oven with a scalded nose, ears, and tail, Mom was returned to us in a plastic baggie, her ashes like the gray dust you'll find when you open up the vacuum. The evening before she drowned, Mom made one last cake. She said we'd frost it in the morning, she had one of her bad headaches and she was going to bed early. The cake was left naked on the counter. It was supposed to celebrate the summer solstice the next day, June 21st, but I guess her death was a new beginning too, for Lizzie and me, for Dad and Boomer. It just wasn't a happy one. It was the start of some changes around our house; Dad said we'd have to learn to adapt. "Sink or swim," he said. I know that would have made Mom laugh. She had a sick sense of humor that way.

If Mom had been alive, I would have joked, "There's something fishy about your death," and that would have been another good one. I was sure parts of Mom had been eaten by the fish in the river, based on what I knew about decomposition. Dad said he didn't want to hear about it when I asked, but he also said he wasn't going to let Lizzie or me see her body before she was cremated.

I thought it *was* fishy that Mom had died by a simple accident. Mom almost never made clumsy mistakes. She was a scientist and scientists aren't careless, so her cause of death felt out of character, unlikely and suspicious somehow. I knew it wasn't the way she was supposed to die. My fifth-grade guidance counselor would tell me that those feelings were part of denial, which she called a normal stage of grief. But as the months passed, I couldn't let it go. I knew there was something we were missing, something un-explained.

I think a lot about the charred rabbit cake, how that was another clumsy mistake. Mom apologized later that night when she tucked me in; she said it tasted much worse than she thought it would.

"I have another birthday next year," I re-assured her. "And the full moon is next week."

"That's my girl," Mom said. "Tough as boiled owl."

"Mom, you know no one eats owls," I reminded her. There are four species of owls commonly found in Alabama, and some-times Mom and I would get up before dawn to go look for barred owls. Most people think that owls mean wisdom, but I read that the Romans thought owls were evil, that they drank the blood of babies.

In ancient Rome, they would have called the burnt cake a bad omen, and maybe the Romans would have seen it all coming: what would happen to my mom, and then what would happen later to my sister, Lizzie, the disasters in store for us.

■ ■ ■ ■

PART I
MONTHS 1 TO 6

■ ■ ■ ■

1.
~~June, July,~~ August

It was August when Mom's body finally showed up, caught in the dam at Goat Rock, twelve miles from home. She had floated across the state border to Georgia, so Dad had to fill out extra paperwork to bring her back to Freedom, the town where we live in Alabama. I wonder sometimes how many miles Mom swam before she drowned; she could hold her breath underwater for a long time. She was an excellent swimmer in her sleep.

We'd already known Mom was dead, of course, we'd felt it for most of the summer. We felt it from the moment we found her swim goggles on the bank of the Chattahoochee River, at the beach down the road from our house, the place where Mom swam. There had been flooding that June, the river running fast and lathered up.

At the police station, two officers took Dad away first to ask him questions, just to be sure he hadn't killed Mom and dumped her in the river. It didn't occur to Lizzie or me then that we might be suspects. It was two years ago; I'm twelve now, but I was still only ten then. Lizzie was fifteen and most people thought she was too pretty to hurt anyone, unless you knew her well enough to know better. The police officer already knew Lizzie.

"Aren't you sad?" the cop asked, handing my dry-eyed sister a Kleenex.

"We knew." Lizzie shrugged.

"How did you know?" He jabbed his finger at Lizzie, almost touching her nose.

"She's our mother," Lizzie said, her hands on her hips. "If *your* mom was dead, wouldn't *you* know?"

I guess that was good enough, because they let us go, and ruled Mom's death an accident.

"Not much of an investigation," I muttered, but Dad shushed me up.

It didn't feel like a case closed, no matter what the Freedom Police Department said. I combed our house for a clue.

"She was a sleepswimmer. She drowned," Dad tried to reason with me, as I rummaged through his bedside table again. "What else is there to know?"

There was a lot left to know. I wondered

what my mother's dreams were about the night she drowned. Did she wake up when the river water filled her lungs or was she still asleep when she died? Did she dream in color or did the water look black as tar?

After we left the police station, we drove to the coroner where Mom was being kept. Dad went back into the morgue, leaving Lizzie and me in the waiting room. He came out a few minutes later, dabbing his eyes, and told us he'd have to go fill out more forms before we could leave.

As soon as he was out of sight, my sister pulled me down the hall by the hand. She said we needed to move quickly if we were going to see Mom. There were signs everywhere that said *No Food* and *No Photography,* but Lizzie was snapping photos with her cell phone anyway with the hand that wasn't holding mine.

Lizzie and I had never held hands before, at least not as far back as I could remember. We weren't those type of sisters. All Lizzie ever wanted to do was sneak out of the house and drink cans of beer with her friends. I'd also overheard her talking on the phone about eating mushrooms in the woods and I wondered how Lizzie knew which ones were edible and not poisonous.

We could see the top of Mom's head, but her face and body were covered by a white sheet. Her hair fell over the edge of the metal table like a waterfall. I didn't want to see the rest of her body, even if Lizzie did; I didn't want to know for sure what the fish in the river had done to her. I'd read that eye tissue is soft and easy to eat. I leaned forward and gagged over a yellow mop bucket.

"No kids back here," a white-coated man said. He was holding up a tiny metal knife. "Where are your parents?"

"That's our mother." Lizzie pointed to the sheet.

I wiped my mouth.

"We were just leaving," Lizzie said, taking one last photo. "Come on," she said, grabbing my hand again.

When we looked through the pictures on the ride home, most were of the green tile floor, but Lizzie had gotten that one shot of the top of Mom's head. We could see that Mom's skull had been dented, probably by a rock in the river. I thought maybe she could have had a seizure that night in the water; that would explain why she had drowned when she was such a good swimmer.

She had had a seizure just once before.

That seizure was supposed to be a one-time thing, but maybe there had been another. I wanted to know what had happened that night. Everything was terrible and uncertain without her.

Dad said there was nothing in the coroner's report about a seizure, and he was sure that autopsies could tell those kinds of things. "It'll always be a mystery," Dad said, which was no comfort at all. "A freak accident."

"Are you scared?" I asked Lizzie.

Sleepwalking is supposed to be genetic, a fifty-fifty chance. It had to be either my sister or me; Lizzie had lost the coin toss. Lizzie had started sleepwalking long before I was born, so it was always normal having two sleepwalkers in the house. I would wake up in the middle of the night to hear Lizzie tinkering downstairs and Mom waltzing down the hall. They never interacted in their sleep, at least not that I'd seen. Two ships passing in the night, Dad used to call them.

On the night of Mom's disappearance, Lizzie had sleepwalked into the shower, curled up in the tub.

"Are you scared?" I asked Lizzie again, because she hadn't seemed to hear my question the first time.

"Scared of what?" Lizzie asked, putting

19

the cell phone down.

"Scared of dying," I said.

"You shouldn't be talking about this," Dad said. "No one is dying."

"No one *else,*" I said quietly, because that was more correct. I knew not to push it any further, or Dad would get mad. I leaned against the truck window, my breath forming a mist on the glass. Then I tried holding my breath as long as I could, pretending I was drowning right there in the truck. It was actually a pretty good game.

Lizzie wasn't a sleepswimmer, she was just a regular old sleepwalker, which didn't seem that dangerous. The strangest thing Lizzie had ever done in her sleep was pee on the houseplants. Boomer always woke us all up when she did it, barking his head off; he knew piddling in the house was what bad dogs did. Once, Mom took a photo of Lizzie squatting over the potted ficus, and she lorded it over Lizzie at breakfast the next day. I'd told Lizzie not to worry, I'd read that alpha female wolves mark their territory by urinating, just like their male counterparts.

"Quit being such a freak," Lizzie had hissed.

"She's just embarrassed that she doesn't

remember," Mom had said to me. "Don't let her get to you."

Mom often said that not-remembering was the worst part of sleepwalking. She believed dreams were important, a gateway to our past lives. Mom tried keeping a dream log, but she could remember the details of dreams only on the nights she'd stayed in bed. If she'd been out sleepwalking, she said, there was this big blank space in the morning where her dream should be.

When they'd first gotten married, Dad had to film Mom until she believed she was sleepswimming some nights. Back then, she sleepswam naked and her hair was dry by morning. "That doesn't sound like me," Mom had insisted, until Dad showed her the video clip. She had been so impressed with herself that she could do the butterfly stroke in her sleep, since she'd never been able to get it right when she was awake.

"Must have been a swimmer in a past life," she'd declared.

Dad used to insist that Mom shouldn't believe in reincarnation because she had a PhD, but that's why I had Elvis Presley's name, even though I was born a girl. Dad always disliked my name, but he wasn't there to sign the birth certificate, so he didn't have a say in naming me. I came early, and Dad was away on business, at the annual carpet trade show. But I never thought Elvis was a bad name, even for a girl. All the teachers in school knew how to pronounce it.

"Elvis is perfect," Mom always said. "She's the king."

"Her name is hardly the weirdest thing about her," Lizzie snarled once.

Lizzie was named after Queen Elizabeth I, but Mom hadn't really thought my sister was the return of the queen of England. Mom had only thought Queen Elizabeth and baby Lizzie had the same tall forehead, but it turned out Lizzie had an ordinary-sized forehead once her hair grew in. So Lizzie was always Lizzie, never Elizabeth, not to anyone. Sometimes Mom would say my sister had Lizzie Borden's former spirit, and that she and Dad had better watch out.

Mom had been 100 percent convinced I had Elvis Presley's hand-me-down spirit. I shared the same birthday with the King of Rock and Roll, January 8th, and that was enough proof for Mom. Elvis had been dead for a long time, but she said some spirits take a break before they come back around. "Like a time-out," Mom explained. "A good kind."

It was Mom's psychic, Miss Ida, who had

taught her about reincarnation. Miss Ida and Mom talked on the phone every Friday. I'd never met Miss Ida; Mom explained that she had become something called agoraphobic in her old age, and she couldn't come visit us because she was too afraid to leave her own house.

"Isn't there a crystal to cure that?" Dad had said.

Miss Ida had predicted that someday Mom would kill herself. She saw it in Mom's leftover coffee grounds, all those years ago, when they first met in Miss Ida's Crystal Shop in Arizona. Lizzie and I hadn't been born yet.

Dad said we shouldn't pay attention to that "New Age lunacy," but Mom used to gently remind us of Miss Ida's premonition often and it was hard to ignore. She wanted us to be ready, I guess. Both Lizzie and I took it to mean that Mom would commit suicide someday, although I thought she would wait to do it until Lizzie and I were much, much older, once we didn't need her so much anymore.

The coroner's report said accident, not suicide, and we thought that Miss Ida's premonition had been wrong. We didn't consider it back then, but there are tons of

23

ways to kill yourself accidentally. Drowning is only one possibility out of a million.

2.

All of our names appeared side by side in the obituary section of the newspaper: *Eva Rose Babbitt is survived by her husband, Frank, and her daughters, Lizzie, age 15, and Elvis, age 10.* I clipped it out and put it on the fridge, so we could remember what had happened to Mom, and that we were her survivors.

"It's going to take us a while," Dad sighed one morning after he'd absentmindedly hollered upstairs for my mom to come down to breakfast. He wiped his hands on his nylon swimsuit; he was still wearing his orange trunks to bed. My parents had always suited up at night because they never knew when to expect an episode, and Dad didn't think Mom should be naked in public. Dad's swimsuit was in better shape than Mom's because his never got wet, not even the hemline. He used to watch her from the shore with Boomer on leash at his

25

side. Mom had said it wasn't really necessary, but she told me once that it was good for their marriage, that time together. She said Dad had a *Baywatch* fantasy, but I had no idea what that meant.

The night Mom drowned, Dad had too much to drink with his bowling league, and he hadn't gotten out of bed with her. In the police statement, Dad said he'd been "dead to the world" that night, which made Lizzie bare her teeth. It was hard not to blame him, at least a little, and my sister blamed him a lot.

"I want to hit you sometimes," Lizzie said once at dinner. "Can I punch you?"

Dad offered up his chin, tapping on his cheek to show her the target. That must have taken all the fun out of it for Lizzie, because she put her fist down. Boomer whined from underneath the table; he hated it when our family got into fights. It was why Mom and Dad took long drives in the truck when they weren't getting along. They always came back happy again, and with Mom's hair needing a brush.

In the months since Mom drowned, Dad had grown pale as a yellow string bean, was nothing like the cheerful dad who used to sing commercial jingles as he got ready for work, the dad who had once wanted us to join a family bowling league. Mom had said that bowling was the most repetitive and dull sport she could think of, so Dad had joined the men's league instead.

"Frank is such a good-natured guy," our neighbors would say to my mother. "A real hometown hero." Dad had grown up in Freedom; he'd inherited the house and the family business, the Carpet World in Opelika, from his father. Dad had been the quarterback at Freedom High, the prom king, and had gotten a full ride to Sewanee, but he'd stayed at home instead to run Carpet World after his dad got sick. Everyone in town remembered how Dad helped out Grandpa, and everyone still said Dad was handsome, even though I thought he was getting kind of old. He was about to turn forty-three at the end of that summer. He was very tall with a square jaw, dark brown eyes, and black hair.

Even before she blamed him for Mom's drowning, Lizzie had never thought Dad was that special, said she didn't see what Mom or anyone else saw in him: he was a washed-up high school quarterback. He worked all the time, but we still weren't rich. He was pretty boring, Lizzie said. He drove a Dodge.

"Carpet World is the largest carpet store

in Alabama," I reminded her, but she only rolled her eyes.

I felt bad for Dad now, not because he was boring, not because his wife was dead, but because of the secret that I knew, the one I'd been keeping to myself all summer. Less than a week before Mom disappeared into the river, I saw her in the back of a trailer with Mr. Oakes, who used to be the speech therapist at Beaver Elementary. I'd gone to see him in kindergarten, when my tongue had seemed too large for my mouth. Now Mr. Oakes worked as the speech therapist for stroke patients at the Evergreen Nursing Home. Evergreen had an animal-assisted therapy program; miniature horses were brought in to cheer the patients up. It explained where Mr. Oakes had gotten the trailer.

In the trailer, Mom had been fully clothed, and Mr. Oakes had been fully naked, and she'd been pretending to milk him. They were laughing and laughing so loud that I heard them from inside and then I could see into the trailer perfectly from my bedroom window. They must have thought no one was home. It was an early release day from school, Mom had probably forgotten.

How could I ever tell Dad or Lizzie about that, how could I put what I'd seen into words? The dictionary said *adulteress, infidelity, extramarital.* Can you divorce a dead person? Dad still wore his gold wedding band. I didn't know if telling Dad would make things better or worse for him, and I didn't want to make things worse.

When Dad wasn't at work, he was sleeping a lot, sometimes crying in his room. He did try to make dinner a couple of times, but usually he let Lizzie do it. Lizzie was a pretty good cook, and I learned how to use the laundry machine.

"What would I do without you?" Dad said, as I handed him a clean stack of shirts. "My sweet Elvis."

Dad wouldn't have thought I was so sweet if he knew the secret I was keeping from him. I wanted to send Mr. Oakes a letter in the mail, to tell him I knew all about him and my mom. I cut up magazines, saving the clippings in an envelope for something like a ransom note. Usually it was just one word, something I'd found in the dictionary. *Bovine* was my favorite so far.

The same day that Dad came back from the crematorium with the plastic baggie of ashes, Lizzie was brought home in a police cruiser. She had gotten into a fight in the parking lot behind the Coffee Shack, and she had broken her best friend's jaw in three places. The policeman said that Megan's family had already declined to press charges, given the circumstances.

"She deserved it," Lizzie said, after the policeman had gone.

"You broke her jaw," Dad repeated. "Megan is your friend."

"Are you wearing lipstick?" Lizzie asked. She reeked of beer.

"Are you drunk, Lizzie?" He wiped his mouth with the back of his hand.

"*You* were drunk," Lizzie said. "And now she's dead."

Dad was wearing lipstick, Mom's old favorite shade. "I know this isn't easy," he said. "But you're making it harder. You're making everything harder." He started to cry, whimpering as he went up the stairs to bed. He was still clutching our mother's remains in his hands.

Lizzie went to bed not long after, with ice on her knuckles. I stayed up to watch a marathon of *Wildlife Encounters with Dr. Lillian Stone.* It was my favorite show; Mom and I used to watch it together. Dr. Lillian went all over the world with her crew filming wildlife; her show was about raising awareness for the conservation of endangered animals and the need for habitat protection.

"I think she's had some work done," Mom almost always said at some point during the episode. "She's turned into such an actress."

Mom and Dr. Lillian had been best friends once, back in graduate school, but they'd lost touch since. They had worked together on a project that involved sewing human hands onto the backs of rats, trying to get the fingers to move again. The research was supposed to help people who'd lost their hands in industrial accidents, or scuba divers whose arms had been cropped by boat propellers. Dr. Lillian and Mom had gone through hundreds of hands for the research. Mom always said she was very thankful to those who donated their bodies to science, but she couldn't do it herself; she said that scientists were too discourteous to the remains.

Another episode of *Dr. Lillian* had just started when Lizzie wandered by in her sleep, and I realized how late it was. I told her to go back to bed, which works with sleepwalkers sometimes. I knew I should go to bed too, but it was an episode I hadn't seen. I felt really terrible that Mom would never see it, because it was a good one: Lillian was saving animals from an oil spill off

31

the coast of Alaska. She scrubbed a young otter with dish soap. The otter squeaked as Dr. Lillian washed him. I wondered if the otter sensed how much danger he'd been in or if he knew he was being saved.

In the morning, Lizzie was asleep in the stairwell; she had never made it back to her bed. I nudged her with my foot until she woke up. "Elvis," she said, groggy. "Bring me my bedpan." It was her favorite line from the one game we'd ever played together, Servant and Master. I was always the servant. I brought her a bowl, and she threw up a little into it.

"You're grounded," Dad said, as he handed her a Gatorade, the purple flavor, her favorite. "But first, get dressed, we're honoring your mother today."

It was August 11th, Dad's birthday, and it felt so odd when there was no rabbit cake to celebrate, nothing like a birthday. We had the aluminum mold, but it didn't seem right to use it, since it still felt like Mom could come home any minute and scold us for touching her things.

What I mean is, Mom felt dead to us, but she didn't really feel gone. She didn't even feel gone after we scattered her ashes along the shallows of the Chattahoochee River.

We had an argument over which part of the river to sprinkle her in, so we put a spoonful of her ashes every quarter mile, until we decided that the current would carry her everywhere anyway.

3.

I didn't ask what Lizzie's fight with Megan Sax was about, but I knew it must have been over something pretty serious when Lizzie asked if she could be homeschooled for the upcoming year. Dad said okay, because it had always been Mom who said no to Lizzie's bad ideas.

Lizzie's friends used to come over on a rotating schedule; Mom said only three girls allowed, *we weren't running a brothel.* Megan Sax was the only girl always invited. I tried to imagine how Lizzie felt about losing Megan, but I didn't have a friend to lose, other than Boomer, and he always came running when I called him.

I didn't know who was going to teach Lizzie. Dad was not a teacher, that had been Mom. She had taught at Magnolia Community College for years, but she didn't like teaching that much. Mom always said she was supposed to be the world's-next-great-scientist, but then she'd met Dad at a bar during her final year of graduate school at Auburn. Mom claimed the pregnancy was the reason she'd gotten stuck in Alabama, but once when Dad was tipsy he told me that that was her excuse, that she'd had trouble finding a job after getting her PhD. "Her references weren't very good," he slurred.

It had driven Mom crazy that Dr. Lillian had gone on to be famous, when Mom said she knew she was the better scientist. Mom frequently pointed out that Dr. Lillian had never gotten married.

With Mom gone, Dad should have known that he couldn't homeschool Lizzie. Carpet World was half an hour away in Opelika, and he was almost never home during the daytime. Before Mom's death, he hadn't come home for dinner most nights, except in the winter months, December through February — the home decorating off-season. But by the time all of this dawned on Dad, the homeschool textbooks had been ordered and Lizzie had been un-enrolled in the sophomore class of Freedom High School. She refused to reconsider.

I knew most of the town would have already heard that Lizzie had pulled out of Freedom High, and about Megan Sax's broken jaw. Last year, everyone had known when Lizzie's first-ever boyfriend, a high school senior named Dave, dumped her. She'd left a wasps' nest in his car, and he'd been stung almost fifty times.

"If he was allergic, he'd be dead," Mom had fumed.

"But he wasn't," Lizzie had huffed. "And I got stung a bunch too, just putting the damn thing in the glove box."

She'd also left a pile of dog poop on his front seat, but Mom hadn't mentioned that. With Lizzie, you had to let some things go.

I came home from the first day of school on August 17th to find my sister wearing Mom's paint-speckled overalls, her hair piled on her head, tendrils falling from her bun like tentacles off a squid. She had baked a chocolate pound cake and cut me off an ink-black slice.

Even when Mom was alive, I was envious of how much Lizzie looked like her, blonde with blue eyes, the same perfect nose and mouth. Mom had been very tall, almost six feet, and the doctor said Lizzie would be tall someday too. Lizzie could fit into most of Mom's clothes, and she had borrowed them even before Mom was dead. Mom's top drawer was overflowing with bras, and

Lizzie didn't have to stuff them to fill them out. Lizzie wore Mom's shortest dresses too, and the purple cowboy boots that had been her favorites.

Mom didn't fit in with the other mothers in Freedom; she didn't wear floral dresses or pastels, no string of pearls on her neck. She wasn't originally from the South, she liked to remind people, she'd moved here from Philadelphia when she was ten. Dad said she used that as an excuse to stand out, but we stood out in lots of ways already. We didn't go to church on Sundays, for one. Mom used to say that women in Alabama only went to church in order to show off their outfits, and that most people could learn more about God from going for a walk in nature. Mom called herself a *spiritual naturalist,* which Dad said wasn't really a religion. She wore mostly black clothing, paired with red high heels or a zebra-print scarf. She loved lipstick in every shade, including electric orange, which made her lips look like two tropical fish swimming side by side on her face.

I wished I looked more like Mom, but I had Dad's big chin and black hair and so many dark eyelashes that they clumped together. I had once tried to dye my hair blonde, but Mom caught me as I splashed the first spill of bleach.

Lizzie slid another piece of chocolate cake toward me.

"So who's your teacher?" she asked, her elbows on the table. Maybe she was interested because the new fifth-grade teacher had been a big town mystery: the usual teacher, Mr. Wagner, had had some sort of breakdown over the summer and wasn't allowed to be near kids any longer.

"Well, she's brand-new," I said. "You never had her."

Our new teacher had come in that morning right as the bell rang. A pair of sunglasses pushed back her hair, which was divided into tiny braids. She was no taller than a fifth grader, and she looked like a babysitter, but she said she was twenty-six when someone asked. She'd written her name on the whiteboard, first and last, Ms. Cassandra Powell.

Ms. Powell was already my favorite teacher because she was the only teacher I'd ever had who hadn't had my sister as a student first, a few years before. Those teachers were nervous that I'd be another Lizzie, another troublemaker. But Ms. Powell hadn't sounded one bit fearful when she called out my name on the roll; she hadn't snapped her neck up to ask if I was Lizzie Babbitt's younger sister. Instead, she'd sung a few lines from "Heartbreak Hotel," snapping her fingers and curling her lip like Elvis the King. She hadn't sounded at all sad while she was singing either, which meant she hadn't heard about my mother's death. I was relieved, because last year when Billy Dickle's uncle died, the whole class had to have a full three minutes of silence for his loss.

"Is twenty-six too young for Dad?" I asked Lizzie, who was sealing the pound cake in tinfoil to freeze.

"Don't be an idiot," Lizzie said, her breath full of familiar acid. "We can't run out and get a replacement. It's not like the time the old TV conked out."

Lizzie was partway right, but I didn't think Dad should go on mourning Mom forever, especially since Mom had been an adulteress. Still, I wanted to be sure that Dad always loved Mom best. Our new television was so much nicer, I didn't miss the old one even a little.

For those first weeks of school, all my classmates looked at me side-eyed, nervous that they might catch whatever causes parents to drop dead. They all knew about my mom, even if Ms. Powell still hadn't heard. Everyone must have felt bad for me, because I always got the best spot during silent reading hour; no one ever tried to contest my space in the beanbag chair. There were perks.

It was coming home that was painful, like picking open a crusty scab. The bus drove right over the Chattahoochee River; I always held my breath over the bridge.

"What are you doing?" Jackie Friskey asked me once. Jackie was our newly elected class president, the nicest girl in school.

"I'm pretending I'm drowning," I said, after I let out the air in my lungs.

"I heard how your mom died," Jackie said. "I'm sorry."

"Well, she was *supposed* to kill herself," I told Jackie, and she nodded but didn't answer. She went back to reading *The Art of Public Speaking for Fifth Graders,* which Ms. Powell had given her for winning the election.

Our house on Watson Hill Road was the second-to-last stop. Our house was white with black shutters, with a covered porch, which Mom had said made it a farmer's cottage. I loved our house. It had a stained glass window in the front door, and you walked from the mudroom into the living room, which was my favorite room in the house. The living room had bookshelves, the TV, Dad's leather chair, and the most comfortable couch. The kitchen was next to the living room, painted bright yellow, and copper pans hung above the stove. Mom had a small messy office off the kitchen, which we weren't supposed to go in, only stand in the doorway if we needed something. On the second floor, my parents had their bedroom, and I had my own bedroom, and Lizzie had hers. We all shared a bathroom, which had a shower over a clawfoot tub.

When I came home, my mom's Honda was still in the driveway. I wiped my feet on the bristled welcome mat so I wouldn't track mud on our nice carpets bought from Dad's store. I dropped my backpack in the front hall to announce my arrival, just like always. Before Lizzie hollered hello from the kitchen, it was easy to forget for a second that Mom was still sprinkled in the river, dissolving like the orange and red flakes we fed to the goldfish at school.

4.
~~AUGUST,~~ SEPTEMBER

I had to meet with the Beaver Elementary guidance counselor for twenty minutes every week, school policy in the death of a parent. Her name was Ms. Bernstein and she collected snow globes. My favorite was a giant tarantula that lay half-hidden in snow until you shook it, or held it upside down; then you could see its fangs.

"Most kids like the Snoopy one," Ms. Bernstein said.

"I like arachnids." I shrugged. "I like all animals, really." This was our first meeting.

"How are you feeling?" Ms. Bernstein asked. Her office smelled like tomato soup.

"Like a bee sting." I turned the snow globe upside down.

"Death is painful." She nodded.

"The tarantula's bite," I said, "is virtually harmless to humans."

Ms. Bernstein explained that the grieving process takes eighteen months, and she drew a timeline on a piece of paper for me to take home. She drew twenty empty boxes instead of eighteen, since she said she wasn't sure when I had started the grieving process, whether it was after my mom had gone missing or after she'd been found.

"Do you think it's suspicious," I asked during that first meeting, "that Mom died in a drowning accident when she was an excellent swimmer?"

"Denial," she said. "What you're experiencing is a stage of grief. You need to work toward accepting your mother's death."

Ms. Bernstein said there were normal and abnormal ways of dealing with the death of a loved one. I didn't know if I was being normal or not. Ms. Bernstein admitted it was a little strange that I was still asking questions about my mother's cause of death.

I worried I wasn't normal because I felt sad, but not as sad as I wanted to feel, as sad as I thought someone with a dead mother should feel. I got out of bed every morning, and brushed my teeth, and walked the dog. I ate Fruity Pebbles for breakfast and they tasted fine. I raised my hand first in class whenever Ms. Powell asked a question. So much was the same as before. "Shouldn't I feel worse?" I asked.

Ms. Bernstein explained that I was experiencing the numbness after loss, and she said it was another expected response, especially for someone so young, someone still learning how to suffer. I asked if that meant that grief would be easier for Lizzie because she was older, and Ms. Bernstein said it was possible but unlikely, based on what she knew about my sister. Ms. Bernstein had been Lizzie's guidance counselor once too, before Lizzie graduated from Beaver Elementary and gone on to Three Rivers Junior High. Ms. Bernstein had tried to get Lizzie placed into an institution for troubled youth, but Mom threatened a lawsuit against the school and Ms. Bernstein quickly changed her mind.

I hung up the grieving chart in my bedroom, tacked it on my bulletin board between an old report card and the glossy photographs of Sumatran tigers that I'd cut out from *National Geographic.* I would cross off every month as it passed.

When I arrived for our next meeting, Ms. Bernstein was with another student, a third grader. She kept a small desk chair outside her door, which she called the waiting room. There was a bookshelf along the wall too, with titles like *Diagnostic and Statistical Manual for Kids!, The Secret Language of*

Eating Disorders, and *Learning to Live with Your Demented Child.*

The third grader was upset about his parents' divorce, and Ms. Bernstein could talk about divorce forever. I read through the *DSM for Kids!* while I waited. It was a list of all the things that could be wrong with a person, the disorders and phobias. There was a whole section on grief, normal and abnormal, uncomplicated and complicated.

"Tell me about normal grief," I asked, once our meeting started, twenty minutes late. "Does a normal grieving process always take eighteen months?"

"There's not a hard-and-fast rule," Ms. Bernstein said. "It's just a guideline."

"Does it depend on how the person died?"

"What do you mean?"

"Would I feel different if Mom had died by suicide, the way she was supposed to?" I felt so stuck on Miss Ida's prediction. I wondered how a psychic could stay in business if she got major details like cause of death wrong.

"Do you think you would feel differently?" Ms. Bernstein sometimes did this annoying thing where she repeated my own questions back to me, without answering them.

"I don't know, maybe."

45

"Maybe." She nodded her head like the Bo Jackson bobble-head that Dad kept on his dashboard.

"I wish we had rescued her," I said. "My dad knows CPR, but he wasn't there to use it."

"It's not healthy to blame yourself, or your father."

"So what is healthy?"

"It's healthy to cry," Ms. Bernstein said. "I haven't seen you cry."

I hadn't cried when Mom disappeared, or when she was found dead, and neither had Lizzie. Mom had always said we weren't a family of criers, not on her side anyway. I had come home crying only once, in the second grade, because I had been the last kid picked on the dodgeball team in gym.

"Well, look at those skinny legs," Mom had said, poking my thigh. "You're not an athlete. Those legs are for reading books. Those legs are for studying."

Mom had hated when Dad cried, and she'd flip off the TV if he teared up over a sad commercial like those ones with starving children in Africa.

Dad was sobbing in his room when I got home from school that afternoon, I could hear him. He came out with red-rimmed puffy eyes and even Lizzie had enough sense not to push it. My sister wasn't evil, just angry, which was a normal stage of grief, according to the *DSM for Kids!* Guilt was another normal stage, and I hoped Dad knew that, that lots of people felt guilty about losing someone.

When my classmates finally stopped tiptoeing around me, they asked me what the worst thing was about having a dead mom. They wanted to know who tucked me in at night, who matched my socks and rolled them into little organized balls. There were a few kids in our grade who didn't have a dad, but everyone else still had a mom. Some dads were divorced, some dads appeared only in old photographs, and David's dad was in Afghanistan, a country that Ms. Powell had to spell on the board when the whole class wrote letters to the troops.

I said that some of the worst things about Mom being dead were that no one woke me up in the morning for school so I had to set an alarm, and no one ever cleaned the microwave so sauce was splattered inside. I told them I had more chores. I said my dad had been trying on different shades of Mom's lipstick, which I felt bad for telling about, but I had gotten carried away with all the attention. Lots of kids knew my dad,

47

since he still had the Freedom High record of most career touchdown throws, so I think the boys were surprised about the lipstick.

I told my classmates how Lizzie blamed our dad for Mom's drowning, even though anyone could have pulled her out of the water that night.

"Is your sister still cracked?" Billy Dickle asked.

"What do you mean?"

"Cracked in the head," Billy said, circling his finger around his temple. "My brother said she was."

"No," I said, because I didn't think that was anyone's business, and besides, Lizzie was really boring these days, baking at home all day like Rachael Ray on TV. She didn't seem to be teaching herself anything in homeschool, but I guess Dad figured that she'd go back to high school eventually.

There was another thing I wasn't honest about, because my classmates wouldn't have understood, but one of the worst things about Mom being dead was that she would never finish the book that she'd been writing. The working title was *The Sleep Habits of Animals and What They Tell Us about Our Own Slumber,* but Mom had mostly called it *The Book.* She'd been trying to get a grant to finish it. Mom had said if I helped with the research, she'd make me a coauthor, or at least thank me on the acknowledgments page.

"Write it yourself," Dad suggested, when I told him how much it bothered me that *The Book* would never be on the shelf in a bookstore or in the library under *Nonfiction, Babbitt.* He had a point, since I was already nearly an official coauthor. I printed out the rough draft and three-hole-punched it into a red binder. I carried the binder around with me everywhere, making notes on the empty pages I had put in the back.

So far, *The Book* had a chapter on the sleep of nocturnal animals, one on diurnal animals, and one on crepuscular animals, animals that stay awake during dawn and dusk. There was a chapter on animals that sleep for more than twelve hours a day (lions, gerbils) and another on hibernating animals (bears, bats, lemurs, turtles).

The chapter Mom had been working on hardest was on sleep-disturbed animals, which she said was work that no one had compiled before, really important science. She said it would open doors and windows for us.

Mom had hated being stuck teaching at a community college, lecturing to uninterested students and growing bacteria in petri dishes. She had really believed that *The Book* would put her name on the map, and she could get a tenure-track position at a university somewhere. We'd have to move, but she said it would be worth it. "No one knows about the sleeping lives of animals," she'd declared. "Everyone wants to know what their dog dreams." Boomer had been awake when she said that, sitting at her feet.

That was something that still bugged me: Mom had always been Boomer's favorite. When she came home, he would jump and wiggle and wag his tail, dash around the living room with excitement, even if she'd just been out to the grocery store. He followed her around the house, except when she was vacuuming; then he'd hide under a bed. He could stare at her for hours with his deep chocolate-brown eyes, measuring her every move. Mom used to say that Boomer would always be her baby, even though he was getting to be an older dog with some arthritis in his hips. We didn't know how old he was exactly, he'd been full-grown from the shelter.

Dad used to take Boomer when he went to watch Mom sleepswim in the river; no matter how late it was, Boomer never turned down an offer to go outside for a walk. I knew Boomer wasn't a heavy sleeper, so the night Mom drowned, why didn't Boomer wake Dad up to go out? Why wasn't Boomer the one to save her? Why wasn't he the hero?

I wanted to believe that Boomer did try to follow Mom that night. He would have trotted down the stairs at her side, run right to the front door to see if she would grab the leash. But maybe, as Mom was leaving the house, she turned to face her beloved dog and held up her hand like a stop sign, the motion for *stay*. Boomer was a good dog. He would have listened.

After Mom drowned, Boomer was sick for days with diarrhea, and we had to feed him white rice and boiled chicken instead of kibble. I didn't think about it until later, but maybe he was sick with guilt.

5.

Boomer didn't even like Lizzie much, but one night he woke me up with a cold nudge of his nose. He knew something was wrong. I found my sister in the kitchen drinking milk straight out of the carton. The milk had gone sour, I could smell it from where I stood. Mom had kept our house clean, and she would have been horrified to see the clutter we left around, the things that molded in the fridge.

I flipped on the light, and Lizzie had that glossed-over look I knew so well, the sleep-walker's gaze. There were food wrappers everywhere; she'd already gnawed her way through a block of cheese and a head of cauliflower. I tried to take the milk carton from her, but she wouldn't loosen her grip. Some of the curdled milk splashed onto the floor, and not even Boomer would lick it up.

"She'll get food poisoning," I said to Dad,

when I woke him up to tell him. "Or regular poisoning." I thought of the jug of blue antifreeze in our garage, the easy twist-off top. I'd read that antifreeze tastes like sugar going down, but then causes vomiting, a heart attack, and, finally, kidney failure.

"She'll be fine," Dad mumbled, still half-asleep.

"Mom wasn't fine," I said, but Dad didn't hear, or he pretended not to.

I went out to the garage for the antifreeze. I poured it into the toilet and flushed over and over until the toilet bowl was no longer tinged blue. There were probably other poisons in our house, but it was a start.

Lizzie didn't look sick when she came down for breakfast, so we didn't tell her what she'd done. Dad cleared all the expired food out of the fridge, and we hoped that maybe the sleepeating was a one-time thing.

But after it went on for a week, after a key lime pie she'd baked earlier that day and a box of Pop-Tarts and a loaf of bread had disappeared, Dad said he'd be the one to break it to her. I was relieved, because there was the time I'd told Lizzie that her favorite sitcom was canceled and she tied me up with a jump rope and filled my mouth with pine needles. I'd started to choke just as

Mom had come running outside.

"We were just playing," Lizzie had said, but Mom had asked me for the real story.

"Lizzie," she scolded. "Don't kill the messenger."

But Lizzie didn't flip out on Dad like I thought she might. She just said: "That makes sense." I guess she'd been waking up the past few mornings with food on her face, in her hair.

"Are you scared?" I asked her.

"I have a fast metabolism," she snapped. "You're the one who will probably get fat like Dad."

Our family doctor said that somnambulatory eating was becoming more common in teenagers, and it wasn't usually very serious. "She's still growing, so she's probably just hungry," Dr. Agee said. "Leave some healthy snacks out."

Dad sighed. "Can I lock her door or something? Maybe use a handcuff?"

Dr. Agee looked horrified. "She will likely hurt herself trying to get out, not understanding why it won't open. And she might break her own arm in a handcuff."

"Okay," Dad said. "Got it. Healthy snacks."

That night, Dad and I waited up together.

I was glad to see Dad taking it seriously, even if he fell asleep in his armchair before Lizzie wandered in, her eyes glossy, crouched forward at the waist. Mom had called it Lizzie's velociraptor walk, because she looked like those dinosaurs in *Jurassic Park*. "Bloodthirsty and clever," Mom had said, when we watched the movie as a family, "just like my Lizzie-bell." When Mom sleepwalked, you could have balanced a book on her head she was so graceful and upright.

Lizzie ignored the carrot sticks and hummus that Dad had arranged, and I followed her as she headed to the cereal cabinet. I took the box from her when she tried to open it with her teeth. I poured the Lucky Charms into a plastic bowl and tried to get Lizzie to the table, but she wouldn't get into a chair. She started whining, loudly. I didn't want to wake up Dad. I sprinkled some of the cereal on the floor in front of her and she went right for it.

Then Boomer came over too, started eating alongside her, until Lizzie lunged for him. She scratched him right across the nose. Boomer bared his teeth for a second, like we were in the dog park, then looked up at me, ashamed. I filled Boomer's dish and gave the bowl to him in the other room.

I didn't know what else to do.

I thumbed through every page of Mom's work in progress, and there wasn't anything about animals that eat in their sleep. In the chapter on sleep-disturbed animals, there were two horses that Mom had observed with parasomnias, which is the medical word for sleep disorders. One horse had escaped from her stall and cantered in her sleep down the highway. The mare was nearly hit by a semitruck. There was a stallion who tried to mate in his sleep, mounting anything that was around. He had killed a stable hand that way.

Mom had found a sleepwalking beagle in Wyoming, had interviewed the dog's owner over the phone. Every night, Larry the beagle stumbled his way around the house, knocking into furniture and smashing his skull into walls. His owner said it was obvious that Larry was asleep the whole time; the dog continued to snore, and his eyelids twitched. After Larry fell down the stairs, his owner had to put up baby gates to keep Larry on the first floor at night.

Then there were the scientific studies to create sleep disturbances in mice, which Mom kept track of in a file on her computer since there were so many of them. I didn't know how I felt about tests on animals, like the ones where scientists put mascara on rabbits or give loads of drugs to mice. But Mom argued that studying animals helps us understand human behavior, because we're all animals, all connected.

"But what if you come back as a lab rat in your next life? With tubes in your brain?" I asked her once.

"I won't be a lab rat forever." She shrugged.

Mom had collected stacks and stacks of books on reincarnation, books with titles like *Past Lives* and *Journey of Souls.* We still kept them stacked next to the bathtub, where Mom liked to read. The books said there were rules about your next life: If you ate meat, you'd be born the next time with bad skin. If you had sex with too many women, either you would come back with diseases or you would be a horse. If you drank beer, you'd have bad teeth. If you stole, you'd come back as an ant. If you ended your life by suicide, you would come back as a defenseless prey animal, like a rabbit or a moth.

I started leaving the porch light on all night, so moths would gather on our front door to be near the glow. I warned Dad not to smoosh them if he came in from work late.

One night, Lizzie took everything out of the pantry and put it on the floor, leaving paths to walk through between the flour and dried beans. It looked like a lot of food, once it was out of the cabinets, even though I'd just said that day that there was nothing to eat in the house. Lizzie also pulled all the utensils out of their drawers, made a big sterling silver pile of forks and spoons and knives. The knives made me nervous, especially the one Mom used for carving the turkey at Thanksgiving. I wasn't sure how Lizzie had gotten into the knife drawer when Dad had a child lock on it.

"What were you looking for?" I asked Lizzie in the morning, as we started to put things back in their places. It looked like she'd been searching for something, tearing the kitchen apart for some missing ingredient.

"You really think I know what I was doing?" Lizzie asked, sweeping some spilt flour into a dustpan. "I was asleep, you moron." Lizzie could be mean in the morning, especially if she hadn't gotten enough sleep the night before. Mom used to say that was normal for teenagers.

When Dad saw the mess, he called a sleep

specialist in Birmingham, since our family doctor had been no help. The sleep specialist was booked solid until mid-November.

"We can handle it until then," Dad said. "It's not an emergency."

"It could be an emergency," I said, thinking of the carving knife.

"If only your mother was around," Dad said, hanging his head in his hands. "She'd know what to do."

Of course I would have liked to ask Mom about Lizzie's sleepeating, but that wasn't an option. I asked Ms. Bernstein instead, since she had a master's degree framed on her wall in the guidance office. She didn't seem to understand my question, but she said that changes in sleep patterns and appetite were to be expected. They were both on her list of *Physical Symptoms of Grief,* another handout she'd printed for me to take home. Ms. Bernstein said she'd lost twenty pounds and barely slept for a whole year after her husband left. I didn't see how divorce was anything like a death. Mr. Bernstein had only moved to the next town and into an apartment complex.

Still, Ms. Bernstein was probably onto something. I didn't have any trouble sleeping, and my appetite was the same as always, but Lizzie had her own ways to grieve.

6.

~~SEPTEMBER,~~ OCTOBER

When I got up to check on her, I found Lizzie working her way through a bag of marshmallows, the Jet-Puffed ones. Her lips were powdered with sticky sugar.

In the morning, she didn't want to talk about how many marshmallows she had stuffed into her cheeks.

"It's called emotional eating," I said. That's what Ms. Bernstein had told me about, the physical symptoms of grief. "There's a lot of information about it online."

"I don't think that's it," Lizzie said. "That's for ugly people."

"You're sad about Mom," I told her. "You're eating your feelings."

"You're sad about Mom," Dad repeated, and tears gathered in his eyes.

"I'm going for a walk," Lizzie said. Boomer raised his head at the word.

"It's okay to be sad," Dad called after her.

"Come back and we'll be sad together!"

But Lizzie didn't come back, and Dad shushed me when I asked him whether marshmallows were still made with bone marrow. Dad seemed to be getting plenty of sleep, but the skin underneath his eyes was purple and sagging, and sometimes he was cranky for no reason. Ms. Bernstein had said it sounded like my father was being morose, which was another word I liked the sound of. I made Mr. Oakes a clipping of that one too.

"Someday I'd like you to tell me about her," Ms. Powell said, when I got back from my guidance appointment. Someone must have finally told Ms. Powell that I had a dead mom.

"Okay," I said.

"When you're ready," she said, before she walked away, which seemed to mean that I wasn't ready yet.

I didn't tell Ms. Powell anything about my mother, because she never asked me again, and I didn't know how to bring it up. I wouldn't have told her about her affair with Mr. Oakes, that didn't seem appropriate for school. I would have told Ms. Powell that there were times when my mother was terrible, and that was where Lizzie got some of her terribleness. Sometimes Mom got such bad headaches that she wouldn't come out of her room for days, and she would ground us for no reason if we were making too much noise. But she had mostly been wonderful. She had been smart and funny, and everyone had looked at her when she walked down the street in the town center.

Sometimes Mom would pick us up at school in the middle of the day; she'd get Lizzie first and then come for me. She would pull up into the SCHOOL BUSES ONLY driveway in her station wagon and lean on the horn until someone from the front office went down the hall to retrieve me from my classroom. The Beaver Elementary principal had said this was disruptive behavior, and had given Mom a talking-to about it. Mom had argued that we were *her* kids, and she could do whatever she wanted with us, wasn't that true?

"Within reason," Principal Witherspoon said.

Mom liked to take us to abandoned farmhouses, ones on the side of the highway with the roof about to fall through. She would pack a picnic, a basket stuffed with pimento cheese sandwiches and potato chips, sparkling cider and brownies, or a rabbit cake if there was something to celebrate. We'd lie in the middle of the barn on our picnic blanket, looking up at the sky through the rotted-out gaps in the roof.

"I love you, my little chickadees," she'd say, sitting up with a stray piece of straw in her hair. "If this barn fell down on us right now, we'd die happy, wouldn't we?"

"Yes," we'd agree, but I'd always cross my fingers when I said that. I didn't want to be crushed to death by a barn, not even during a moment when I was feeling happy.

I would have told Ms. Powell about rainy days, when Mom built forts with me, using the kitchen chairs and the clean sheets. And then there was the time that Lizzie and Mom and I showed up at Dad's carpet store dressed as burglars with nylon stockings pulled over our faces and squirt guns for weapons. Dad hadn't thought it was funny at all, especially since there were customers in the store.

Mom always said Dad worked too much, that he was a workaholic. She blamed that on his mom, the grandmother we'd never met. That grandmother had run off with another man right after our grandfather got sick, and soon Dad was left with the house and the store and no family at all, until he found Mom.

"He's always taken the job too seriously,"

Mom said sometimes. "He should have gone to Sewanee, and he would have if it weren't for that witch."

"But then he wouldn't have met you," I reminded her, since they'd met in Alabama.

Dad's mother wasn't dead, she only lived in Texas, but Mom claimed she might as well be because she was *rotten to the core.* "She's only still standing," Mom had said, "like the dead elm tree out back."

Dad had wanted to cut that tree down, but Mom hadn't let him because she liked the patterns the beetles made in the bark, their tunnels and elaborate mazes. Mom said everything was weird if you looked at it closely enough, like how sound waves could snuff out a fire, how worms could live when you cut them in half, how oysters made pearls with their tongues, and how someday science would help people live for hundreds of years. She'd said if we had the money now, we could clone Boomer and have a whole house full of identical border collies who were all very good boys.

I would have explained to Ms. Powell about Mom's psychic. We never told Miss Ida Mom had drowned, but I'm sure she already knew.

I would have told Ms. Powell that my mom was supposed to commit suicide, about what Miss Ida had seen in the coffee grounds. I wouldn't have been able to explain to Ms. Powell, or to anyone, why Miss Ida had been wrong.

In their phone calls, Miss Ida had given Mom instructions on everything: from how to cut her hair to how much exercise to get. She had taught Mom how to put leeches on her body to reduce anxiety, had told Mom to put herself upside down every day in a headstand.

Miss Ida had dictated what color we painted the rooms in a house she had never seen. About a year before Mom drowned, Miss Ida mailed another paint sample and Mom painted the master bedroom a deep dark green, almost black.

"It's my terrarium," Mom had declared, when she finished the job. She put plants around the floor beside the bed, on the bookshelves, and on the windowsills. Every plant died within the following month, except for one lonely philodendron. "I never did have a green thumb," she'd sighed. Mom always kept the curtains drawn in her room, and there hadn't been enough sunlight. I thought a scientist with a PhD should understand about chlorophyll.

Even if she couldn't keep a plant alive, Mom would have known what to do about

Lizzie. She would have stopped the sleep-eating in its tracks. Then again, I was pretty sure that Lizzie was sleepeating only because Mom wasn't there; Ms. Bernstein said that Lizzie was stuffing herself at night because she missed our mom. I felt jealous that Lizzie missed Mom so much that something physical was happening to her. Nothing was happening to me, nothing had changed, at least nothing noticeable. Ms. Powell hadn't known I had a dead mother until someone in my class told her, and she was my favorite teacher.

7.

I thought Dad would stay morose forever, until the afternoon that he came home with the bird, a hyacinth macaw. The parrot was perched on his shoulder like Dad was a pirate, and had already pooped down the back of Dad's gray suit jacket. I recognized the parrot immediately: the blue-and-yellow bird had been in the front window of Debbie's Petland for years; I thought Mr. Debbie owned him. His name was Ernest Hemingway. I raced to the cabinet for a box of saltine crackers.

"What's this?" Lizzie asked.

"Hello," the bird said, in Mom's voice.

Boomer growled, the fur bristling up on his spine. I'd never seen him growl at Mom.

"Holy shit," Lizzie said.

"I know." Dad was bug-eyed.

"Holy shit," the parrot repeated, still using Mom's voice. "I know."

Mr. Debbie had called Dad's office at

Carpet World. Mr. Debbie said the bird was good at imitations, and it was one of the reasons Ernest had been returned to the pet store three times, but this was a new thing. The bird was using Mom's voice. It was a little suspicious, but Mom did get Boomer's food from Debbie's Petland.

"You should at least hear him," Mr. Debbie had insisted over the phone. "I'm so sorry for your loss."

So Dad had gone to the pet store with the green awning and the glass cages of puppies, one of the few stores in the Freedom town center, besides the Coffee Shack, the butcher's, the hardware store, and Suzy Sundaes. The bird had whistled when Dad walked in.

"Gimme kiss," said Ernest Hemingway, and my dad passed out cold on the tile floor of the pet store. When he woke up, he tried to pay for Ernest, but Mr. Debbie gave him the parrot free of charge.

"So the bird is possessed?" Lizzie asked.

"Something like that," Dad agreed, as the bird shifted his weight from foot to foot, bobbing his head.

"Mom did love going to Debbie's Petland," I said. Sometimes we went after school just to look at the puppies, and we'd always stop to say hello to Ernest when we first came in the door.

"That's true," Dad said.

"Want a cracker?" I asked Ernest, and he bobbed his head.

After Dad said I'd given the parrot enough saltines, I went upstairs to the bathroom. None of the reincarnation books said what you had to do to return as a hyacinth macaw.

But of course I knew that the parrot wasn't Mom reincarnated. Ernest Hemingway was already seven years old, it was written on the papers Mr. Debbie had given Dad. Macaws can live for sixty years.

I could hear Dad in his room, talking to the parrot behind the closed door.

Dad was growing attached to the bird.

"He's really a sweet pet," Dad said, on our third day with Ernest.

It only took a week before Dad started bringing Ernest into work with him.

"Isn't that illegal?" Lizzie asked. "Against health code?"

He argued that the parrot gave Carpet World a new credibility; hadn't we seen *Aladdin*? Wasn't there a parrot in *The Arabian Nights*? Dad said he knew that Ernest would help the Persian rug sales go up.

Dad always insisted we get Boomer the

70

cheapest dog food, the kind Mom said was made of dehydrated horsemeat, but he came home with bags of gourmet birdseed. He built Ernest a perch next to the headboard of his bed.

"See how easy it was for him to replace her," Lizzie said. She snapped her fingers. "The merry widow."

"I think men are widowers," I said, but it was true that Dad had become completely enamored with the parrot.

I liked the parrot, I just didn't like the way Dad was acting. He was smitten. And it made me feel mixed-up when I listened to Ernest, both happy and sad. He said some normal parrot words and phrases like *cracker* and *pretty bird,* but some were things Mom might have said, like *hurry up,* or *I'm ready,* or *dinnertime,* or *I love you.*

"There are African grays that know thousands of words," I told Dad at dinner, watching the hurt spread across his face.

"Ernest is smarter than most people," Dad said.

"Her body's not even cold," Lizzie grumbled, which didn't make sense because Mom had been cremated. She didn't have a body anymore, not even a skeleton left. But it was true that Mom hadn't been dead for that long, even if sometimes it seemed as if she'd been dead forever. It had been four months.

I found a section of the *DSM for Kids!* called "Hallucinations of Loss." It said over 60 percent of kids who have lost a loved one will experience a hallucination, most often *the ghostly image or the voice of the deceased. It's a common reaction,* the book said, *although more likely to happen during times of stress.*

I wondered if that was why we were hearing Mom's voice in the parrot, but that didn't make sense, since Mr. Debbie had heard her voice too. The pet store owner wasn't grieving Mom, or at least I didn't think he was.

I wished I could see Mom's ghost, I wished that could be my physical symptom of grief. I thought maybe it could happen on Halloween, Mom's favorite holiday. She used to do whatever she could to make our house look haunted; there were still fake-blood stains on our porch that wouldn't wash out.

But Mom's ghost didn't show up on Halloween and Lizzie decided we weren't going to go trick-or-treating that year. She said we were too old for it and she started dinner. I wanted to remind her that I was five years younger than she was, but I decided not to say anything.

When Dad came home, he was carrying a huge bag of candy. He was wearing the mask from my costume from *The Sound of Music,* the musical that we had put on the year before in school. I had been a mountain goat, a nonspeaking, nonsinging part. Mom had tried to get me recast as a nun or a von Trapp, but I'd insisted I wanted to remain a goat.

"Smells delicious," Dad said, pushing the goat mask up on his face. He always dressed up for the staff party at Carpet World.

"It's a Cajun chicken casserole."

"See, some birds aren't so lucky," Dad said to Ernest, tickling him on the chest.

"I bet parrots are delicious," Lizzie said, setting down the casserole dish and taking off her oven mitts.

"Shush," Dad said.

"You started it."

We all sat down at the table, with the parrot perched in an old high chair from the attic. "Doggie want a cookie?" Ernest asked. He dropped a piece of okra onto the floor, and clucked when Boomer didn't touch it. Boomer wouldn't come within six feet of the bird.

"Isn't this nice," Dad said, digging into

the casserole. "I think things are really starting to come together for this family."

"Everything still seems pretty shitty to
me," Lizzie said.

"Eat your dinner," Ernest said, the way
Mom would've, and it was Dad's turn to
whistle then.

8.
~~OCTOBER,~~ NOVEMBER

On the date of Lizzie's appointment with the sleep specialist, Dad packed up Ernest in his carrier cage, and we all drove together to Birmingham. Dr. Monroe gave Lizzie a full examination plus an MRI scan, but he didn't find any physical problem. He read his diagnosis checklist aloud.

"Are you depressed?" he asked.

"My mother died," Lizzie said.

"We're all depressed," Dad added, even if that wasn't totally true, not for him, not since the parrot had arrived.

"Are you bulimic?" the doctor asked. "Anorexic? Do you have heartburn, indigestion? Any allergies?"

In the end, Dr. Monroe prescribed Lizzie an antiseizure medication that he said had been proven to help with nocturnal eating. "I know she doesn't have seizures," he explained, "but drugs don't only cure the things they were designed to cure."

"Mom had a seizure once," I said. "Are those genetic too?"

"Sometimes." The doctor nodded. "But that's not Lizzie's current problem."

"Any other suggestions, doctor?" Dad asked.

"No television before bed," Dr. Monroe said, peering over his glasses, giving Lizzie a half smile. As we walked out, Dr. Monroe gave Dad a business card for St. Cloud's Hospital for Women, in case things got any worse.

Dad and I stayed up together to watch Lizzie that night, but again he fell asleep in his armchair. When he woke up with a stiff neck, he told me he was going to bed.

"Don't wake her up," Dad said. "I tried to wake your mother up once. She scratched my cornea. I had an eye patch for a week."

"Wake up," the parrot repeated, nuzzling into Dad's neck.

So I stayed up alone, and Lizzie didn't even get out of bed. Sleepwalkers don't sleepwalk every night, I'd known that before, but I still wanted to keep watch. I drank almost a liter of Mountain Dew, played solitare on the laptop, and continued my research on Mom's book.

Mom had been curious as to how prolonged darkness affects sleep, and she was planning to look into studies of the naked mole rat. An herbivore native to desert regions of East Africa, the naked mole rat lives in colonies deep underground, and almost never sees sunlight. Mom had ordered a whole book on the animal, a five-hundred-page brick, *The Compiled Studies of the Naked Mole Rat.*

Naked mole rats have an extremely slow metabolic rate, less than half of other rodents, and they have a different kind of hemoglobin — a type more efficient at capturing oxygen. They need less air to function. A lot of the time, the tunnel system of a naked mole rat colony is sealed, with no hole to the surface.

A person drowns because there is not enough oxygen in the body, in the brain. You could hold a naked mole rat underwater for thirty minutes, and the animal would be fine once it emerged.

Mom could hold her breath for five minutes and seventeen seconds; I'd timed her in the bathtub once, sometime right after Nana died. I thought Mom could have held the world record for holding her breath underwater the longest, but I checked Lizzie's *Guinness World Records* book, and the record belonged to a Danish man who had set the twenty-two-minute record in a fish tank full of sharks.

Mom spent a lot of time in the tub after her mother's funeral. For those weeks, after school, I'd sit on the toilet lid and read to her. I'd been in the advanced reading group in my first-grade class.

"My heart hurts, Elvis," Mom groaned, but she clutched her stomach, above her belly button.

"Are you an octopus?" I asked, flipping through a magazine with a giant Pacific octopus on the cover. An octopus has three hearts, the article said; I thought maybe one heart was in the stomach.

"I'm a submarine," Mom said and slid under the water. If one heart failed, the octopus died.

"Your mother will be better soon," Dad said from the doorway. He walked up to the tub and Mom emerged for air. "Honey, you're a prune."

"I'm a peach pear apple banana. Close the door."

Every morning, Mom would fill the bath with fresh water as she read the newspaper, dipping the bottom of the pages in the water, letting the ink run. She balanced her coffee cup in the soap dish. Lizzie and Dad had to take most of their showers in our outdoor stall, which we usually used only after we went swimming in the river and there was sand in our suits. But I was allowed to bathe with Mom three times a week. She'd wash my hair and hum this one song from *The King and I* that we had played at Nana's funeral.

One Monday, when my bath time was over, Mom climbed out of the tub after me. She wrapped herself in two towels, one on her head and one around her waist, leaving her breasts exposed.

"Your body only lets you hurt that much for so long," she said.

The next night, after a long afternoon nap, I stayed up again to watch for Lizzie. It was two in the morning when I heard the screen door slam. Lizzie had rarely gone sleepwalking outside the house; that was something Mom did. Maybe Lizzie was using the sleepwalking outside to feel closer to Mom, trying to act like her, an imitation. I hoped Lizzie wouldn't go down to the river.

I pulled my sneakers on and ran out to the driveway. It was pitch dark, and I had to go back inside for a flashlight; I hadn't been prepared for her to go outside. I wandered through the woods waving my flashlight around, wondering if sleepwalkers could see better in the dark. A branch scratched my face, and I was about to give up and start back home when I heard screams coming from our neighbor's backyard.

I found Lizzie sitting in their chicken coop, the hens huddled in the far corner, squawking in alarm. I shined my flashlight on her, and she looked straight at me. She smiled, her pupils huge.

"Lizzie, come out of there."

She cracked an egg in her hand; the yolk ran down her wrist.

"Lizzie, I mean it," I begged. "Lizzie, go back to bed." It seemed stupid to say that, so far from her room, but I hoped it would work before our neighbor came out with his gun. "Come on, back to bed. Back to bed."

Then Lizzie licked the egg off her arm, like a bear would lick a paw soaked in honey. The egg's mucus dripped from her chin.

"Salmonella!" I cried. I opened the gate, got on my knees to crawl into the coop too, but Lizzie kicked dirt in my face. Then she threw an egg at me, it hit me in the eye, and I backed out of the cage. I wiped the yolk from my face as she laughed. You are supposed to gently lead a sleepwalker by her elbow back to bed, but how could I gently lead Lizzie anywhere? I shined the flashlight on her again. She broke another egg in her hand, made a loud slurping noise as she swallowed it. I gagged, hard, like a cat trying to bring up a hairball. It was too much for me.

It wasn't the first time we'd broken into the neighbor's chicken coop. It was something we'd done with Mom last Christmas, when the grocery store was closed and we were out of eggs. Mom had wanted to make a rabbit cake, she'd said we couldn't celebrate without one, she always said that. So Mom had kept watch, and she'd sent both Lizzie and me into the coop to gather eggs. The chickens went berserk. Then we all ran, our pockets full of eggs, even though we only needed two for the cake. It was one of our best memories.

"Lizzie," I tried one more time. "Come home." She acted like she couldn't hear me.

I'm not sure how long I watched my sister. I was hoping she'd wake up, I guess, although who knows what would have happened then. Eventually, I backed away and walked down the neighbor's long gravel driveway, shivering though it wasn't really cold. I hugged myself and tried not to think of my sister back in the chicken coop, or of the time Mom had made us steal eggs, and the way we laughed and laughed when we made it home safe. My chest ached.

A naked mole rat cannot feel pain, I remembered. It is one of the reasons naked mole rats are studied so extensively in labs. The rodents are missing some neurons or something, scientists aren't sure, but you can dribble acid directly on their skin and they won't even shudder.

In the morning, there were eight eggs on the kitchen table, in the fruit bowl. They were different shades of white and brown and even bluish, not all clean white like the ones from the supermarket. When Lizzie got up, I presented the eggs as my proof, told her what I'd seen. She still had a feather in her hair.

She ran to the bathroom and retched over the toilet, but nothing came up. I stood in the doorway while she curled up on the bathmat, her head between her knees. Mom would have sat on the side of the tub and rubbed her back, but I didn't think Lizzie would want me to do that.

"Dad's going to freak," she said. "He's going to send me away."

"To where?" I asked, but I realized I already knew. Dad still kept the business card from Dr. Monroe in his wallet. I didn't think we were ready for a last resort.

"I've heard what happens at places like that," she said. "Mom told me." I could see the fear in Lizzie's eyes.

"We won't tell him," I said. "He doesn't have to know."

Lizzie held out her little finger to me, and I accepted the pinkie-swear.

Of course I knew that I should tell Dad that Lizzie had been sleepwalking outside. She could drown; she could get hit by a car. Dad really should have been the one to stay up to watch Lizzie at night, but he probably didn't want to be blamed again if another sleepwalker went missing. If Lizzie's body was found twisted in a ditch off the highway, the blanket of guilt would fall on me.

9.

My grades in math were slipping because I kept falling asleep when we were supposed to be doing worksheets on long division.

"Are you eating breakfast?" Ms. Powell asked. "At least a granola bar?"

After I fell asleep on my desk for the third time, Ms. Powell sent me to the nurse's office.

"I'm sure it's mononucleosis," I told the nurse. "Or my thyroid."

"What kind of kid are you?" the nurse asked. "Lie down over there. I'll call your mother."

"Father," I corrected her.

Dad had to leave the carpet store to come sign me out from the nurse's office and take me home.

"Is it the flu?" he asked. He didn't know that I'd been staying up at night to watch out for Lizzie. It had always been easy to slip something by him. Mom would have noticed I wasn't in bed.

"It could be the flu," I said.

I was already falling asleep in the truck, letting Dad talk. He said it had been kind of a slow day, except that our neighbor Paul Greenburg had come in and ordered wall-to-wall carpeting for his upstairs bedroom. "Paul said we're lucky we don't raise chickens," Dad said.

I snapped awake. "What?"

Paul Greenburg had told Dad that his coop and three others in the area had been raided in the past two nights. I breathed in. I hadn't even heard Lizzie leave the house, I must have nodded off.

"I didn't know foxes ate eggs, but Paul said foxes are notorious egg thieves," Dad said. "Sometimes they hunt in groups. What's a group of foxes called? A herd? A pack?"

"An earth. An earth of foxes."

"You're amazing," he said, smiling, because he didn't know I was lying to him, didn't know that I knew exactly what had happened to the missing eggs. "Well, I guess they'll have to buy eggs at the supermarket like the rest of us."

Before bed, I told Lizzie what Dad had told me. "They all think it's foxes," I explained.

"You're off the hook."

"But why am I doing it?" Lizzie was lying on the floor of her bedroom, looking up at the ceiling, her hands on her stomach. "How can I stop?"

"I don't know. Maybe you've been dreaming you're a fox."

"Elvis," Lizzie said. "Stop being stupid."

"I'm just kidding. Just trying to be funny." I turned to leave the room.

"Elvis, wait."

"Yeah?"

"Do you think Mom was dreaming when she drowned?"

"Maybe," I said. "Sure."

"I don't like to think that she was afraid when she died."

"I don't either."

"I hope she was still dreaming. I hope she didn't know what was happening."

"Maybe Mom dreamt she was a fish, and she thought she had gills."

"Or an alligator," Lizzie said.

"Alligators breathe air," I pointed out.

But then I remembered that alligators always look like they're smiling, so sometimes I still try to picture Mom drowning like that, floating down the river and grinning with all of her teeth.

10.

It was halfway through November, month five on the grieving chart, and I couldn't figure out how to stop Lizzie from sleepwalking. I read online that there are only a couple of ways to keep a fox out of a chicken coop: you can install an electric fence or you can sprinkle coyote urine around the area. A fox will not cross a boundary that smells strongly of a larger animal. Of course I didn't really believe Lizzie was a fox, but I thought it was worth a try to see if those tricks would work on Lizzie too. I couldn't put an electric fence around our house, so I ordered a half gallon of coyote urine on Dad's account from Amazon.com.

"That smells awful," Dad said, when he found me with the watering can outside of Lizzie's room.

"It should," I said. "It's urine." I told him that it would help Lizzie stop sleepwalking, or it would at least keep her in her room. Since I didn't tell him about the chicken coop, I guess the idea made less sense to him than it did to me. He snatched the watering can away.

"Who told you that would work?" he snapped.

"At least I'm doing something," I said. "You aren't doing anything."

"What else can I do? I took her to the doctor. I took her to *two* doctors."

I stopped there because I remembered what Dr. Monroe said we should do as a next step if things got worse. I imagined what the house would be like without Lizzie, and without Mom too: it would be like a desert island, abandoned and lifeless. I pictured the rooms of our house filling with sand.

I got a book out from the Freedom Public Library, *Sleep Walking and Moon Walking* by Isidor Isaak Sadger. Moon walking, Sadger explains, is when you sleepwalk under the influence of the full moon. Moonstruck is another word for this state.

While I was reading, Mrs. Reasoner, the librarian, pointed out that the book was published in 1920, and there had been many advances in science in the years since.

But I thought Sadger's information was pretty good; it said that sleepwalking is classified as a "nervous disease," which means it comes from the mind. The author said that a sleepwalker is trying to work out some problem from her current life in her dreams.

The book also had another theory that I thought was interesting: Isidor Sadger wrote: "Too much sex, or too little for that matter, can turn any woman into a noctambulist." That is one of the Latin words for sleepwalker; somnambulist is another. Mrs. Reasoner said I should "absolutely not believe that bullshit," and I was surprised that a librarian would swear to a kid.

Late that night, I realized there was someone who could tell me if Mom had been having too much sex, or too little. I took Mom's cell phone from her office, we'd left it on its charger all this time, and went up to my room. I found him listed in her contacts under *The Tongue Doctor*, which she had called him when he'd been my speech therapist.

"Tell me from the start," I demanded, after Mr. Oakes picked up. I tried to enunciate every word I said.

I didn't mean to fall asleep after I hung up

the phone, but I woke up a couple of hours later to yelling from the kitchen. I went running downstairs to find Dad holding Lizzie by the waist. She had oven mitts on both of her hands, and she appeared to be trying to climb into the oven.

"Turn the stove off," Dad yelled. All four gas burners were on full-blaze. The oven was set to 450 degrees. There was so much in the kitchen Lizzie could hurt herself with: knives, household cleaners, the oven.

I saw then that the rabbit cake pan was out on the counter, and Lizzie had cracked a half-dozen eggs inside. She had also set the table with the good china, and somehow she hadn't broken one plate.

"Leave it," Dad said, when I started cleaning up. "She should see it tomorrow."

"You could have set the house on fire," Dad scolded Lizzie in the morning. "You could have set *yourself* on fire."

I didn't think I was supposed to be part of the conversation, but I peeked into the kitchen from the other room. Dad was holding a little white business card. It had to be the one Dr. Monroe had given him.

"Daddy," Lizzie begged, though both of us had grown out of calling him that years before. "Just give me another chance. I'll get better, I promise. I'll fix it."

"You can't blame her," I said, stepping into the room. "She was asleep." It was my fault, I wanted to say, I should have been watching her. I didn't want her to be sent away to St. Cloud's. I didn't want another member of our family to go missing.

"Another chance," the parrot echoed, and I know that helped.

"Okay," Dad sighed, "one more chance." He fed a grape to the parrot. "Keep taking your meds."

"Thanks, Elvis," Lizzie said, giving me a one-armed hug.

I borrowed the credit card and overnight-express packages filled our mailbox by noon the next day. I ordered *Eyes Open Hypnosis,* a self-hypnosis kit that promised to curb your smoking, gambling, overeating, or sleepwalking habits. It came with head-phones, a back massager, and a bonus cof-fee mug. I bought a leather dream catcher from Horsefeathers.com.

I also hid the rabbit cake pan underneath my bed, where Lizzie wouldn't find it. It was another happy memory that I didn't want her to wreck.

11.

"I don't know if it's better or worse that they're really in love."

It was our Tuesday meeting, and Ms. Bernstein wasn't talking about Mr. Oakes, even though that was one thing I'd found out during the short phone call with him last week, that he had really loved my mom. Ms. Bernstein was talking instead about the affair her ex-husband had had with her sister, which was why Ms. Bernstein was divorced. Her sister was expecting a baby.

"I don't know either," I said.

"You're right," she said. "I am alone but I am not lonely." She repeated that last part several times. It was what she called her divorce mantra. Sometimes she made me chant it with her, and I did kind of like doing that.

When I called Mr. Oakes, he hadn't wanted to talk to me at first, but then he said, "You know, what the hell, I can't tell

anyone else about it, and *you* called *me.*"
He told me that he and my mom had been
seeing each other for about three months,
which was long enough for two people to
fall in love, he assured me. They had connected on Craigslist, the same website
where we had sold our moth-eaten couch.
Mom had put up a personal ad.

"What did it say?" I asked, but Mr. Oakes
was sure I shouldn't know.

"It's really an adult website," he said. "You
can't call here again. I'm trying to move
on."

I'd agreed that I wouldn't call him again
as long as he admitted that Mom hadn't
loved him back, that it had been a one-sided
thing.

"You know," Mr. Oakes had sniffed, "I'm
not sure she did. She never said it back."

That made me feel a lot better and I hung
up the phone. I decided not to tell Dad or
Lizzie about what I'd learned from Mr.
Oakes, they would be too upset. I wasn't
even going to tell Ms. Bernstein. She was
judgmental about extramarital affairs.

Ms. Bernstein had finished chanting her
divorce mantra, and she asked me about
dinner the night before; she always wanted
to know what I'd eaten. I said that my sister
had made shrimp and grits, but it must not

have been enough food for Lizzie because that night I'd watched her eat a stick of butter rolled in sugar.

"I think your obsession with Lizzie is hindering your own grieving process," Ms. Bernstein said, when I told her that the hypnosis tapes weren't working.

"I'm not obsessed with her, I'm trying to take care of her."

"Siblings of the mentally ill often ignore their own problems, and you've been conditioned to believe your needs are not important."

"Mentally ill?" I shook my head. "She's not mentally ill. She's a sleepwalker."

Ms. Bernstein didn't talk at all for a minute, until finally she said it was good that Lizzie was cooking our meals. "Sharing regular meals is an important part of collective grief," she said. "It's healthy for a family to get into that routine."

Healthy and unhealthy. Normal and abnormal. I had borrowed the *DSM for Kids!* from Ms. Bernstein's shelf. I was confused by a sentence in the book that read: *There is no wrong way to grieve, but if you believe your grief is abnormal, seek professional help immediately.*

I asked Ms. Bernstein if she could clarify *normal* and *abnormal,* and she sighed. I'd asked the question a few times by that point, and I guess she was tired of answering. Ms. Bernstein had banned a few topics from conversation in her office, like how a coroner knows for sure that a death was an accident and not a suicide.

"Abnormal grief means someone who never gets over the loss," she finally said. "Nothing changes in the client, nothing improves. But you'll get over it, honey, don't worry. Most people recover from a major bereavement."

"How do I know when I'm over it?" I asked, because I still didn't know any other kid with a dead mom. I had the grieving chart, but not a lot of other guidelines to follow. Ms. Bernstein was looking at the framed photo of her ex-husband on her desk again.

"You'll just know," she said.

That night, Lizzie made a big mess of the pantry, pulling out all sorts of ingredients onto the counter. She took out a large bowl and made a mixture of flour and yogurt, sugar, food coloring, and milk. She cracked seven eggs into the batter. Then she pulled Dad's gout medicine from the cabinet, and dumped all the pills in and stirred.

"Oh no," I said, once I realized what that

meant, how much pain Dad would be in. Dad had been diagnosed with gout the year before, and he'd been pretty ashamed about it. "It's supposed to be for fat guys," he said. "Or old people."

"You're not fat," Mom said then. "Or old. It's genetic. You're still my hunk of beef." He lifted her onto the kitchen counter for a kiss then, the same kitchen counter that Lizzie was making a mess of now.

I picked up the empty orange pill bottle, and the print on the side was pretty clear about the danger of an overdose. I thought we had hidden all the household poisons, but we hadn't considered Dad's gout medication a poison. I'd just read in a pamphlet in Ms. Bernstein's office that drug overdoses are the second most common tragic teen deaths, second only to car accidents. I tried to take the mixing bowl from my sister, and she pushed me down, knocking me to the floor. She was strong in her sleep.

"Lizzie," I pleaded. "You'll *die.*"

Lizzie picked the bowl up off the counter, put the goop into the freezer, and headed back to bed. My chest lifted in relief. I opened the freezer and dumped the purple slop in the trash.

In the morning, I'd have to tell Dad what she'd done, would have to explain why his pills were missing. When he didn't take his meds, his gout acted up, and he could barely walk down the stairs. His stiff movements scared me; I didn't like to think of my dad as an old man.

Dad was mad about the gout pills, and he warned Lizzie that she had two strikes.

"Are you trying to poison yourself?" I asked her. "Are you trying to poison us?"

"Sleepwalking isn't like that; I'm not *trying* to do anything. No one understands."

"I understand," I said, but of course I didn't.

12.
~~November,~~ December

By the end of the week, Dad was back on his gout medication and in a much better mood. He bought a barbecue smoker for the backyard, a Big John E-Z Way Roaster. He said he'd always wanted to have a winter pig roast, and Mom had never let him. He ordered a two-hundred-pound swine from a farmer in Georgia. Dad said we'd go pick it up on Saturday, after we went to Dad's friend's funeral.

"I've realized that life is short," he said; that was why he'd bought the smoker.

One of Dad's bowling buddies had died, a heart attack. Dad had stopped going to bowling night since the alley didn't allow the parrot, but he insisted he was still part of the team.

"Bernie's wife died last spring," Dad told us. "That happens to men; strokes and heart attacks the first year after their wife goes. My doctor gave me a pamphlet, how to keep stress low."

"Good thing Ernest gives you something to live for," Lizzie said, but I think it was sarcastic.

"Good thing," Dad agreed.

On Saturday, we walked through the staggered rows of gravestones to get to the plot near the back of the cemetery. I read the epitaphs, engravings that read *Gone to Sleep with Jesus,* or *My Love Will Not Let Me Go.*

"I love the cemetery. It's every holiday at once."

I saw what Lizzie meant. Some gravestones were decorated with Pilgrim hats and turkey drawings left over from Thanksgiving, which we hadn't celebrated this year. There were Christmas wreaths looped around many of the headstones, and some were draped with strings of Christmas lights. Other more forgotten gravestones were decorated with little ceramic chicks and fake silk tulips for Easter, and there was an empty heart-shaped box of chocolates at the base of another grave, and a Mardi Gras mask wrapped around the statue of an angel.

Dad was wearing a suit. Lizzie and I wore black dresses, and Lizzie held the helium balloons she'd bought at the grocery store that read *I'm Sorry for Your Loss.* "I can't believe they sell those," Dad had said, but he'd let her buy them.

There were about twenty people at the funeral, sitting in white plastic chairs around the casket, which looked like it was made of balsa wood. Elvis Presley's casket was said to have weighed 650 pounds and been too heavy for four men to lift.

The groundskeeper drove up then on his riding mower. Boomer had picked up a little stuffed bear off the gravestone of a Vietnam War soldier, was shaking it violently between his jaws, but the groundskeeper was more upset by the balloons Lizzie had tied around her wrist.

"No balloons in the graveyard," the groundskeeper said, "and please don't kiss the headstones." On the walk in, I had been kissing all the headstones marking the graves of children. I noticed that lots of babies had died in the 1800s.

"The balloons are for him," I protested, pointing to the casket.

"Balloons kill wildlife," he said, taking off his workman's gloves. I hadn't thought of that. He reached into his back pocket and pulled out a knife. Then he grabbed the balloon strings and stabbed the biggest blade on his Swiss army knife into each of the three helium balloons. He handed Lizzie their limp silver carcasses.

"Let's get started then," Father Tillman announced to the crowd. He gave a speech, or I guess it's called a sermon, and everyone said a silent prayer for the deceased. It was nice, I thought; we hadn't had anything like that for Mom. There was music even, a shrill recording of bagpipes playing "Amazing Grace."

I decided then that I didn't want to be cremated. I wanted to go into the ground, skin and all. I wanted a copper-lined casket, like Elvis Presley had. I wanted someone to come decorate my tombstone during the holidays, to leave silk flowers and Christmas ornaments. Maybe Lizzie could do it, if she outlived me.

We went straight to Hog's End Farm after the funeral, and the farmer said he was going to throw in a few jars of pickled feet as a thank-you for buying a whole hog. He said most people around here wanted bacon or sausage prepackaged now, and no one was buying whole pigs or even half pigs. He had a lot of extra pig feet on hand.

The farmer gave us a tour of the farm, which had won several prizes in *Butcher's Paper* magazine. A new litter of piglets had just been born, squirming and pushing one another with their tiny forked hooves, fighting for a space at their mom's teats. The sow kept her eyes closed the whole time, flicking her short tail. There was a heat lamp set up in the stall, since the farmer said piglets born in December can get sick if they're cold.

"Where's Papa going with that ax?" Dad said, in a horror show voice. It was the first line of *Charlotte's Web,* Mom's favorite book.

The farmer helped Dad load the Saran-Wrapped pig into the truck. He explained that our hog would have to cook for twenty-four to twenty-six hours, which would mean roasting it overnight. He wished us good luck, and gave us each a jar of pig's feet, and a big bag of dried pig ears for Boomer to chew.

On the drive home, Dad stopped to buy a new set of sharp knives to remove the fat from the pig. He also needed a half-dozen bottles of barbecue sauce and yellow mustard to rub on as a marinade, and a few rolls of aluminum foil. The farmer had recommended injecting the pig with apple juice, but Dad had no idea where to get a meat syringe.

"Pigs are as smart as three-year-old children," I said, while Lizzie, Boomer, and I waited in the back of the truck in the Stop 'n' Save parking lot.

"I'd eat a kindergartener." Lizzie smiled, slapping the hog on its side.

"Ew," I said. "I wouldn't."

"You've always been the good sister."

"You're the brave one," I said. "And the pretty one."

"I'm not so brave."

"You are."

"Remember how you asked me after we left the morgue if I was scared?"

"Yeah."

"I'm scared now," Lizzie said, stroking the pig next to her.

"Of what?"

"That I might do something really bad in my sleep."

"Worse than the poison gout cake?" That was what we'd started calling the slop she had made earlier in the week. It had almost become a family joke.

"Yeah," she said. "Worse."

We could see Dad coming through the parking lot then with his hands full of groceries. "Don't tell him," she whispered. "Pretend everything is fine."

"Okay," I said, and we pinkie-swore on it.

That night we sat in lawn chairs, all

bundled up in blankets, watching the black barrel of the smoker. Lizzie snuck me a beer, my first beer ever, although I knew Lizzie had been taking Dad's Bud Lights for years. I didn't like the taste much, but the bubbles popped yellow explosions on my tongue.

13.

In the morning, I felt better than I had in a while, more clearheaded after sleeping eight hours. I decided I'd tell Dad about what Lizzie had said in the truck, that she was scared. I'd pinkie-sworn I wouldn't, but she seemed like she really needed help. Dad was our remaining parent; he should be the one to deal with it.

But when I went into Dad's room, he grabbed me into a bear hug. He was wearing a holiday sweatshirt with a Santa on the front, and the house stunk of bacon grease. Boomer's tail wagged so hard his whole body wiggled. I had not seen either Dad or the dog that happy since before Mom died. I didn't want to ruin it.

We went into Lizzie's room together, and Dad jumped up and down on her bed like a little kid. He yanked off her covers, but Lizzie snatched them back. She was half-naked under there, so Dad looked away fast.

She told us to leave her alone, said we could go check on the pig without her.

"It still has a few hours to go," she mumbled, pulling her covers back from Dad. "Wake me up then."

"Okay, grumpy," Dad said. "Let's go, Elvis."

I'd never seen Lizzie that tired. She was almost always out of bed before Dad and I were, usually in the shower or making breakfast. Maybe Lizzie remembered a sliver of the night before. Maybe she had a new strange taste in her mouth, something lingering on her tongue. Maybe she wanted just one more minute of rest before Dad and I would see what we saw.

Brilliant blue feathers were dusted around the kitchen. Dad grabbed a feather off the counter and screamed.

Dad stormed back toward Lizzie's room. I didn't try to stop him, didn't hold on to one of his legs. I turned on the sink and tried to wash a cluster of feathers down the drain. I saw that she'd plugged the oven in; I dreaded what I would find in there.

"Hello," said Mom's voice from inside the trash can, followed by a rapping. "Hello, hello." I opened the silver lid. Ernest was sitting in the trash, plucked half-bald, not a scratch on him. If Lizzie had a taste in her mouth that morning, it was only the fluff of parrot feathers, or the copper taste of her own blood.

Later that afternoon, a Pepto-Bismol-pink van with a fluffy white cloud painted on the side showed up in our driveway. Dad had felt bad after he'd found out that Ernest was still alive, but he still made the phone call to the hospital.

"Two months is no time at all," Dad promised, as the two men restrained Lizzie. They'd had to take the hinges off the bathroom door to get to her; she'd locked herself in. When they opened the door, she looked like a wild, cornered raccoon.

The website said that St. Cloud's specialized in addictive disorders and depression. Lizzie would be put in the girls' ward, which was for ages twelve to seventeen. I didn't know what they did with crazy girls under twelve; maybe real craziness set in later.

I wouldn't be twelve years old until after month eighteen on the grieving chart, and that was a whole year away. Then again, it had been six months already, so the year might go by quick.

"It's going to help her," Dad said. "It has to. She's a danger to herself and to others."

We were in way over our heads; I knew we

needed a last resort. I just wished we had something better than to send her away to St. Cloud's. Lizzie wouldn't even look at us when they carted her off.

I hoped Lizzie wouldn't stay mad forever. Maybe like an otter pulled from an oil spill and then drenched in Dawn dish soap, she hadn't known she was being saved.

■ ■ ■ ■

Part II
Months 7 to 12

■ ■ ■ ■

14.
~~December,~~ January

We weren't allowed to visit Lizzie, weren't allowed to call. We could write letters and send care packages, but there was a long list of things we weren't allowed to send: toenail clippers, shoelaces, razor blades, sharp or heavy objects of any kind, magazines or books, photos or baked goods, anything that might remind her too much of home. Flip-flops had recently become off-limits, after one girl had tried to use the rubber straps to hang herself.

Lizzie didn't respond to any of Dad's letters, but she sent me doodles that she made in her art class; there were several sketches of Boomer.

"Why would she draw Boomer?" I asked Dad. "She doesn't even really like Boomer."

"He's her dog too," Dad reminded me.

She sent a self-portrait, one of her and Boomer together. In the drawing, Lizzie is feeding Boomer a huge steak. *Why are you doing this?* Boomer thinks, in a cartoon bubble.

I pinned Lizzie's drawing on the wall next to my grieving chart, but I didn't know what she was trying to say. The Beaver Elementary art teacher said not all art had meaning, but I knew Lizzie meant something by the picture. I just couldn't figure out what.

Dad was still wearing Mom's lipstick when he thought nobody would notice. He wore her bathrobe around the house too, changing into it as soon as he got home from work. He carried Ernest around in his arms; the half-naked parrot was always looking for a warm spot. Dad asked one night if maybe I could make Ernest a sweater. "A late Christmas present?" he asked.

"I can't knit."

We had not celebrated Christmas. It had come and gone like any other Monday, except with more pork sandwiches.

Dad went out the next day and bought an argyle sweater at Debbie's Petland. It was meant for a miniature Yorkshire terrier or one of the smaller Chihuahuas. "But look!" Dad smiled. "Look how well it fits!" Ernest toddled in a little circle.

New Year's Eve came, and New Year's Day, and then my birthday on January 8th. I turned eleven, and there was no rabbit cake for the first year ever. I waited for Dad to say something that morning, but he went to work with the parrot dressed in his new tiny sweater, his wings poking out through the sleeves. Dad wiped off his lipstick before he left the house, using some of Mom's cold cream. I felt sadder and lonelier than I ever had before. Mom would have woken me up with cake and presents, and Lizzie would have at least remembered.

The morning newscaster on TV wished Elvis a happy birthday, but she meant Presley. I didn't see the point of celebrating a dead person's birthday. We hadn't celebrated Mom's when it had come in the fall. I pinched my arm and wondered if I really had been Elvis Presley in a past life, his soul trapped in my skin. Mom used to say that I could expect challenges, consequences that came with possessing Elvis Presley's former spirit. Some mornings she used to fill a plastic pill canister with M&M's and Skittles. She'd tell me to remember to take the whole bottle or else I'd get the blues.

"You'll give her diabetes," Dad had warned as Mom sorted out the yellow candies. She always said yellow was the happiest color, said that was a fact proven by several studies. I was supposed to eat the yellows first.

I didn't know if I was depressed now, but I did miss Lizzie. I had let Dad send her away without a fight; I'd probably pay for it once she got home.

At school, we were building a life-sized sarcophagus of King Tut. Lucy Wiggins and I were in charge of the gold paint. Lucy had long red hair, and a birthmark over her left eyebrow that looked like a butterfly. When Lucy brushed her hand against mine, a shiver ran up my spine, but it was a good feeling, a good shiver. It felt nice to be touched. Lucy's mother let her wear makeup to school, and she was wearing this plum-purple lip stain that made her look like a dead person.

"Do you know that *narwhal* is Danish for corpse whale?" I asked her.

"What's a narwhal?" Lucy asked, dipping her brush into the Dixie cup of gold paint.

"You know, the whale with the horn on its head. Like a unicorn whale."

"My brother is crazy too," Lucy said. "I think that's why Ms. Powell paired us together."

"Girls," Ms. Powell said. "King Tut needs more gold leaf on his forehead."

I was building up the courage to ask Lucy what kind of crazy her brother was when

114

the bell rang. Everyone else rushed out to recess and I walked down the corridor for my regular meeting at the guidance office. Ms. Bernstein was napping when I got there, her nyloned feet up on the desk.

"Ah," she said, after she'd woken up and asked what I'd been up to. I told her I was still reading *The Compiled Studies of the Naked Mole Rat.* It was the longest book I'd ever read.

"Naked mole rats can live for thirty-two years in a zoo or laboratory," I told her. "And close to that in the wild."

"Oh yeah?" she asked. There was a little dried spit in the corner of her mouth.

"They live in colonies," I explained. "Sometimes up to three hundred rats. There is one breeding female, the queen, and then three breeder males. The rest of the naked mole rats are divided into two classes: warriors and workers. The social structure is like a beehive. That's very rare for mammals."

"Let's talk about your mother for a moment," Ms. Bernstein said.

"My mother wanted to put the naked mole rat in the book she was writing. A whole chapter for them."

"What did your mother do for a job?"

"She was a biologist."

"She studied these rats?"

"It's a naked mole rat, not a rat. Entirely different animals. They aren't rats *or* moles. They look like bald guinea pigs."

Ms. Bernstein nodded, writing down more notes on her chart.

"A queen naked mole rat will regularly kill some of her workers," I explained, "in order to assert her power. Every time a naked mole rat dies, the social structure of the colony shifts."

"How do the mole rats decide who is a queen?" Ms. Bernstein asked.

"No naked mole rat is born a queen. Dominance must be won. It's a fight to the death."

"Oh," she said. The timer on her desk dinged, which meant our meeting was up.

Going through Mom's research helped me feel close to her, especially after I discovered that the last hundred pages of *The Compiled Studies of the Naked Mole Rat* were scribbled with Mom's handwriting. At first I thought that was strange, since none of the studies in the back of the book were about sleep, or about prolonged darkness.

Scientists had found that naked mole rats do not get cancer, and some articles said that naked mole rats might be the key to

116

curing the disease in humans. The research found that the cells of naked mole rats never clump into tumors because of a sugary goo produced by their skin called high molecular weight hyaluronan. It was pretty complicated, but *The Compiled Studies of the Naked Mole Rat* explained it pretty well, and Mom had already underlined the most important parts.

"Did Mom ever have cancer?" I asked Dad at breakfast.

"She had a mole removed once," he said. "But it wasn't cancerous."

Dad was wearing Mom's bathrobe; he had finally stopped sleeping in his nylon swimsuit. Ernest was having trouble perching on Dad's shoulder because the robe's fabric was so slick.

"Do you think I could get a copy of her medical records?"

"Probably," Dad said. "But I know everything about your mom, so just ask me."

I felt my face turn red, because Dad didn't know everything about Mom. He didn't know about Mr. Oakes, about her affair. Who knew what else she'd been hiding?

15.

A week went by with no mail and then Lizzie sent a postcard, her handwriting so small that Dad couldn't read it even with his glasses on. It didn't help that she'd written the postcard in red crayon either, the wax not as precise as a pen. The postcard said a girl had a seizure, right in front of everyone. Everyone was watching *Finding Nemo* when one girl fell off the couch and onto the floor, her mouth frothing, her whole body twitching, her eyelids fluttering back. Lizzie wrote: *It was like a bird was set free in her brain.*

"A bird set free in her brain," I repeated, after I read the card out loud to Dad.

Lizzie hadn't been home when Mom had her seizure that one time, but it had looked like that: a bird flapping madly around in her body. One minute Mom was standing in the kitchen, and the next she was flailing all over the ground. Mom stayed overnight in the hospital, and the next morning she came home fine.

"The doctor wasn't sure what happened. He thinks it was stress-related," she explained. "So someone else can do the dishes tonight."

A bird in the brain was a much more interesting diagnosis than high stress levels. I knew it couldn't be a *real* bird, but I kept picturing juncos and finches, swallows and ravens, and birds even larger.

Ms. Bernstein had said once that Lizzie's handwriting was the mark of someone severely disturbed. I wanted to know if it was showing any signs of improvement, so I brought the postcard to our next meeting.

"How is your sister?" Ms. Bernstein asked, as I sat down in the leather chair facing her.

"Fine," I said. I showed her the postcard.

"Did the girl die?"

"She didn't say."

"It seems like important information."

I shrugged. I told Ms. Bernstein I'd seen Megan Sax at the Coffee Shack, where she worked, and that her jaw had healed completely.

"Are you afraid of your sister?" Ms. Bernstein asked.

"No," I lied, or at least it felt a bit like lying.

"Are you afraid of *becoming* like your sister? Or like your mother?"

It seemed like a dumb question when she knew the options were

1. crazy, or
2. dead.

I knew I didn't want to be dead. But I also knew I wanted to be like Lizzie, at least in some ways. Lizzie had once had lots of friends who loved her, before she'd broken her best friend's jawbone. I bet Lizzie had made friends at St. Cloud's. I bet she wasn't lonely without me.

"I think you're afraid of developing your sister's mental problems, and we need to eradicate that fear or you'll never feel in charge of your own life," Ms. Bernstein said, setting the clipboard aside. "Can I tell you a secret, Elvis?" She looked at me straight on. She made excellent eye contact, which they probably taught her in therapist school.

"Okay," I said, tracing my fingernail through the white sand of Ms. Bernstein's tabletop Zen garden.

"I live alone," she said. "I'm divorced, I've told you that."

"I know." Ms. Bernstein had seen Mr. Bernstein and her pregnant sister at the

Laundromat, and she had cried throughout our meeting last week. I had suggested she buy a laundry machine for her house, so she wouldn't have to go to Fat Betty's Wash & Dry, but she'd said I was missing the point.

"Listen, Elvis." Ms. Bernstein leaned toward me. "Sometimes I'll wake up in the middle of the night and hear a noise, and I'll think that a serial killer or a burglar has broken in. I'll panic for a minute and then I think — what's the worst that could happen? They'll kill me. I'll die. That's it. As soon as I imagine the worst, I can go right back to sleep. Works like a charm."

"They could torture you," I offered. "That might be worse."

Ms. Bernstein then requested that I meet with her every day, not only once a week. She said it seemed like I had a lot on my plate.

As I tried to fall asleep that night, I listened for a serial killer or a burglar, and wished I were afraid of the same things Ms. Bernstein was afraid of.

Without Lizzie, it was so quiet I could hear the bones of our house creak in the wind. I turned on the radio and closed my eyes, but could still see the neon-green glow of the clock in the cracks of my eyelids. A doctor hosted the radio program, and he was taking medical questions from callers. I fell asleep as the doctor soothed a hysterical woman with a strange tumor growing on her ribs. The tumor had grown long black hair, and the woman was sure she could feel a tooth in the mass.

That was the way Mom should have died, by some strange and incurable cancer. She shouldn't have died doing the same thing she did on countless other nights, something part of her regular routine. It wasn't like her, and that bothered me.

In the morning, I knew there was someone I needed to talk to, and her number was still taped next to the phone in our kitchen.

"Hello, welcome to Miss Ida's psychic hotline," said a robot voice. "The charge is three dollars a minute." I entered Dad's credit card number, and the phone started ringing again, and a real person picked up.

"Miss Ida speaking."

"It's Elvis," I said, as quietly as I could. Dad was upstairs doing his stretching exercises.

"Babbitt or Presley?" she asked, as if it were a serious question.

"Babbitt," I said.

"Ah," she said. "This again."

"What?" I'd never called Miss Ida before.

"Lizzie called me already."

"When? Why?"

"She was very upset about sleepwalking."

"What did you tell her?"

"I told her that she was working through both her worst fear and greatest desire."

"What's her worst fear?"

"Becoming your mother."

"And what's her greatest desire?"

"Becoming your mother."

I remembered why I called. "Miss Ida, do you know how my mom died?"

"Well, she drowned, didn't she?"

"What about the coffee grounds? You predicted Mom's death would be a suicide, that's what we were supposed to be ready for."

"Plenty of people have committed suicide by drowning."

"So it *was* a suicide?"

"Or it was an accident. Or a murder."

"A murder?"

"The point is, we can't be sure."

"So the coffee grounds aren't accurate?"

"We can always change our fate. Everyone's life has several possible paths."

"I don't understand."

"I once saw a vision of your mother's name on a television screen, listed in the credits. So even though Eva was never an actress, she could have been if she took a different life path. It makes sense. She was very beautiful."

I thought of Dr. Lillian Stone, and wondered if that really could have been Mom, if things could have been different. "Miss Ida, do you know what really happened that night?"

"I can't look into the past, and I can't talk to the dead. I'm not that type of psychic."

What type of psychic are you then? I wanted to ask, but I didn't. I'd been the one who liked Mom's stories about Miss Ida, about how she could read your aura or voodoo an old boyfriend. "What do you *think* happened?" I asked instead, because Miss Ida must have had an inkling. "Do you think it was an accident?"

"Most times, people die and it's no one's fault," Miss Ida said. "We will always wish there was something we could have done. Elvis, that's natural."

There those words were again, *natural* and *unnatural, normal* and *abnormal.*

"You can believe whatever you want about that night. It won't bring your mother back."

"Gee, thanks," I said, before I hung up.

I couldn't believe that Lizzie had called

124

Miss Ida, and that she hadn't told me about it. I wished I could ask Lizzie, in person, not in a letter, but she was at St. Cloud's. I wished Lizzie hadn't hidden things from me, that she had trusted me. Then again, I had never told her about Mom's affair with Mr. Oakes. I had secrets too.

Another postcard arrived. It was, again, written in crayon, but this one was more legible. *I'm in heaven,* she wrote. *Can I come home?*

"If she's in heaven, what does she want to come home for?" Dad asked, reading over my shoulder. I didn't understand either, and I wouldn't get it until a long while later. Dad put the postcard on the fridge underneath a magnet, like it was something to be proud of, a report card or a drawing. He hung the card glossy side up, a photo of a brick building that looked like a prison. *St. Cloud's Hospital for Women,* it read. *Rebuilding lives and families since 1878.*

The *DSM for Kids!* claimed suicidal tendencies were genetic, passed down the same way sleepwalking was, or blonde hair and blue eyes. In the week before Mom disappeared, she'd acted completely normal. We'd gone to the farmers market and bought seed packets; she had said we should start planting more vegetables, fewer flowers in our garden. She was making plans for the future, which the *DSM for Kids!* said was a good sign. But maybe she was suicidal, like her father. Miss Ida had admitted it was a possibility. Mom could have committed suicide, staged it to look like an accident.

I'd pretty much forgotten how our grandfather had died, since Mom had never really talked about it. He'd shot himself in the middle of his own sixty-fifth birthday party, and now I realized we had a family history of causing our own deaths, and that meant Lizzie was *high risk.* I'd seen Lizzie nearly poison herself with Dad's medication, but I hadn't considered that a suicide attempt.

I called St. Cloud's front desk and said I thought Lizzie Babbitt, a patient in the girls' ward, should be placed on suicide watch.

"Who am I speaking with?" the woman on the other end asked.

"Elvis," I said.

"And I'm Elton John," she said, and hung up. When I called back, the phone just rang and rang.

After I gave up on calling St. Cloud's, I searched Mom's office for a suicide note. I'd looked before, in the weeks Mom was missing, but maybe I hadn't been thorough. I flipped through all of her books, in case she'd tucked a note in the pages. I felt a little guilty that I was digging in her personal belongings, but not that guilty. She had been the one to leave it all behind.

16.

January was National Shakespeare Month, and Ms. Powell wanted everyone in the class to memorize a sonnet. I decided I would perform a monologue from *Hamlet* instead, after I found the book in Mom's office, some of the pages dog-eared. In the play, Ophelia falls into the river and drowns, but everyone thinks it was a suicide. It happens offstage, so no one can be sure.

"That's enough, Elvis," Ms. Powell said when I was halfway through my oral presentation, holding the human skull I'd borrowed from our storage closet. "They'll read it in high school."

So even Ms. Powell had her limits. She said I should stick to the assignment from now on.

We had the fourth- and fifth-grade winter concert, and during rehearsal the music teacher, Mrs. Cote, asked me if I would mind lip-syncing most of the words.

"Elvis is tone-deaf," Lucy Wiggins said. "It's not her fault."

"She's retarded or something," Aiden Masters added.

"Her mother died," Jackie Friskey said. "And she's not retarded." Jackie usually called the word "retarded" the "R-word."

"She's not singing," Mrs. Cote said firmly, and she made Aiden Masters go sit in the hallway for name-calling, but she didn't send him to the principal like she should have. I agreed to lip-sync, said it was no problem, and I felt happy that my classmates had defended me. I knew Mom would have stormed into Mrs. Cote's office and demanded that I be allowed to sing, that I be given a solo, so I was glad, for one small moment, that Mom wasn't around.

Before the concert, Jackie Friskey came up to me in the girls' dressing room and gave me one of her red roses out of the dozen she had. There was a card on a plastic stick in the middle of the bouquet that read: *We love you! xo Mom & Dad.*

"You can have the card too," she said when she saw me staring at it. "It's not my mom's handwriting. The florist did it."

I clutched the single rose's stem, noticed

it had been dethorned. I thought of Mom's handwriting, what I had searched for in the days before. A nice, neatly written letter that told me she loved me and Dad and Lizzie and Boomer, that she was sorry she was doing this to us.

"Thanks," I told Jackie. "It's great."

I didn't sing one note, just mouthed the words, and the parents gave a standing ovation at the end. After the encore, I found Dad in the front lobby by the bake sale table, surrounded by three divorced moms. Lizzie would have called them *vultures* if she'd been there; she said that about any women who talked to Dad. I pictured the moms pulling meat from Dad's bones.

"Where'd you get the flower?" Dad asked, once I pulled him away. I had held the rose for the entire concert, but it hadn't lost any petals or wilted.

"A friend," I said, and hoped no one else in Ms. Powell's fifth-grade class overheard. Everyone knew Jackie Friskey wasn't my friend, including me. She was just trying to be a good class president.

"A nice friend." Dad smiled.

I'd once overheard Dad tell Mom that he was worried that I didn't seem to have any friends. "Really, Eva," he'd said. "Don't you think Elvis should spend more time with other kids?"

"I think that's pretty common in kids who live in rural areas," Mom had said. "That's what you get for living in the middle of nowhere."

Freedom, Alabama, wasn't really the middle of nowhere. We had big fields and the woods, sure, and horses and cows, but if we drove half an hour to Auburn we had a mini-golf course, a mall, and both a Waffle House and a Red Lobster. We had a bowling alley and the water park, even if the water park had been closed last summer, and we had the second-largest zoo in Alabama. It wasn't like we were Laura Ingalls Wilder or anything.

But maybe now it was normal that I didn't have any friends. No one else in my grade had a dead mother. Maybe it was too hard to be friends with the bereaved, because Dad's old high school football buddies never came over to the house like they used to, even though all of them lived nearby. Dad had quit the men's bowling league. He didn't have any hobbies after work at all anymore, except talking to the parrot and wearing Mom's lipstick and her old sweaters around the house.

"It helps me feel close to her," Dad explained about the clothes and the lipstick, when I asked him why.

After I finished *Hamlet,* I took *Macbeth* from Mom's office. Lady Macbeth has a sleepwalking scene in the play, in act 5, and shortly after that she kills herself. Maybe suicide has always been more common in sleepwalkers. I couldn't find anything on the internet to confirm whether that was true.

In *Macbeth,* the doctor says that the sleepwalking disease is "beyond my practice," but that he knows that some sleepwalkers die "holily in their beds." I thought that meant the rest of the sleepwalkers, the unholy, the ones like Lady Macbeth, must commit suicide. Of course that play was written a long time ago, but Shakespeare was a genius; everyone knows that.

17.
~~JANUARY,~~ FEBRUARY

I was feeling defeated, as if I'd never find out any more information about the way my mother died, when I came home from school to a refrigerator-sized box on our porch. It was from a return address I didn't recognize. I went into the kitchen and brought out the box cutter and sawed the cardboard apart slowly.

Inside the box, a statue of Jesus was sitting cross-legged, his hands on his knees. Each of his fingers was made of a small dried fish, a herring probably, pressed into clay. The statue was wearing blue jean overalls, real ones — OshKosh B'gosh. His head was tilted toward the sky, his eyes Coca-Cola bottle caps, his whole face covered in individual fish scales.

"It's beautiful," I said, when Boomer barked at the statue.

The Jesus statue wasn't exactly a clue about Mom's death, but I thought it was a beacon of hope, a sign that I would figure it all out someday. Jesus was considered to be a savior by a lot of people; he could be mine too.

The fish scales flickered when the light hit them. Jesus had a child's blue plastic rake for a mouth, an abandoned beach toy. The rake's teeth stuck out in a snarl. Did the real Jesus ever snarl? His nose was a red-speckled calico scallop shell, his ears two nearly identical moon snails.

To tell the truth, I only knew it was supposed to be Jesus because I'd been there when Mom bought it. She had been waiting for the statue ever since we went to the Magnolia Community College Craft Fair last spring.

At the fair, Mom had gone looking around the booths for someone who could build a sculpture she'd seen in a vision during her meditation class. She finally settled on a boy with hair down to his shoulders. He was selling wooden carvings.

"Hi Professor Babbitt," the kid had said. "I'm in your Bio 101 class."

"Oh." Mom had twenty-four students in each of her two classes, and she had a policy against learning their names. She said it made her *biased in her grading if she knew which of her students looked like idiots.* "Do you work on commission?" she asked.

"Yeah, sure," he said. "I mean, I haven't, but I would. But it has to be Jesus. I only do Jesuses."

"Or would the plural be Jesi?" Mom smiled.

"I'm not sure, Professor Babbitt, since there's really only one. I'm a member of the College Christians Club. We're going to Haiti on a mission trip for spring break, and we could use another faculty advisor, if you're interested."

She agreed the statue could be a Jesus, which surprised me. Most of the sculptures in our house were fertility statues, round-bellied, ample-breasted women, Venus of Willendorfs.

Mom kept talking. She described her vision to the sculptor. She said she wanted the man, the Jesus, to be made out of dried fish, seashells, gray clay, and beach trash. She wanted him to look as though he'd walked straight out of the ocean.

"That's so weird, Professor Babbitt," he laughed. "You're awesome. I'll definitely do it. I'm taking a class on taxidermy, so preserving the fish for the sculpture will be a piece of cake."

"I didn't know we taught taxidermy," Mom said. "Fascinating."

"Naturalistic Taxidermy 301," he said. "It's only offered in the fall."

"This one's not a Jesus," I interrupted, holding up what looked like a wooden dog.

"That's a lamb," the kid said. "Self-portrait." He then extended his hand to Mom. "My name's Soda."

"I've got big plans for you, Soda," Mom said. "Masterpiece plans." She always knew what people needed to hear.

I wished Mom had stuck around long enough to see the Jesus statue. I lifted it and dragged it into the house. I could carry it on my own without much of a problem; the statue was lighter than it looked. The torso was made of papier-mâché. I took it all the way upstairs.

"What in the hell is that?" Dad asked, meeting me at the top of the stairs.

"It's Mom's statue," I said. "It cost seven hundred dollars."

"Sheesh," he said. "That is ugly."

Dad wanted me to leave the Jesus statue in the hallway, where someone was sure to trip over it in the middle of the night on the way to the bathroom. I volunteered to keep it in my room.

"You're sure? It's creepy," Dad said.

"It was Mom's."

136

In the dim light of my room, Jesus did look creepy, so I arranged a pile of stuffed animals around the cross-legged statue. I thought I was too old for toys, but Dad wouldn't let me throw the stuffed animals out and I was secretly glad I still had them. I couldn't find my favorite, Mr. Tequila the orange tabby, so I put another stuffed cat near the top. I'd read that felines could ward off evil spirits. I wished we could have a real cat, but Dad was allergic. Our fifth-grade class was on a campaign to get Ms. Powell to bring her cat into school for a day. Langston was an elegant tortoiseshell cat, named after a poet. He had his own website.

Even after I'd hidden most of the Jesus statue, the whole pile was disturbing. Many of the animals were missing their plastic eyes. Boomer liked to chew those off, leaving white cotton stuffing spilling out of the sockets.

That night, I lay awake staring at the wallpaper, my back to the statue. I thought about Jesus biting into my neck with his plastic rake teeth. I thought about his fish-head fingertips running down the length of my body, measuring me. Maybe he'd want to crawl into bed. "Scoot over," he'd say. "I'm chilly." He'd press his cold toes against my ankles. Jesus's feet were two stuffed rainbow trout, one fish bigger than the other. My left foot was half a size larger than my right too; I usually wore an extra sock to balance it out in my shoes.

I got out of bed and lifted up Jesus by his overall straps and moved him into Lizzie's empty room. Ocean Jesus wasn't my savior. Maybe he was just another thing Mom had left behind to haunt us, like her voice in the parrot, like her unfinished book.

18.

Dad and I had started getting takeout fried chicken and biscuits almost every night, since no one was around to tell us how unhealthy that was. Dad let me watch the Animal Network as we ate, and we'd watch TV until Dad fell asleep in his chair, Ernest nestled in his lap. I always walked Boomer one more time before I went to bed.

One night, when Dad came home with the yellow takeout box, I realized how much I'd been enjoying these nights, and I felt really guilty. I wondered what kind of food they served at St. Cloud's.

"I bet the food's pretty good," Dad said, when I asked him. "It should be, for what they're charging me." He handed me the box of chicken and turned on the TV to the Animal Network. Ernest pecked at his buttered biscuit.

Wildlife Encounters with Dr. Lillian Stone wasn't on that night, so we watched an hour-long program called *Animal Wars,* a show that I usually avoided because of how violent it was. It filmed animals as they hunted. A lion attacked a zebra, a mongoose decapitated a cobra, a barn owl swooped down on a mouse. I covered my eyes each time something bad was about to happen, and asked Dad to tell me when to open. Dad said I shouldn't feel too bad for the victims, because not many animals die of natural causes anyway. That was something Mom had told him once when he was upset after running over someone's pet poodle.

After a string of commercials, we watched a troop of chimpanzees cannibalize another primate. The group of chimps ambushed the red colobus monkey, a cuter and fluffier primate species. The chimps used their fingers, trying to tear the little monkey apart. I shut my eyes again.

"Lizzie is going to be okay," Dad said then.

I wasn't sure why the monkeys had made Dad think of Lizzie, but Ms. Bernstein had warned me that Lizzie might not be okay, as if I didn't already know that. Every time I went to our meetings, Ms. Bernstein asked about the girl who had the seizure at St. Cloud's, the one Lizzie had written home about. She said it sounded like a drug overdose.

"You need to be ready for when Lizzie comes home," Ms. Bernstein said. "She may be a very different person. It's a good idea to find out what things are like for her now. If she's seen someone die, that would be very traumatic."

"We saw Mom," I said. "At the coroner."

"Someone Lizzie's own age," Ms. Bernstein said, as if she was annoyed.

Three days before Lizzie's release from St. Cloud's, Dad asked me to clean her room, since it badly needed dusting, vacuuming, fresh sheets on the bed. I hadn't spent any time in Lizzie's room while she'd been at St. Cloud's, except to move the Ocean Jesus statue in there. Ocean Jesus smiled his rakish smile at me when I entered the room. One of his fish fingers had fallen off so I threw the lacquered herring into the trash.

I filled a bucket with warm soapy water and rubbed a sponge on the wooden surfaces. I alphabetized the books on her shelf. I made Lizzie's bed and fluffed her pillows. The girls weren't allowed to have pillows at St. Cloud's. They were listed as both an *unnecessary luxury* and a *possible safety hazard* since pillows could be used to suffocate another St. Cloud's patient. I was sure that Lizzie had missed pillows.

141

She must have missed her clothes too, since she had been allowed to take only three changes of clothes with her and she had packed in a rush. Her closet was full to the brim. I ran my fingers over her corduroy jacket, her summer dresses. If she never came back, all these nice clothes would be mine, I thought, for one ugly second.

When I went downstairs to get more Clorox wipes, I found Dad in the living room reading Mom's unfinished manuscript in my red binder. I must have left it out.

"You've been working on her book," he said when he saw me. "I hadn't realized."

"Just a little." I blushed. The only really good thing I'd added to *The Sleeping Habits of Animals* was a study on dolphins.

"She was so proud of you," Dad said, dabbing his eyes.

Researchers had found that whales and dolphins sleep with one eye open, with half the brain shut off, the other half awake, so that the mammal can go to the surface to breathe every fifteen minutes. When a dolphin gives birth to a calf, the mother doesn't seem to sleep at all for the first month — keeping both eyes open at all times, watching out for predators. I knew Mom would have liked that research; it showed what mothers sacrifice.

She had been a really good mom, that was why we missed her so much. That was another thing that didn't add up: if my mother had killed herself, she had gone against her maternal instincts. Mothers don't abandon their young that often, not most mammals anyway.

"She was proud of Lizzie too," Dad said. "She was so proud of both of you."

Sibling rivalry *is* a big part of the natural world, in many mammals and birds too, and I hoped that explained why there was a part of me that didn't want Lizzie to come home.

Before Lizzie was discharged, the St. Cloud's doctor warned us not to talk about Mom too much. He said that it would stir up some bad feelings.

"Of course it brings up bad feelings," I said. "Our mother is dead."

I wanted to ask Lizzie about the phone call with Miss Ida. I wanted to know if Lizzie thought Mom might have killed herself, and I wanted to know if Lizzie felt at all suicidal. But the doctor gave us a list of things we shouldn't discuss with Lizzie while she was in what he called a *delicate state.* Suicide was second on the list, and death was listed first.

When Lizzie arrived home, she promised

Dad that she wouldn't sleepwalk again, not ever. "Cure-all," she said, poking a fork into her Styrofoam cup of noodles. She had cut her long blonde hair off into a bob, or her roommate at St. Cloud's had, and they'd gotten in a lot of trouble for stealing scissors from the therapist's office. Lizzie's hair was uneven on one side. "I hadn't noticed," she said, when I pointed the lopsidedness out.

19.

~~FEBRUARY,~~ MARCH

I waited for Lizzie to lash out. I waited for her to tell me that she hated my guts for letting Dad send her away, or maybe she would say that she'd missed me. But she didn't say much of anything. Instead, she slept on the couch most of the day.

It had been Lizzie who always ate the last piece of pie. It had been Lizzie who always got *failure to cooperate* comments on her report card. It had been Lizzie who stole beers from the fridge, Lizzie who hid an active wasps' nest in the glove box of a car. It had been Lizzie who had to be sent away to St. Cloud's for two whole months.

But my new sister, or the girl who said she was my sister, washed the dishes, and she never broke them. She put her wet towel back on the rack after she showered; she didn't leave it on the floor. She rarely went outside, and when she did, she always wore her shoes. She cleaned our parrot's cage three times a week, and changed his water every morning. Ernest's feathers were still growing in, but he chattered to Lizzie as she laid down fresh newspaper.

"Sweetie," he'd say, when she was done. "Don't you bite!"

In their monthly phone call, Ms. Bernstein explained to Dad that kids with after-school activities were less likely to fall into depression. I eavesdropped on their conversation from the phone upstairs, my hand over the receiver so they wouldn't hear me breathing.

"Elvis would also benefit from some time away from her sister," Ms. Bernstein said. "She's very caught up in Elizabeth's mental problems. It's not healthy."

"Her name is Lizzie," I said into the phone, before remembering I wasn't supposed to be on the line.

So that was how Dad decided to sign me up for the volunteer program at the Serengeti Park Zoo.

"You love animals," Dad said, showing me a map of the zoo. "And I need you supervised."

I'd never been to Serengeti Park. It was only fifteen minutes away, halfway between Freedom and Opelika, but Mom had said she didn't like it there so we'd never gone. She'd argued that while cages were fine for some animals, they weren't okay for the wild ones. All animal species had been wild once, I'd reminded her. Dogs were the first animals to be domesticated by humans, which made perfect sense. Boomer liked other dogs, but it was clear he liked us best.

"Unless . . ." Dad said, "you'd rather join a sports team or a club."

"It's fine, Dad," I said, crossing my arms, pretending not to be excited. I would have started acting depressed much earlier if I'd known I'd get sent to the second-largest zoo in Alabama every day after school and all day on Saturdays.

On the first day of the Serengeti Park enrichment program, we got a prison-orange T-shirt that said *ZooTeen* on the back. Most of the ZooTeens were sixteen or seventeen, ordered there by a judge; Dad had gotten me special permission to be the youngest ZooTeen they'd ever had. There was a van that picked up the volunteers from the high school and junior high, and they had to make a special stop at Beaver Elementary just for me. The boys wore pants too big for them and the girls wore shimmery blue-green eyeliner, the color of a peacock's tail. Our supervisor, Pamela, told us we'd have to write a three-page report on our experience, due by the end of the first ten weeks.

Pamela showed us how to clean the tree kangaroo cages. Each cage was two inches deep with pine chips that needed to be shoveled out and replaced. The wood shavings stuck to my shoelaces. The tree kangaroos stayed curled in their hammocks while we cleaned.

Then we fed broccoli sprouts to the bongos, a kind of striped antelope that lives in the jungle. Pamela explained that bongos don't have top teeth, only cheek teeth and bottom teeth. She said you could put your whole hand in a bongo's mouth and it couldn't bite you so that it hurt. Their noses were soft and wet like a cow's.

I knew that Lizzie wouldn't remember to take Boomer out during the day, and Dad would be at work, so I walked the dog for thirty minutes every Saturday morning before Dad drove me to the zoo.

"You're getting well versed in picking up poop," Dad laughed, when he saw me swinging a plastic bag full of Boomer's warm dung. In only two weeks at the zoo, I had learned that snake poop is white and runny, much like bird droppings. I learned that gorillas and rabbits eat their feces, so that they can better digest their food a second time. I knew that cleaning the waterfowl enclosure was the worst assignment at Serengeti. We had to drain the cement pond and hose it down and the smell was so bad we had to do it before the zoo opened.

The ZooTeens learned about feeding too. We chopped vegetables, peeled hard boiled eggs, doled out bowls of ferret chow, mixed in live mealworms for special treats.

"You should get paid for this," Dad said, when I told him about the buckets of fish chum we fed to the crocodiles.

"You signed me up," I reminded him.

But I liked the zoo just as it was. The rest of the ZooTeens ignored me, so I could always sneak off to the wooden viewing platform at the giraffe enclosure. The giraffes could come over to the tower and be at eye level with you, seventeen feet up. It wasn't open to the public, hadn't been since the male giraffe, Harrison, had gotten sick. He had a disease that caused him to lose weight fast, dropping to 1,700 pounds, bone-thin for a male giraffe; a healthy one should weigh between 2,500 and 3,000 pounds. An article on Harrison had been in the newspaper and that had helped with fund-raising. The zookeepers were optimistic. I always offered Harrison a banana and sometimes he'd take it, wrapping his long purple tongue around my hand.

There was always something to do at the zoo; extra volunteers were usually needed in Rodent Tunnel, the underground exhibit lit only by dim red light. The other ZooTeens said Rodent Tunnel was spooky, but I liked it down there. It wasn't all rodents either; there was a den for the foxes and the skunk, and those animals had cages on the surface as well, doggie doors to connect them to their outdoor enclosures. There was a long row of mouse cages, and a few moles.

I did try to avoid Rodent Tunnel on Wednesdays. The mice we had on exhibit in Rodent Tunnel bred too fast, so we fed them to the other animals, but that wasn't the part that bothered me. It was the way we killed them that I couldn't stand. The zoo had a no-live-prey policy because, on occasion, a mouse could kill a snake, or pull too many feathers off the kingfisher. We got most of our prey frozen in shipments from a company called Mice Direct, but it didn't hurt to have extras.

The instructions were to dump one of the mouse cages, shavings and all, into a garbage bag. You then squirted in some carbon dioxide from an aluminum tank, the kind you would use to fill up helium balloons for a birthday party. You tied the Hefty bag closed. Sometimes it took the mice hours to die; you could hear them peeping.

When I found out about Wednesdays in Rodent Tunnel, I came home and told Lizzie. She was sitting on the couch, watching a reality show about teenage mothers.

"It's terrible," I said. "They suffocate slowly." I told her about the trash bag, and I started crying then, and I was so embarrassed; we weren't a family of criers. But Lizzie didn't even look away from the screen.

"Can I watch *Dr. Lillian*?" I asked, once I stopped sniffling. "She's on now."

"No," Lizzie said. "I'm watching something."

She's mentally ill, I thought to myself. Ms. Bernstein had said that should be my new mantra every time I tried to deal with my sister.

I got up regularly in the night to check if Lizzie was still in bed. A habit like sleepwalking is hard to break, harder than quitting smoking; that was what the self-hypnosis CD said, the one I'd ordered

151

online. I'd listened to it while she was gone. Mom had never wanted to stop sleepwalking. She'd said it was good for the spirit, but she had thought all sorts of things were good for the spirit: pickled vegetables, stretching first thing in the morning, pretzels dipped in spicy mustard, and Dolly Parton's records, especially the songs Dolly had written herself.

There was a Halloween years ago when Mom had dressed both Lizzie and me up like Dolly Parton, with big hair-sprayed bangs and country music outfits, makeup heavy on our faces. Mom had to pick us up early from school that day, because of the socks in the push-up bras we were wearing.

"Dolly Parton has a genius-level IQ," Mom had screeched at Principal Witherspoon, who put his hands over his ears like he was a little kid.

I wanted a genius-level IQ too, but I'd never been tested, other than the national assessment tests we had in school. Mom had said what really mattered was how hard you worked; Dolly Parton composed thousands of songs to get her career. I'd already written my ZooTeen supervisor three reports on the care of different species at the zoo, even though Pamela told me over and over that the after-school enrichment program only needed the one, and most people never completed theirs.

The zoo had a small library where I could do my reports as well as my research for Mom's book. I was in the middle of reading *The Reference Guide to Porcupine Anatomy and Behavior* when I came across a section of the book dedicated to relatives of the porcupine. A hedgehog is not actually a porcupine cousin, despite appearances, and the book got that right, but there was a text block about the echidna, or the spiny ant-eater, known in Australia for its four-pronged penis. The book was wrong there: the echidna is *actually* a closer relative to the platypus than to the porcupine, since both are egg-laying mammals, *monotremes*. Porcupines are rodents, and give live birth. They are bona fide cousins to the naked mole rat. I made a note to write to the publisher.

While I was mucking zebra stalls, I tried not to think about my sister, since equine animals are especially sensitive to fear and stress. I had missed Lizzie so much when she was gone, although I hadn't told her that, not yet. There was something so weird about her. I didn't know how to talk to her. Her eyes were dark and vacant, like the windows of an abandoned house. Her lips were chapped so badly I thought she might have a vitamin deficiency of some kind.

One Friday, before school, I asked Lizzie if she wanted to walk me to the bus stop. I thought some fresh air could be good for her. She hadn't been showering, and was lying on the couch with her hand in a box of Apple Jacks.

"No, thanks," she said.

"Gimme kiss," the parrot said.

"Ernest, tell Lizzie to wake up."

"Sweetie," Ernest said. "Sweetie."

"Huh?" Lizzie grunted.

"I know you called Miss Ida."

"Who?" she asked, still dazed.

"I know you called her, and she doesn't know how Mom died either. She doesn't know what happened that night."

Lizzie started shivering violently then, as if she'd been left out in the cold all night. Maybe that was what the doctor meant when he said she'd have a bad reaction. It freaked me out, to be honest, and I'm ashamed about what I did next. I threw a blanket over her, and I left for school.

20.

I came home that afternoon to find Lizzie's roommate from St. Cloud's curled up on the couch with her. Her name was Vanessa and she was older than Lizzie, had just turned eighteen. She had a tattoo of a rattlesnake around her neck and she told me she was a pathological liar.

"You're a what?"

"As part of my recovery, I'm supposed to tell new people I meet. It means I lie a lot of the time."

"Okay," I said. "Thanks for telling me."

"Vanessa's nice," Lizzie said in a dreamy voice. "Hey, what's that in my room?"

"What's what in your room?"

"It's a man," Lizzie said. "A silver man."

"It's a statue," Vanessa said. "Made out of fish. I saw it when I put my suitcase down in there. I asked Lizzie about it; she said she'd never seen it before."

I had forgotten to move Ocean Jesus out

of there before Lizzie came home from St. Cloud's. I'd forgotten about him completely. She had been sleeping in that room with him every night for weeks and I don't know how she hadn't noticed. He was in plain sight, sitting cross-legged in meditation by her desk just across the room from her bed.

"It's the statue Mom had commissioned," I said, feeling pretty spooked that Lizzie hadn't felt Jesus's red bottle cap stare. "I can move it back into my room."

"No." Lizzie shook her head slowly. "He's magnificent. Thank you."

"Okay," I said. "He's yours."

When Dad got home, Lizzie told him that Vanessa was staying for a week, that she'd just left St. Cloud's. Vanessa jumped in then, explained that she had checked herself out of the hospital when she turned eighteen, with her doctor's blessing. She told him too that she was a pathological liar.

"Okay," Dad said, looking overwhelmed. "We're always happy to meet Lizzie's friends."

Vanessa and Lizzie didn't move much all weekend, just lounged around watching old Tom Cruise movies. I joined them for *Vanilla Sky*. Lizzie laughed at the part when Tom Cruise smothers a woman with a pillow as she thrashes and thrashes for air.

"Kind of a dumb tattoo," I told Vanessa when we were alone Monday morning in the kitchen while Dad and Lizzie were asleep.

"Oh yeah?" she asked, like she wasn't mad about it at all.

"Do you know what's wrong with my sister?"

"They yellow-wallpapered her," Vanessa sighed. She explained that that was what the girls at St. Cloud's called it when a patient was frequently administered electro-shock therapy. "Fried her brain."

"Are you telling the truth?" I asked.

Vanessa shook her head full of dreadlocks. "Nope."

Snake hair, I thought.

"Fine," Vanessa said. "Here's the truth: she's on too much medication. She'll go back to normal if they cut her dosage."

"The pills make her better," I said, because Lizzie hadn't had a sleepwalking episode since she'd been home, as far as I could tell.

"Do they?" Vanessa asked, jutting out her chin defiantly, like Lizzie used to. I took a glug of Coke straight from the family-sized

157

bottle. The soda had gone flat.

"So what's stupid about my tattoo?" she said, as she peeled a clementine.

"Well, a rattlesnake wouldn't strangle you around the neck, they're venomous snakes. They're not constrictors, like a boa or a python, for example." The zoo's green anaconda liked to wrap his two already dead rats in his coils and soak them in his water tub for hours before he swallowed them.

"Who says I want to be strangled?" Vanessa countered, before stuffing the rest of the clementine into her mouth. "You know," she said, once she was nearly finished chewing, "it's okay if you were glad she was gone."

"Who?"

"Lizzie. It's okay if it was kind of nice when she wasn't around. She's a hard person to live with, I know. I love her, but she's not easy."

"*I* love her," I said, as if loving someone were a race.

When Vanessa and Lizzie came down for dinner that night both of them were missing their eyebrows.

"That looks bad," Dad said. "Ugly."

"It feels good," Lizzie said dreamily, stroking her smooth forehead. "I look like my-self."

"Sorry, Dad," Vanessa said. "I got carried away."

"Don't call me Dad," Dad huffed. "I'm not your dad."

Vanessa explained that she had a hair-pulling disease, said it was a reaction to stress. Before St. Cloud's, Vanessa said, she used to pull out her own hair and make birds' nests by placing the tangled clumps in a tree. She said a starling laid eggs in one.

"You're lying again," Dad said. Vanessa had told us to call her out on it whenever she lied.

"Maybe she isn't," I said. "Starlings don't always build their own nests. They often steal from other birds."

"I'm not lying about the hair-pulling disease," she said. "That part is true." She explained that her dreadlocks were sup-posed to be a type of therapy for her. She could build something with the hair on her head. "The eyebrows were what we call a relapse," Vanessa said. "I'm so sorry."

"I'm not mad," Dad said, blushing. "Not if it's really a disease."

"I feel beautiful," Lizzie said, looking at her reflection in the curve of a spoon.

■ ■ ■ ■

The next day, I was eating lunch on the giraffe platform when Pamela, the ZooTeen supervisor, cornered me. I was worried I had cleaned one of the cages wrong. Some of the animals were allergic to pine shavings and needed aspen chips instead. But Pamela said the whole staff was impressed with me and asked why I was in the enrichment program anyway, since I was such a smart kid.

"My guidance counselor didn't think I should spend too much time at home with my sister. She just got back from the hospital."

"Ah," Pamela said. "I'm sorry to hear that. Is she still sick?"

"Sort of," I said. "It was a mental hospital."

"Huh," Pamela said. "Sounds like my brother."

"What happened to him?"

"Never mind, it doesn't matter," she said, shaking her head. She handed me a white bucket full of butternut squash chunks to give to the giraffes. "You should be good to your sister," she said before she climbed off the platform.

The two females ate the cubes greedily, shouldering each other out of the way, but they both backed up once Harrison approached. Harrison took one piece from me and dropped it into the dust. He nosed my chest, leaving a long string of snot on my ZooTeen shirt.

"Harrison," I said, putting a cube in my mouth, "watch me." I'd never heard of a person eating raw squash, but I figured it couldn't hurt me. The chunk was spongier, sweeter than I expected.

Despite my demonstration Harrison dropped the next cube. I chewed up another squash chunk, spat it back into my palm, and held it out, fingers flat. Harrison rested his lips in the orange puree, but he didn't lick it or eat it. The sign tacked up to the side of the tower said Masai giraffes eat up to seventy-five pounds of vegetation a day.

I wasn't sure why it mattered to Pamela that I was nice to my sister, but it was easier to be near Lizzie with Vanessa around. Lizzie was less like a lump of clay. She had facial expressions again. She looked more awake without her eyebrows.

"Earth to Lizzie," Vanessa would say, when Lizzie spent too long staring at the ceiling.

A week after Vanessa arrived, Lizzie asked Dad during dinner if Vanessa could move in with us. She still hadn't unpacked her little red suitcase.

"Oh," Dad hesitated. "I don't know if her parents would like that."

"I'm abandoned," Vanessa said. "A regular Orphan Annie. My stepfather thinks I'm still in the loony bin, and he'd try to kill me if he knew I was out."

"Are you lying?"

"No."

"Then sure," Dad said, cutting into the steak that Vanessa had made. "Stay as long as you like."

I wished I could be the one to wave my hand in front of my sister's face, remind her that she needed to remember to blink. I was jealous that Lizzie responded only to Vanessa, but somehow I liked Vanessa too.

21.
~~MARCH,~~ APRIL

Pamela gave me some more responsibilities, since she said I was such a good worker. One of my new tasks was to feed Nacho and Yoyo, our two California black bears. Bears are omnivores, so we gave them buckets of vegetables and dog chow, a cattle leg bone to chew on, and a platter of several fish, salmon or trout. Our bears were well-fed, so they wouldn't eat all of the fish, just the brains and skin, the fatty parts. A hungry bear will eat the entire fish, discarding only the intestines. It made me feel good that our bears never had to feel real hunger.

Once I was done arranging the food in different parts of the enclosure so the bears would have to hunt a little to find it all, I locked the cage door behind me and held my ID badge up to the scanner, which let the bears out of their sleeping chamber. They came galloping out, heading straight for the plate of fish.

Nacho and Yoyo had both been raised as circus bears. We tried to treat them as wild animals now and never went into their enclosure when they weren't locked in the sleeping cave. Pamela told me that sometimes you could catch Yoyo doing her dance routine, standing on her hind legs and rotating in a circle. Yoyo the Ballerina Bear had been her stage name. She'd been kept chained up when she wasn't performing.

Pamela said that Nacho's only skill was that he could smoke cigarettes, several at a time, blowing the smoke out of his big round nostrils. He'd drink vodka too, gallon jugs of it. The circus had said Nacho was unusable after he'd drunkenly mauled the trainer, which was why the circus had given both of the bears to the zoo. Once at Serengeti Park, Nacho had been forced to quit smoking and drinking cold turkey, which must have been hard, but at least he had Yoyo with him.

"Good girl, Yoyo," I said through the cage bars while she bit into her salmon. She looked up at me and waved her paw. It was another circus trick.

I was not happy when I came home from the zoo one afternoon and saw the rabbit cake pan resting on its aluminum haunches on the kitchen counter. Lizzie must have found it hidden underneath my bed. She knew my hiding places, even if her brain was fried.

"What's wrong?" Vanessa asked when she saw my expression as she sprayed PAM into one side of the rabbit mold.

"The rabbit cake is sacred in our family," I said.

"Nothing's sacred," Lizzie said, unwrapping a stick of butter.

"I don't think she should use the stove," I said to Dad, trying to remind him that Lizzie had almost burned the house down in her sleep.

"Leave them to it, Elvis," Dad said. He was sitting at the table doing the books for the store. "I could really use some cake."

Vanessa and Lizzie decided that they'd make two rabbit cakes, one for us to eat after dinner and one for their friends back at St. Cloud's. I sat on the kitchen stool to watch. When Lizzie pulled the first cake out from the oven, its head fell off, lopped right over to the side. *Don't be alarmed if the head falls off,* the rabbit cake recipe noted, the one Mom had circled in her *Country Living* cookbook. *Reattach with a hatpin.*

"What's a hatpin?" Lizzie asked. The head was in the rabbit mold, the rest of the body

165

perched on the counter.

I went upstairs to grab a few of Mom's old bobby pins, but stopped when I found long blonde hairs tangled in their pinchers. *Maybe they aren't Mom's,* I thought as tears welled up in my eyes. Lizzie could have borrowed the hair clips; my sister was always taking things that weren't hers.

"I miss her," I said to Boomer. He whined, and I realized he probably hadn't been walked all day.

Lizzie yelled from the kitchen, said that she'd fixed the rabbit cake with frosting. I wiped my eyes, and reminded myself we weren't a family of criers, not on Mom's side anyway. I came downstairs to see that the whipped icing wasn't much of a fix. Lizzie insisted it would taste the same.

"No," I said. "It won't."

Lizzie wasn't listening, her head halfway in the oven.

For the second cake, Lizzie and Vanessa mixed an unopened bottle of Tylenol and two permanent markers into the batter. Vanessa said that was how people used to sneak metal files or shovels into prison. I asked how Sharpies would help the St. Cloud's girls escape.

"They aren't trying to escape," Vanessa said. "Not most of them, anyway. Our friend

Colleen likes to sniff markers."

"What's the Tylenol for?" I asked. We had tons of Tylenol in our medicine cabinets, since Mom bought a new bottle practically every time she went to the supermarket.

"Headaches, duh," Lizzie said. At least Lizzie could still roll her eyes, I thought. She wasn't broken completely.

Vanessa explained that Tylenol was forbidden at St. Cloud's, even for period cramps. They were afraid of overdoses. But Vanessa said that overdosing on Tylenol is a terrible way to try to die. It is painful, slow, and rarely successful. Most girls at St. Cloud's wouldn't bother with the attempt, not when there were better drugs for suicide.

I wasn't thrilled that Vanessa and Lizzie knew the best drugs for suicide. "What about the girl who had the seizure during *Finding Nemo*?" I asked. "What drug caused that?"

"Antidepressants," Vanessa said. "That one was the hospital's fault, a bad mix of pills. Her family is going to sue the pants off of St. Cloud's."

"She died?"

"In my arms." Lizzie looked off into the distance of the other room. "I felt her spirit leave her."

"Lizzie has had a rough time with it,"

Vanessa said.

So Lizzie had seen another girl dead, someone her own age, like Ms. Bernstein had warned. Maybe that was what was so wrong with her; maybe that was why she'd turned so strange, so alien.

I wondered what it had been like, to watch the girl die, to feel her spirit leave. I pictured a stream of birds flying from the girl's open mouth after the seizure stopped, one bird after the next. The birds that had been in her brain could be free now, balancing somewhere on a black line of telephone wire.

I stayed up Googling all of the causes of seizures: epilepsy, drug overdoses, low sodium levels, venomous snakebites, high blood pressure, a brain tumor.

I clicked on the link to the brain tumor page. Other symptoms of a brain tumor included chronic headaches, changes in sexual activity, and new religious beliefs. Mom had suffered from migraines, was always popping pain relievers. She was having an affair with Mr. Oakes, a new sexual activity. She had ordered a Jesus statue, even though she'd never seemed to care much about Jesus in the years before.

"Yahtzee," I said to myself.

I ended up on the message boards at LivingwithBrainTumors.com. The user Stephanie9866 asked when she should tell her family, and how. She got 184 replies. Another user, LuvingHusband, posted that his wife was planning on killing herself to escape the last few horrible months of life with a brain tumor. LuvingHusband was looking for a doctor who might help his wife. No one had replied.

From my previous research, I knew that cancer was considered one of the best reasons to kill yourself. So maybe my mom had known she had brain cancer, and she wanted to beat it to the punch, staged her death to look like an accident. If she'd had a tumor in her brain, a lump the size of a bird's egg, it would explain her seizure, her affair with Mr. Oakes, her interest in the naked mole rat's natural resistance to cancer.

It would explain a lot.

"You have no basis for this conclusion," Ms. Bernstein said, at our next meeting, when I told her about the brain tumor. "Elvis, you're not a doctor. Where did you get this idea?"

I told her about the conversation I'd had with Lizzie and Vanessa, about the girl who had died. I said I'd then researched the causes of seizures, since Mom had once had a seizure too.

"You need to remember that your sister is mentally ill, and her friend Vanessa must be as well." Ms. Bernstein added that anyone who had been on a tour of St. Cloud's could tell you how troubled the patients there were.

"They let you take a tour?" I asked. "They don't allow visitors."

"I'm a medical professional," Ms. Bernstein said.

"When did you visit?"

"A few years ago."

"What was it like?"

"It wasn't so bad," Ms. Bernstein said, but I could tell that she was lying. Vanessa had told me that people look up and to the right when they lie. "Elvis, I want you to keep this brain tumor theory to yourself, okay? Your father doesn't need this right now. I want you to forget about it."

"Okay." I nodded. "That's fine." I needed more proof before I could tell Dad anyway, if he was going to believe it.

"Elvis?" she said, when I was halfway out the door. "Don't trust your sister, or her friend. You're smarter than that."

I didn't know what Ms. Bernstein had

against my sister, and I liked Vanessa; she didn't seem that mentally ill to me. She asked Dad about Carpet World and me about school, and she knew every single fact about Tom Cruise, even his favorite color. When she saw the *Guinness World Records* on the shelf, she said she knew someone who had a world record for most tennis balls held in a human mouth. The record was three, although a dog in Texas could fit five.

"You can make a record for almost anything," Vanessa said, as she flipped through the book. That got Lizzie's attention, and by the end of the night they'd decided they'd be world record holders by this time next year.

"Record holders in what?" I asked.

"We'll think of something," Vanessa said.

"Yeah," Lizzie added.

"I think it's a great goal," Dad said. "Something to shoot for." Vanessa reached over and put her hand on Dad's knee.

Late that night I heard noises in the kitchen, and I thought Lizzie was having another sleepwalking episode. I tiptoed down the stairs, a disposable camera in my hand, wanting to make sure I had proof.

But it was Dad who was out of bed, and

Vanessa too. I froze on the last step, and peeked around the corner into the kitchen. Dad's shirt was off, the parrot perched on his bare shoulder. Vanessa was wearing one of Lizzie's bikini tops and her SpongeBob SquarePants boxer shorts.

"Close your eyes," Vanessa said, moving closer to Dad. "I can be your wife."

"Close your eyes," the parrot repeated.

Vanessa unhooked her bikini straps.

"Vanessa, stop it," Dad said.

She pulled her boxer shorts down to her ankles. She had freckles on her butt cheeks, as if she'd been naked out in the sun.

"You're a kid," Dad said. "Put your clothes back on."

"I'm old enough." Vanessa took the last two steps between her and my father. I was about to scream.

But it was Ernest who shrieked first. He flew up off Dad's shoulder toward the ceiling fan, then dive-bombed Vanessa's head. He attacked her gnarled lumps of hair, beating her face with his wings.

I dropped the Kodak camera. It flashed when it hit the floor.

22.

Vanessa left on a Greyhound bus in the morning; she said she had an aunt she could stay with. That afternoon, Lizzie gave one of her pills to the parrot. I saw her do it, but there wasn't time to stop her. I ran to Ernest, and tried to make him spit it out. He opened his beak, as if he wanted to show me that the pill was already gone.

I raced into Dad's room, where he was fumbling with a tie in the mirror. He hadn't worn a tie since Mom was alive; she had always tied them for him, every morning. It hadn't occurred to me that he didn't know how to do it himself.

"Lizzie," I gasped. "Lizzie has been bad again."

Dad threw his hands in the air, dropping the tie onto the ground. But I knew there was something in his gesture that was jubilant too, before he knew her victim was Ernest.

We called the local vet, but she was not helpful. "I have no experience with that medication," she said. "And I'm a dog-and-cat-only veterinarian. Rabbits, hamsters, gerbils, sometimes."

So I called Pamela, and she gave me the number for the zoo's exotic animal vet. I introduced myself into the phone receiver in one giant breath, and Dr. Rotherwood said he remembered me from when the ZooTeens did a backstage tour of the zoo's animal hospital.

"Thanks for the tour," I said, and then launched into the list of the pill's side effects in humans.

Dr. Rotherwood said the parrot would be fine, but I could speed passage of the pill through Ernest's digestion track if I gave him milk of magnesia, five to ten drops in his beak. "You can bring him to the zoo on Monday, if you still want me to check him out," Dr. Rotherwood offered, before he hung up.

Monday was two days away. Ernest lay like a baby in Dad's arms, his gray talons curled in.

"It was good enough for me," Lizzie said from her roost on the couch.

For the rest of the weekend, Dad was in the

armchair cradling Ernest, feeding the bird squirts of water with an eyedropper. I thought Ernest might be faking it, remembered how easy it had once been to get Mom to think I had a fever just by putting a hot towel on my face for ten minutes. The bird liked tummy rubs.

Lizzie stayed in her room for two days. I made peanut butter and jellies for everyone, doled the sandwiches out separately. Dad gave most of his to Ernest, tearing the bread up into tiny pieces so he wouldn't choke on the peanut butter.

I thought it was clear by the end of the weekend that Ernest wasn't going to die, but Dad still dropped me off at the zoo early Monday, along with Ernest in his carrier cage. It was a good reason to skip school, I thought. I went to the vet hospital, a little red house behind the stables. There was a sick camel out front, his legs folded under him. Dr. Rotherwood wasn't in yet.

I walked toward the giraffe-viewing tower, since I had two bananas in my backpack. There was a yellow construction crane parked in the middle of the exhibit, peering over the trees like a mechanical giraffe. When I reached the tower, I saw Harrison lying sideways on the ground, a blue tarp wrapped around him, a harness fastened to his chest. I held the carrier close and ran down the stairs to the front gate.

Dr. Rotherwood was there to let me in, swinging open the metal fence. He didn't try to stop me when I bent to sit by Harrison's head, or when I stroked his bumpy face. The older a male giraffe gets, the more lumps grow on his forehead, formed by calcium deposits.

"Whatcha doin'?" Ernest asked, chewing on the bars of the cage.

"Harrison's body starved him," Dr. Rotherwood explained to the newspaper reporter who was already there. "His stomach wouldn't let him absorb the nutrients in food. He could eat and eat and eat but it wouldn't matter at all."

"Peracute mortality syndrome," I said. "Wasting disease."

"Star student." Dr. Rotherwood pointed at me.

Ernest made clucking and whistling sounds.

"Will the other giraffes miss him?" the reporter asked.

"We know elephants and chimps mourn their dead, that's what they say. But the female giraffes were out there this morning, nudging him, licking him."

I put my ear to the ground and lifted Harrison's whiskered lips to look at his black-purple tongue. Like bongos, giraffes have no top teeth, only a row of grooved bottom front teeth and their cheek teeth far in the back. I closed his mouth, and then I kissed him, right on his velveteen nose.

After the newspaper reporter left, Dr. Rotherwood and a few workers used the mechanical crane to lift Harrison's body over the fence, but then they needed to fit him in a truck in order to drive to the crematorium. An entire giraffe doesn't fit in a truck, not even a Dodge Ram.

One of the workers took out a chainsaw and that's when I lost it. I climbed on Harrison, gripping around his neck with my hands and my legs, and screamed that they'd have to saw me apart first before they chopped up Harrison. It took Dr. Rotherwood and two other men five minutes to pull me off since I kept biting at their hands. Once they'd pried me off, I spat on Dr. Rotherwood. I was aiming for his face, but I hit his lab coat, a big foamy loogie on his breast pocket right above the stitching of his name.

23.

Pamela said they'd welcome me back with open arms in a few months, once everyone cooled off a little. They said I needed some time to rest, to recover from what I'd seen. Pamela said everyone understood, everyone had been emotional that day. She said there was no reason that I should have had to be there that morning.

So after school, I was left home with my sister, which was okay. I didn't feel ready to see Harrison's empty pen, and I knew someone probably should be keeping an eye on Lizzie. Dad had taken her in for an appointment, and the doctor said we could lower her dosage.

"What if I start sleepwalking again?" she'd asked the doctor. He'd closed the door to the exam room, and I didn't hear the rest of their conversation. Lizzie wasn't sleepwalking again, not yet anyway. After a week, she was much more alert. Her reaction time was better. You could toss something to her and she would catch it.

She was baking at least three rabbit cakes a day, sometimes as many as six. She didn't frost some of them, and I felt bad for those ones, looking like those hairless sphinx cats. Others were elaborately decorated, with marzipan eyes and soft pink ears and marshmallow fluff for tails. The rabbits were everywhere, on top of the microwave, in all the cabinets. The goal was to be in the *Guinness World Records* for the most rabbit cakes ever baked, which meant we didn't get to eat them.

"They need proof," Lizzie explained. "I want to get to a thousand."

Dad loved the idea, and brought cake ingredients home from the Stop 'n' Save every night; he said it was cheaper than sending her back to St. Cloud's. After the first twenty cakes, Lizzie ran out of space to keep the cakes in the kitchen and started stacking rabbits in our bathtub. Dad went out and bought a chest freezer. He rolled it in on a dolly, and put it on the porch. Lizzie asked me to get inside to try it out. My whole body fit, and it wasn't plugged in so it wasn't cold.

"A little-sister freezer, a fifty-rabbit fridge," Lizzie chanted. "It's perfect."

I no longer minded that Lizzie was using Mom's cake pan. Lizzie was acting more like herself again, finally, so I told myself this was a new beginning, a lucky one. Baking during the day could be the thing keeping her from sleepeating at night. Maybe I never should have hidden the rabbit cake pan underneath the bed where Lizzie couldn't find it; then maybe she wouldn't have attacked the parrot in her sleep.

"I'm sorry, Ernest," I said to the parrot, giving him a shelled peanut.

The constant cake smell in the house drove me nuts, and I wanted sugar all the time. Sometimes I'd microwave a Twinkie and eat it with my eyes shut, pretending it was a rabbit cake. I picked up a fork one morning and held it over a cake, one I'd named Lemondrop, but Lizzie snatched the utensil by its prongs and chucked it across the kitchen. Dad didn't look up from his section of the newspaper, but I thought I saw him smile a little. He hadn't liked to see Lizzie acting brain-dead any more than I had.

While the rabbit cakes baked, Lizzie studied for her homeschool exams. The state sent the package of tests in the spring and you had three days to complete them and mail them back. She read her history textbook and the SparkNotes for *Of Mice and Men.* I was surprised to see her suddenly taking it seriously. Maybe it was because of Dad's suggestion that he re-enroll her in public school for next year. "One year of home-school might be enough," he'd said. "Don't you think?"

Lizzie told Dad she'd rather drink Drano than go back to Freedom High, and she took the drain cleaner out from under the sink to show that she meant it.

"Okay," Dad said, his hands in the air as if Lizzie were pointing a gun at him. "You're the boss."

Serengeti Park had six rabbits kept in a hutch behind the Safari Grill. We used them for the educational programs on Saturdays with the smaller kids, the youngest groups. Two of the rabbits, Steven Tyler and Oscar, were biters so they never left the hutch. Jessica Rabbit and Punk were the non-biters, so we'd take them into the air-conditioned barn and make the kids sit in a circle while the two bunnies cautiously crawled around. Rabbits will only really hop when they're comfortable, otherwise they crawl or they dash away in a panicked zigzag pattern.

There was a chinchilla kept in with the

rabbits too, a sweet one named Fisher. Fisher was not a biter, not even when the hair dryer got too hot on his skin. It was my job to blow-dry Fisher whenever it rained, since a chinchilla's fur is so dense that it'll never dry on its own. Fifty strands of fur sprout from a single hair follicle on a chinchilla. For humans the ratio is one hair to one follicle. A wet chinchilla will grow mold.

I was telling Dad about Fisher at breakfast when Lizzie said I could shut up already about the zoo, especially since I didn't work there anymore.

"You should look up what *temporarily on leave* means in your dictionary," I huffed. "It might be on the homeschool exam."

"Be nice," Dad warned.

Ernest interrupted the fight with a loud squawk. "You bad dog," he scolded. The dog lifted his ears. I was careful never to say *bad dog* to Boomer, and I never heard Dad or Lizzie say it either. But the parrot said it, sometimes directing it at the dog, or at Lizzie or me.

"Do you think Ernest knows what it means?" I asked.

"Sure," Dad said. "Absolutely he does. You know he doesn't like the dog."

I wondered if the parrot's voice sounded

like Mom's to Boomer. Dogs' hearing is sharper than ours, so maybe Boomer detected a difference in pitch. I hoped he knew that they weren't the same. I didn't want Boomer to think Mom had turned on him somehow, not when he had loved her the most.

Mom had always argued that Boomer was the best dog he could be. We weren't supposed to yell at him, he was too sensitive. "He's trying to be good," she'd say. "He's making an effort." Then she'd bury her face into his white tummy, weaving her fingers into his fur. Boomer's tongue would loll out of his mouth, his eyes wild with pleasure.

I wondered what Mom would think, about me getting kicked out of the zoo, about Lizzie refusing to go back to school, about the rabbit cake project. *We are trying to be good,* I thought.

Without the zoo, I was *at liberty,* as Mom used to say during semesters when Magnolia Community College didn't assign her any classes. With all this free time, I told Ms. Bernstein, I could do more research into Mom's mysterious death.

"It's not a mysterious death," Ms. Bernstein reminded me.

Dad had made me an appointment with

our family doctor for a checkup, and I saw that as an opportunity. After the nurse checked my blood pressure and weighed me, she left me in the exam room to change into a paper gown. I slipped into the hallway and went to the file cabinet, where I looked under *B* for *Babbitt.*

"What are you doing?" someone asked behind me. It was Dr. Agee.

"I have a right to know my medical history, and I want to see my mother's chart," I said. "Come on, Charlie." Mom always called our doctor by his first name.

"It's not in there," Dr. Agee said. "We keep the records of deceased patients in another room, and I'm not telling you where. Your father has seen the file. You can talk with him." His eyes drifted to the waiting room, where Dad was reading a magazine.

"You've seen Mom's medical chart?" I asked Dad on the ride home.

"Sure," he said.

"Was she sick when she died?"

"She was healthy as a horse."

So maybe Mom had gone to another doctor for diagnosis of the brain tumor. That would make sense. I'd heard Mom say once that she thought Charlie was kind of a dope.

Every day after school, I did more research on brain tumors, on suicide rates for cancer sufferers. When it got too depressing, I went downstairs to watch Lizzie bake. She was using *The Southern Cake Bible* to try out new recipes: a hummingbird cake, a chocolate cake called Mississippi mud, and then she went on a red velvet kick for a while. She bought box after box of red food coloring.

It was her sixteenth birthday on April 26th, and there were rabbit cakes all over the house, but she said we couldn't eat even one. She said first the rabbits would be in the *Guinness World Records,* and then someone would probably want to exhibit them in a museum, the Smithsonian maybe — she heard they organized new exhibits all the time. She said there was a 115-year-old wedding cake displayed in England, preserved in a box of silica gel, so she knew a long-term exhibit was possible.

"But that cake smells so good," I begged. I wanted to celebrate birthdays the same way we used to.

"You'll get over it," Lizzie said.

24.
A̶p̶r̶i̶l̶, May

When the homeschool exams arrived in the mail on May 2nd, Lizzie put commas in the wrong places on her writing composition. She was a terrible speller, and didn't have the best memory either. Dad said I absolutely was not allowed to help her, and I'd be in major trouble if I did.

Lizzie remembered very little about what had happened in World War I, other than that mustard gas had been used for the first time. In the biology section, I saw that she'd mislabeled the pancreas as the spleen on the drawing of a frog's digestive system; she was supposed to have dissected a frog at some point during the school year. I would have let her use my virtual dissection software, but there was nothing I could do about it now.

By Saturday, the homeschool exams were on their way back to the Alabama Department of Education, and Lizzie and I were playing poker. She had learned to play at St. Cloud's and she was teaching me. Lizzie said we had to start betting for money right away or I'd never learn. I had my piggy bank out on the table.

The phone had been ringing over and over all morning. Dad was usually the one who picked up, but he was at work doing inventory. The ringing didn't quit, so I finally answered it as Lizzie shuffled the deck.

"I'm calling about the statue," the caller said. "I'd like to have it back."

"Have what back?"

"The statue."

"What?"

"Jesus. I sent it a long time ago, but I want it back now. I need to borrow it for something."

"Uh." I wasn't sure whether I should hang up.

"The Jesus made out of fish? And clay? This is the artist, the sculptor. My name is Soda."

"I remember you."

"Awesome," Soda said. "I'm outside."

"Outside?" Jesus's invisible fish fingers tickled up my spine.

"I'm in the driveway. Can I talk to your dad?"

"Hey," Lizzie said. "Who's on the phone?"

"It's Mom's artist guy. He made the Jesus statue."

"So? Tell him to shove off." Lizzie took the phone from me. "What do you want?" Soda must have told her, because then she said: "And what will you give us for it?"

"It cost seven hundred dollars," I reminded Lizzie.

"What do you mean you're in the driveway?" Lizzie said into the phone, and then went to open the door. Soda was there in the driveway. He was taller than I remembered, skinnier too. He was wearing a T-shirt that said *Phish* on it, and stained beige cargo pants and Birkenstocks. He was wearing a rope as a necklace. I wondered if he had finished with community college, if he'd moved on to Auburn University, like Mom's smartest students did.

"Whoa, it's a mini-Professor Babbitt," he said when he saw Lizzie. "I'm sorry for showing up like this. I didn't think I'd have the guts if I didn't just come here and talk to your dad in person. I was going to knock on the door, but I chickened out. Your dad scares me."

"Why?" I asked, because no one was ever afraid of my dad. He was the hometown hero.

Soda ignored my question and explained that he wanted the sculpture back for an art show, one he was doing next month. He said it was the best thing he'd ever made, that our mom really brought something special out in him.

"That'll be seven hundred dollars," Lizzie said.

"I don't have any money," he said, holding his palms up as if to show us how poor he was.

"Well, we need something," Lizzie said. "We don't give out favors."

"We don't?" I asked.

"I have a boat," he offered. "I can't give it to you, but I could take you out on the boat. We could go fishing. I could show you where I caught the fish for the Jesus statue."

"Interesting," Lizzie said.

The Gulf Coast was only an hour and a half away from our house in Freedom, but I hadn't been to the ocean since before Mom died. It didn't seem like a good idea, but I really liked the ocean.

"What do you think, Elvis?" Lizzie asked.

"Can we bring the dog?" Boomer was on the couch in the living room, chewing on one of the pillows, which he did when he hadn't been getting enough walks.

"Sure, if you bring the Jesus too," Soda

said. "I'll help you carry it, no problem."

"No boys in the house," Lizzie said, and then she winked. "We'll get it for you. We'll be right back."

"So you'll come?" Soda asked.

Lizzie shrugged. "We've got nothing better to do."

We left Soda in the driveway, closing the front door behind us. "He's kind of cute," Lizzie said. "Jesus Christ protect me from porn, fornication, and lust. A girl at St. Cloud's taught me that prayer. That's only part of it, but I forget the rest. Something, something, Holy Ghost, amen!"

"So you think we shouldn't go?"

"Of course we should go," she said. "That prayer is a joke."

"Dad would —"

"I'm the babysitter, we're going."

"I'm not a baby," I said, and I knew now I had to go. I did want to see the ocean.

Lizzie and I carried Ocean Jesus down the stairs. The parrot wouldn't shut up, racing back and forth between the perches in his cage. Dad hadn't brought him into work that day because the office had to be fumigated for carpet fleas. "Bad dog," Ernest rattled. "Clever bird. Wow. It's okay, it's okay, it's okay."

Soda put Jesus in the front seat and

strapped him in. The back seat was full of buckets of seashells, and it smelled like rotten fish in there. Soda left the buckets in the driveway to make room for us, but the smell wasn't any better. "Pull your T-shirt over your nose," he suggested.

Boomer sat on my lap to stick his head out the window. Lizzie stuck hers out too, to escape the stench that had soaked into the vinyl seats.

"You'll get gravel in your eyes," I scolded. "You'll get beheaded by a stop sign."

"No I won't," she said, squinting her eyes in the wind.

Soda turned up his music then, so we couldn't talk much. He drove us to the Silver Sand Motel and Marina, which was on Lake Guntersville, forty-five minutes away. The motel was painted pink and blue, and every room had its own potted plant hanging down in front of the door.

"I thought we were going to the ocean," I said. "You didn't get those fish from a lake. Those are saltwater fish."

"Next time," Soda promised. "The boat's here now. And I did catch some of the fish here. All of the fingers, in fact."

"Is this a love motel?" Lizzie marveled at the motel's sign. "A pay-by-the-hour place?"

"No way, man," Soda said. "It's eighty

191

dollars a night, ninety if you want a kitchen-
ette. No pets allowed, sorry, and no AC
units left. Clean carpets, clean sheets."

"You work here or something?"

"Yeah, yeah I do. I inherited the place
from my parents. Front desk, shuttle driver,
maid service: I'm an all-around motel man.
Big weekend coming up, NASCAR race."

"I thought you were an artist," Lizzie said.
"What a let-down."

"It's really nice," I said, though I was
disappointed too.

"I'm a young business owner. Well, my
uncle owns it, officially, but he's never
around, he lives down in Florida. It's not all
mine until I turn twenty-one."

"So you do have money," Lizzie said.

"Not much," Soda said. "Not seven hundred dollars for the statue I made."

Soda parked in a staff parking spot. He
said we'd have to leave the statue in the car,
because Jesus might dissolve if he got wet.
We left him buckled in.

Soda led us down to the docks. His motorboat was at the end, the smallest one. He
asked us to put on life jackets, including the
dog. The carpet squished under our feet
when we jumped in.

"A leak," Soda apologized. "Carpet's got
mildew. But it won't sink, scout's honor."

He gave us both fishing rods. We'd never been fishing before but he said it wasn't hard. He would cast for us, and then it was just a waiting game.

We drove the boat out, bouncing against the waves. We were going so fast that Boomer's lips pulled back and showed his teeth, or maybe that was a real dog smile.

Soda slowed the boat and turned off the motor. He threw the anchor down, and then looked over at Lizzie. She had put her legs up on the side of the boat, sunning them.

"You really look a lot like your mother," Soda said.

"Yeah," Lizzie said. "I've heard."

"What happened to your eyebrows?"

Lizzie had a rash of acne where her eyebrows were just starting to grow back in.

"My roommate shaved them," Lizzie said. "She likes cutting off hair."

Soda looked at me.

"I'm not her roommate. I'm her sister. She had a roommate at the mental hospital where she lived for two months," I explained. I didn't see why Soda shouldn't know everything.

"Ah," Soda said. "My mom died too, a few months ago. I got a tattoo of her." He pulled up his pant leg. There was a tattoo of Marilyn Monroe on his calf. "I know it looks like marlin," he said, pronouncing it like the fish. "But my mom really looked like that, when she was young. She died in the motel, room fourteen. I'll show you when we get back."

"She's still there?" Lizzie said. "Is this like that old scary movie?"

"No, no, no," Soda said. "It's only the bed. The hospice bed, not the motel's one. It's a rental. The company keeps calling to ask for it back. Mom was also missing her eyebrows by the end."

"I'm not dying," Lizzie growled.

"It's good that you feel that way, man," Soda said.

"Did your mom name you Soda?" I asked.

"Nah, Phillip is my given name," he said. "My friend named me Soda because I'm always dispensing advice like a goddamn advice-giving vending machine, that's what he said. But you know, I've been taking advice now, I'm more open to that." Soda tugged on our fishing lines, which hadn't been nibbled on. "You know what my friend says — my friend Bill, who moved into room twenty-two after his wife left him — you know what he says? He says the only way you get over somebody is if you don't sleep where they've slept. Too much is absorbed during your sleep, and if you're breathing in their leftover spirit, you're not gonna move on."

Mom had slept in all the rooms in our house. She'd slept in my room when I was sick with a fever, and she'd done the same for Lizzie. She'd fallen asleep on the couch in our living room many times. She'd even slept in the hallway and on the kitchen floor when she didn't make it back to bed after sleepwalking. Our entire house was full of her leftover spirit, but I would never want to move away.

"I killed her," Soda said.

"What?" I jumped up in the boat. He was confessing to killing my mother.

"My mother needed a kidney," he said. "And it was my fault she died." I realized I had misunderstood, and I felt relieved, but also disappointed. I thought we were going to solve the mystery.

"You didn't give her a kidney?" Lizzie asked. "Don't we have two?" I was surprised Lizzie knew that, after the way she'd filled out her homeschool biology exam.

"I had the surgery, I gave it to her. But her body rejected it and she died."

"So you didn't kill her."

"I did. I didn't mean to, but I did. I meant to save her."

"I wish I'd saved my mom too," Lizzie

said. "But at least you tried to. I didn't do anything to save mine."

We were all quiet, and I stared at Lizzie. I had only heard her blame Dad before, never herself. I hadn't known that she felt guilty too.

"We had an affair," Soda said, looking down at the boat's spongy carpet. "Me and Professor Babbitt."

"No," I said, putting my hands over my eyes.

"I was her boy toy," Soda said.

"Soda," Lizzie said, sternly. "Phillip. No one wants to hear the things you're saying."

"I'm so sorry, I've been really sorry. I told your father in that letter I sent, but he never wrote back." Soda started to cry big sloppy tears, and sat down on the bench seat at the back of the boat. "I wanted to talk to him about it." It made sense now, why he'd said he was afraid of Dad.

Lizzie and I moved away from Soda, toward the steering wheel. Boomer jumped up onto the driver's seat. Dad had never mentioned the letter.

"I wish we could catch a fish so we could slap him with it," Lizzie said.

Soda held his knees to his chest as he cried.

"How old are you?" I asked.

"Nineteen," he said to his knees.

"Gross," Lizzie said. "That's way too young."

My father was at home breathing in Mom's spirit at night like a spider creeping down his throat and I knew that Mom would've laughed if Lizzie slapped Soda with a fish, as its eyes bulged and its red gills throbbed. People were so cruel to each other I couldn't stand it. I picked up the fishing rod Soda had given me and I threw it into the lake.

Soda had stopped crying, but he was still mad about the lost fishing rod. He refused to give Lizzie the key to the boat.

"I can drive," Lizzie said.

"Don't make me swallow it," he said, when Lizzie came after him for the key.

"You couldn't," she said. "The keychain is huge." He removed the key from the chain and held the key over his mouth.

"It would mess up your intestines," I said. "It could puncture your stomach lining. Lizzie, tell him."

"I'm an adult," Soda sighed, putting the key into his pocket. "A small business owner. I'm not going to eat the key; I just need a minute. You owe me a fishing rod."

"Okay, sure," Lizzie said. "We'll get you

another."

"Why don't you tell us about your affair," I said. Now that I'd calmed down, I needed to know. It might help me figure out Mom's death.

"If you really want me to . . ."

I nodded, told him to go on. Lizzie fiddled with the crank on her fishing rod, as if she didn't care whether he told us or not.

"Well, after she ordered the statue, I used to go to her office with every new fish I taxidermied. The first ones weren't very good, pretty messy. She said she liked to see my progress. And then we started talking, about my mom, about my classes, about a lot of things."

"Why did she want a statue of Jesus?" Lizzie asked. "Mom wasn't a Christian."

"She was a spiritual naturalist," I said, even though I didn't really know what that meant. I knew she believed in reincarnation, and in a God of some form.

"My mom wasn't that religious either, not until she got sick, three years ago," Soda said. "We started to go to church together. I got really into it, started making the Jesus carvings. After she died, the church really saved me."

I remembered when Ocean Jesus had arrived in the mail, how I'd thought he would be my savior. Maybe Mom had wanted something to protect her from cancer, and that was why she'd ordered the statue. Or maybe she wanted someone to protect her family once she was gone. "Soda, did she ever mention any health problems?"

"What does that have to do with any-thing?" Lizzie asked, turning to me.

"No, she didn't," Soda said. "But we did talk a lot about my mom's illness, about how dialysis works."

"Did my mom seem to know a lot about dying?"

"Sure, she knew a lot about dying," Soda said. "She taught biology." He said that last part as if it were something I didn't already know.

Then Lizzie yelled that she felt a tug on her fishing line. She had her line dangling in the water, from when Soda had first cast it. Soda leapt up and grabbed the rod over Lizzie's shoulders. He was hugging her, basically, his hands on top of hers.

"It's a big one," he said. The rod bent forward as Soda cranked the wheel, fast as he could.

"His mouth is getting cut up," I said, but I knew Soda couldn't just let the fish go, not until he reeled him in, otherwise the fish would have the hook lodged in his jaw forever. Lake Guntersville didn't look that clean; it was probably not a good place for a wound to heal.

The fish came out of the water all of a sudden, burst through the surface, flapping his tail madly back and forth. Boomer's ears perked up in surprise, but he didn't make a move toward the fish.

"It's a chain pickerel," Soda told us, grabbing the fish in his hand. The fish was long and thin, a yellow silver, with sharp little teeth you could see when he opened his mouth. I waited for Lizzie to slap Soda with the fish like she'd said she would.

"I've never caught a fish before," she marveled, wiping her hands on her jeans.

"Pickerels are nasty fighters," Soda said, pulling the hook out of the fish's mouth. "They eat each other. I've heard you can slice open a pickerel and find another pickerel in the stomach, and you can open up the eaten pickerel and find another. Man, so much for family, right?"

"Can we see?" Lizzie asked. "Cut it open."

"Let him go," I demanded. "Let him go now."

"I don't eat pickerel. Too many little bones." Soda tossed the fish back into the water and the pickerel swam away fast as he could, disappearing into the murky depths.

"Thanks," I said, though I only half meant it. I hadn't forgiven Soda, not for anything.

"Let's catch another," Lizzie said, excitedly. "One with bigger bones."

The sun was low in the sky and Lizzie hadn't caught another fish. I tried to ask more questions about Mom, but Lizzie told me to stop bugging Soda and he didn't seem to have the answers I was looking for anyway. Soda gave me bags of peanuts to eat; he had about a hundred tiny pouches stashed in the boat.

Soda and Lizzie had moved to the back of the boat, were talking and laughing. They were taking turns smoking from a colorful glass pipe.

"I thought you were a good Christian boy," Lizzie said, when Soda first took out the bag of dried leaves.

"From God's green earth."

"Are those drugs?" I asked, but no one was paying attention to me.

"You're really funny," Lizzie said, putting her hand on Soda's shoulder. He was telling her about everything he'd ever found left behind in the motel after checkout, including a blow-up doll and a live goat.

"She really had sex with you?" Lizzie asked.

"Sex?" Soda said. "No, no, not sex. She kissed me." He pointed his finger to the side of his mouth.

"Yuck," I said.

"That's not an affair," Lizzie honked. "That's not even a kiss."

"It was too," Soda muttered. "I told her that I was giving my mother a kidney and she kissed me. She called me Superman."

"Are you a virgin?" Lizzie asked.

Soda blushed and looked down at the water where the pickerel had swum away.

I realized then that my sister was not a virgin. She must have done it with Dave, her first boyfriend. That was probably why she'd been so mad when Dave broke up with her right before he left for college. I'd read in one of Lizzie's *Cosmopolitan* magazines that rejection after sex makes women crazy. It was no wonder that Lizzie had filled Dave's car with wasps.

I was on my third packet of honey-roasted nuts when we saw a motorboat headed toward us, cutting through waves so fast it was tilted high in the air. Sirens came on; blue lights flashed.

"Is that a police boat?" I asked. "Do they have those?"

"Yeah," Soda said, putting his hands into

his pockets. Boomer was still in the driver's seat, wearing his lemon-yellow life vest, only now he was barking.

Our dad had called the police when he got home from work and saw we were gone. I was surprised that he did it; he didn't usually care if we were out of the house during the day, but he said later that Ernest had been acting weird, reciting some prayer over and over, and that was enough to make Dad nervous. Dad always listened to the parrot.

The police had looked through our phone history at the house and found Soda's number. They plugged that into Google and his phone number was listed on the motel's website. It was the number you'd call if you wanted to book a room, so it was easy enough to find us. The police handcuffed Soda right there on his own motorboat.

Before the police boat took us back to land, Lizzie and I wrote down exactly what had happened on the yellow legal pads the officers gave us. We were asked to rate Soda's dangerousness on a scale from one to ten, with ten being the most dangerous. We both gave him a two.

Dad wasn't in the police boat, but the officers said he was waiting for us back on the dock. Once we were on land, Dad hugged both Lizzie and me like he'd thought he'd never see us again. He had already taken Ocean Jesus out of Soda's car and propped him up against a dock piling. The parrot sat on the statue's shoulder, pecking fish scales off of Ocean Jesus's face.

"Get that bird off the art," Soda said, wiggling in his handcuffs.

"He's a member of the family."

"I'm sorry, man," Soda said, turning his shoulders to face Dad. "I'm so sorry about Professor Babbitt. I wanted you to have the Jesus statue anyway, but now I need it back for this one art show . . ." Then a police officer pushed Soda into the back seat of the cruiser. Lizzie waved as they drove away. Soda couldn't wave back because of the handcuffs, but he smiled.

While Dad filled out more paperwork, Lizzie and I waited inside the front office of the Silver Sand Motel. An elderly woman, one of Soda's employees, asked if we needed a room, didn't seem to notice the police cars outside. We said we didn't, so she went back to her romance novel. Boomer hopped right up onto the couch, and we didn't scold him even though he was wet and there was sand in his fur and he'd get the cushions dirty. There was a rack of brochures for places to see in Alabama. Lizzie took one of each.

The office was decorated with taxidermied animals, wall-to-wall. It was mostly mounted fish, but there were also several squirrels and rabbits, a fox, three mounted deer heads, and, above the computer, a small black-green alligator. Its marble eyes stared down at us, its mouth a permanent grin.

25.

Soda wasn't charged with kidnapping, since we had gone with him willingly, but he was sentenced to eight weeks in state prison for the amount of marijuana the police found in the rooms of the motel. Lizzie was upset about the charges, said the police should spend more time arresting real criminals.

"He *is* a real criminal," I mumbled. I didn't really believe that, but I didn't like that Soda did drugs.

Dad wasn't concerned with the case; he was more concerned with how freaked out he'd felt when he'd found the house empty that afternoon. He insisted on having family dinners every night, and told Lizzie he'd do the cooking. He made pimento cheese sandwiches, shuffling around the kitchen in Mom's old fuzzy leopard-print slippers.

Dad was bending over backward to keep Lizzie occupied. He ordered her three new rabbit cake pans off eBay, so she could quadruple her production. He rented the extra walk-in freezer at the butcher's, and Lizzie and Dad transported the cakes down there twice a week. Lizzie began filling out the application for a world record holder.

"Projects kept your mother happy too," Dad told her. "That's why *The Book* was so good for her." Dad started to cry then, and Lizzie told him to go into the bathroom if he was going to do that. "So much like your mother," he sniffed.

I'd been neglecting work on *The Book*. I started going to the public library after school to work on it, since I could no longer work in the library at the zoo. When I tried to work in Mom's office, Lizzie would come in to read aloud another article on the war on drugs and prison sentences, or ask me to proofread one of her letters to the editor of the newspaper about marijuana legalization. I needed quiet to focus on Mom's book. I was stuck on the chapter on hibernation.

From the library computer, I wrote to some of Mom's old coworkers at Magnolia Community College asking if they had any advice on where I could get a grant for my research. I even wrote an email to Dr. Lillian Stone. I found Dr. Lillian's contact information listed on the *Wildlife Encounters* website, and I attached Mom's draft of the book. I got an email back immediately that read: *Due to the high volume of mail we receive, Dr. Lillian cannot reply personally, but you should try to catch her on her next book tour! Thank you for the support.*

And not one of Mom's old coworkers responded to my email, and then Lizzie insisted on coming with me to the library, which I knew would make working impossible. Lizzie asked the librarian a ton of questions about the law books, and complained they really should have more books on criminal law. Lizzie finally bugged Mrs. Reasoner so much she made Lizzie go out and wait on the porch until I was ready to go.

On our bike ride home, Lizzie and I went by the river. Some girls in my grade were there, splashing around in the shallows. Jackie Friskey was wearing a floral bikini and she had gotten braces, her mouth shining silver when she laughed. She looked like a real teenager. She waved when she saw us, and Lizzie took one look at her and said Jackie had definitely already gotten her period.

I only had a few weeks left as a student at Beaver Elementary, and I knew middle school was going to be terrible, even before I saw Jackie Friskey in a bikini. I wished there was some way I could feel better prepared for the sixth grade; maybe I could spend all summer growing a pair of boobs. I'd read you could eat more dairy to make puberty speed up a little, because of the growth hormones they give to cows.

Lizzie was not at all prepared for what came in the mail in a manila envelope: she hadn't passed the Alabama homeschool evaluation, so she'd have to go back to public school in the fall and repeat her sophomore year at Freedom High.

"No," she said quietly, as she read the letter.

My sister had been suspended from Freedom High four times before, in only one year. The school had a six strikes policy; after that, students were expelled for good. Dad said there was no way he could sell enough carpets to afford private school.

"Be my little spy," Dad urged, giving me the thumbs-up, after Lizzie went upstairs to sulk. Freedom High and Three Rivers Junior High were right next to each other; they shared a football field and a track. Lizzie and I would take the same bus.

After the initial shock of it, Lizzie wasn't as mad about going back to school as I thought she'd be. I waited for her to take out the Drano from under the sink again and threaten to drink it, but she turned happy for some reason and was sweet a lot of the time. She let me beat her a few times in poker, and I won back part of my allowance.

"It's going to be fine," she said, when I asked her what junior high would be like, but I could see in her face that she wasn't telling the truth. It wasn't going to be fine.

I already knew Three Rivers Junior High was a big disappointment for any nature lover, because there was only one river in town and the Chattahoochee wasn't all that near the school. There was only a small marshy swamp behind the gym, which separated the middle school and the high school. Lizzie told me that science classrooms were sometimes allowed to collect tadpoles from the marsh for dissection, but otherwise students were not supposed to go back there. She said there was a rumor that the high school principal had set free a bunch of water snakes in the marsh to keep kids out. "Cottonmouths?" I asked. Cottonmouths, also known as water moccasins, are the only venomous aquatic snake in North America. Lizzie said she wasn't sure.

"You're in fifth grade for two more weeks and then you've got all summer," she said.

"Don't worry about middle school now."

I was happy I'd have all summer to do research for Mom's book, and to continue poking around into the details of her death. *And soon I can go back to work at the zoo,* I remembered. Pamela had called and said Serengeti was short-staffed in the summer with so many people on vacation, so if I was *emotionally ready for it* I could come back to volunteer after school let out. I'd already gotten an invitation to the unveiling of Harrison the giraffe's memorial statue, and I was thankful not to have been forgotten.

26.

We were nearing the anniversary of Mom's death and the end of my fifth-grade year. I didn't have proof that Mom had killed herself, but I'd read that undiagnosed brain tumors were found in 2 percent of routine autopsies.

I rode my bike to the coroner and went to the reception desk.

"Most states do not require you to report brain tumors found after death," I said. "But I deserve to know. I am Eva Babbitt's daughter."

The receptionist went to get someone, and a man in a lab coat came out. He was the one Lizzie and I had run into in the morgue. I was surprised when he agreed that I deserved to know what happened during my mother's final examination. He pulled out Mom's file and told me to sit down.

"I didn't check for a brain tumor. We didn't do a full autopsy."

"Why not?" I asked, horrified.

"A full autopsy is expensive and time-consuming. It's very difficult to prove what happened with a water death, especially if the body has been submerged for some time," the coroner explained. "So we usually assume it's death by misadventure, and after what your dad told me about her sleep-walking . . ."

"Misadventure?" I slammed my hands on the table. "It wasn't an adventure."

"It just means it was an accident."

"But anything could have killed her, if you didn't do an autopsy. She could have committed suicide."

"Your father said she wasn't depressed."

"People commit suicide for other reasons than depression."

"Do they?"

I ignored him. "What about murder? Could she have been murdered?"

"I think it's most likely that she drowned by accident," the coroner said.

"What do you know," I spat. "You didn't do a full autopsy. You didn't even do your job."

I was so mad when I came home from the coroner but I couldn't tell Lizzie or Dad what had happened there. Dad would be angry that I'd ridden my bike on the highway, and neither of them knew about my brain tumor theory yet. I didn't have any evidence to present, and I wasn't sure Lizzie could handle it if I did. The St. Cloud's doctors said that patients often relapsed after four or five months, that we should keep a special watch over Lizzie.

"She seems good," Dad told the doctor when he called to check in. "She's baking." Lizzie had baked 413 rabbit cakes so far.

"What's the record?" I asked Lizzie.

"What do you mean?" she asked, piping white icing along the edge of one of the rabbits.

"I mean how many rabbit cakes did the current record holder bake?" I asked.

"I'm not sure it's an official record," Lizzie said. "How many do you think Mom made?"

In her whole life? I didn't know. Mom had owned that cake pan for a long time. I wondered how many world records had gone unrecorded. How did you really know yours was the world record and not just the only one someone had bothered to write down?

"You snooze, you lose," Lizzie said, when I asked her that question.

Lizzie heard back from the Guinness

214

World Records office by email. They said to notify them immediately when she finished her project, and they wished her the best of luck in reaching her goal. The email suggested that Lizzie finish the one thousand cakes as quickly as possible, so that they could feature her in next year's book. That meant Lizzie wanted to speed things up, so she said I could help.

"The designated froster," Dad called me, pounding his fist into his open palm as if it were a baseball glove. Lizzie decided that not all the cakes should be frosted, but most of them should be. I researched frosting ideas on the American Rabbit Breeders Association website. The ARBA listed the possible colors of rabbits: black otter, sable marten, blue, tricolor, champagne, fawn, lilac.

"I've never seen a lilac rabbit," Lizzie said, peering at my notes. "Or a blue one."

I found that, in ARBA terms, blue wasn't a sky or cobalt or turquoise blue but rather this rich, silver-gray color. A lilac rabbit was a softer gray, a shade that was popular in some of Dad's contemporary rugs, the ones imported from Sweden. Dad had a lilac-gray rug in his bedroom.

I wanted to try out the different tones of gray on the cakes, but Lizzie gave me only three bowls of frosting to work with and told me not to muck them together: a chocolate brown, a cream-cheese white, and a buttercream frosting dyed black. There was pink piping for the ears and nose, but not enough to cover a whole cake. I rolled a few cakes in coconut shavings, to give them that fuzzy Angora look.

While we worked, I thought about something Ms. Bernstein had said in a recent meeting. "Have you thought," Ms. Bernstein had said, pushing back her glasses, "that Lizzie is trying to replace your mother? She's baking like her. She's dressing like her."

"My dad's dressing like her too sometimes," I'd reminded her.

I didn't think Lizzie was trying to be my mother; she wanted to be a world record holder. She wanted to do something in a way no one had done it before. There were lots of other world records about cake, but Lizzie wasn't impressed by the world's tallest cake, the world's smallest cake, or the world's most expensive cake. Lizzie said anyone could make a single cake. "Who wants to be anyone?" she asked, and she had a point.

I received my elementary school diploma,

and both Lizzie and Dad came to the ceremony. Everyone else in my class had new clothes for the event, the hems of pink dresses and polka-dotted bow ties peeking out from underneath the black graduation gowns. I had decided I'd wear Mom's old bathing suit underneath the gown, since it was bound to be hot in the auditorium.

"Are you naked under there?" Ms. Powell whispered, stopping me before I processed across the stage.

"No," I said, and showed her the straps of the suit. Ms. Powell was still my favorite teacher, but it wasn't much of a contest. Most teachers I knew seemed hardly to like kids at all.

We got takeout chicken for dinner that night, since Dad knew it was my favorite. It *was* my favorite, but I felt guilty about it, remembering when Lizzie was in the mental hospital and Dad and I were eating takeout.

Lizzie dropped a wing bone in Boomer's dish.

"Mom says he'll choke on those," I said, trying to pull the bone out of Boomer's teeth. He clenched down as hard as he could, but rolled over onto his back, which he did whenever he knew he was being naughty. I straddled his belly, trying to wedge the gray bone loose.

"What do you think wild dogs eat?" Lizzie scoffed. "Boneless chickens?"

"Fine," I said, releasing Boomer's jaw. "He's not a wild dog, but fine." I looked up, and Dad was crying.

"What's wrong?" Lizzie asked.

"Mom *says,*" Dad said. "Elvis said Mom *says.*"

At my last guidance session, Ms. Bernstein and I had checked off May on the grieving chart together, eleven black *X*s since Mom had been dead.

Ms. Bernstein had given me the tarantula snow globe as a parting gift. She'd given me a quick hug too, even though she'd always said there was a strict no-touching policy in her office.

27.
~~May,~~ June

On the first day of summer vacation, I found a letter in the mailbox from Alabama Men's Penitentiary, elaborate doodles all over the envelope. It was addressed to Lizzie. The next day, another letter arrived. Lizzie didn't seem surprised by either one.

"How many have you already gotten?" I asked.

"So I've got a pen pal." Lizzie shrugged. "Big deal."

She asked me if I wanted to drive down to the butcher shop with her to fill the walk-in freezer with another batch of rabbits.

"Sure," I said, "if we can get ice cream after." Lizzie wasn't supposed to drive without Dad in the car, but we were only going a mile away, to J&M's Meat Market in Freedom town square.

As we loaded the car, Lizzie admitted that Soda had been writing her daily letters ever since she'd sent him some photocopied pages out of one of the criminal law books from the library.

"He's great," she said. "He's really smart, and funny. He tells me what Mom was like as a teacher."

"Don't forget he's a drug addict."

"Give me a break, Elvis. I didn't know you were a moron."

That hurt my feelings, so I didn't say anything else to her as we finished loading up the rabbits, but I don't think she noticed. Lizzie drove a little too fast to the butcher's, and she parked in back of the shop. It was a 97 degree day; my forehead trickled with sweat as I watched Lizzie fumble with the padlock on the walk-in freezer behind the butcher's shop. Lizzie wore the key around her wrist like it was a charm bracelet.

"Have you ever heard a rabbit scream?" I asked. I wanted to remind Lizzie that I wasn't a moron, there were lots of things I knew about that she didn't. Rabbits scream when they are in fear for their life, and the rabbits at the zoo used to shriek whenever a zookeeper walked Susie the bobcat past their cage. Susie walked well on a leash; she didn't even seem to notice the rabbits until they screamed. "They sound like a banshee."

"I've never heard a banshee," Lizzie said in a way that let me know I was annoying her. We unpacked the cakes in silence, stacking them on the shelves in neat rows. It was a huge walk-in freezer, and I could see how it would fit 1,000 cakes someday, if she ever made it that far.

I wanted Lizzie to be in a good mood again, because I wanted her to buy me an ice cream at Suzy Sundaes. "Lock me in," I suggested. It seemed like we'd been having fun just a minute ago. She'd been telling me her secrets. "Lock me in, like you did with the chest freezer."

"Okay," Lizzie said, her face brightening. "Okay."

I stepped up into the meat locker, and stood on the red rubber mat. When Lizzie closed the door it was darker than it ever was in my room at night. I blinked slowly, to see if my eyes would adjust. With my eyes closed, I could hear the rabbits. They weren't screaming, but they were making a lot of noise. Not cake noises either, real rabbit noises. They were snuffling around the corners of the freezer, digging against the walls, gnawing on the wooden shelves. I felt whiskers against my leg, a tiny-clawed paw on my sneaker.

I heaved my full body weight against the

freezer door and tumbled out onto the pavement, gravel digging into my knees.

"Jesus," Lizzie said. "I didn't get it locked."

"They're alive," I gasped.

"What?" Lizzie asked, wrinkling her brow.

I told her what had happened, but when we looked back into the freezer, the rabbits were just cakes again.

"You're such a little freak," Lizzie laughed, and locked the padlock on the freezer. Then she turned and walked into J&M's Meat Market, a bell jingling on the door to signal her arrival.

We left the car where it was and walked over to Suzy Sundaes. I was still shaken up from what had happened in the freezer, and then we ran into Megan Sax and three other girls whose names I couldn't remember. The four of them were wearing their Coffee Shack uniforms. They were all smoking cigarettes, except for Megan.

"Hey Looney Tune," one of the girls snickered as we approached. "How's the nut house?"

Megan Sax looked down at her pink-and-white sneakers, but she laughed with the rest of them.

"Hey Megan," Lizzie said, loudly but not

screaming. She pulled a raw sausage out of the brown bag she was carrying from J&M's Meat Market and held it up. "I heard this is what your dad's dick looks like." Lizzie took a bite of the red speckled sausage and then spat it out into the dirt.

The other girls laughed, but Megan's face puckered and she started to cry. Lizzie walked right past her, and I followed, wishing I'd never asked for ice cream.

When we got home, I flipped frantically through the *DSM for Kids!* I was upset about what Lizzie had done with the sausage, but I was also worried that I had seen the rabbit cakes come to life. I didn't want to be crazy too.

I found the "Hallucinations of Loss" chapter in the grief section. If it was completely normal to see the ghost of Mom, could that explain the cakes coming alive? I felt more afraid than I would have if I'd seen Mom's ghost; I had no idea if this was normal or abnormal. The *DSM for Kids!* didn't have the answer.

I made Boomer sleep on my bed that night. He was supposed to stay on the floor and off the furniture, but it was a rule not even Dad obeyed. I'd seen Boomer kill a squirrel once. He broke its neck by shaking it back and forth in his jaws before he disemboweled it, and then he rolled in its guts. I figured he could do the same to a rabbit, but I slept fitfully.

In the middle of the night, I heard Lizzie's footsteps in the hall, her feet loud as hooves. She was sleepwalking again.

28.

I didn't want to break it to Lizzie that the sleepwalking had started back up. Maybe she already knew, by a feeling she had in the morning, but I wasn't brave enough to ask.

"Why are you so mad at Megan?" I asked her instead.

"She abandoned me."

That sounded pretty dramatic, but I guess Lizzie probably did need her best friend in the months after our mom went missing. I had played fetch with Boomer for at least an hour every day that summer.

"You broke her jaw," I reminded her. "In three places."

"She deserved it," Lizzie said. "You should have heard the things she said to me."

"Like what?" I asked.

"Like what?" Lizzie imitated me. "Why do you have to know everything?"

I wanted to ask Lizzie about Mom's death

again. I didn't want her to start shivering, but I had to talk to her about it. "The coroner didn't do a full autopsy of Mom."

"What?"

"I went down there to ask questions. He doesn't really know what happened to Mom. He just guessed."

Lizzie gave me an irritated look. "The police said it was an accident."

"Since when do you trust the police?"

"Leave it alone, Elvis. You're beating a dead horse."

I knew that expression, I'd looked it up years ago when Mom used it. It meant to keep working on something that had already been resolved. Another way to say that, an older phrase, was to *slay the slain.* I really didn't like that idea. I didn't want to kill Mom over and over again.

I wasn't going to tell Dad about the coroner, not when it had gone so badly with Lizzie, and I wasn't going to tell him about Lizzie's sleepwalking either. He might notice on his own, but I wasn't going to be the reason she was sent back to St. Cloud's.

Luckily, Dad's mind was on other things. He was "focusing on himself," he said. He saw a new therapist on Wednesdays and then, every Tuesday and Friday after work, he applied a homemade honey-oat facial and let it set while he watched *Dr. Lillian Stone* with me. He let Ernest peck off the dried oat flakes.

"We're compadres," Dad said, ruffling the bird's feathers, which had finally grown back. Ernest dropped a fleck of oatmeal into Dad's forest of chest hair.

Dad's new therapist, Dr. Judy, was encouraging him. She said it was okay if he wore lipstick sometimes, whatever helped him feel less alone. "It's called psychological resilience," Dr. Judy explained during a family therapy session, one Dad had requested. "It means how well someone can go on after tragedy or trauma."

"I am going to get back into the dating game," Dad announced in the middle of the session with Dr. Judy. "I think it's time to get back out there. I have opened an online dating profile," he continued. "You won't have to meet anyone unless it's serious."

Dad did have a new computer, a silver laptop. He'd been spending a lot of time on the computer, that I'd noticed already. I remembered Mom's personal ad, the one Mr. Oakes said she'd put on Craigslist. I'd gone to the website to try to find it, but Craigslist took the old ads down.

"That's great, Dad," I said.

Dr. Judy gave me a rainbow sticker. "It's wonderful that you can recognize that your father is a person too, someone with needs."

I wondered if Dr. Judy and Dad would end up dating.

"I think we're all doing really well." Dad smiled. "Given the circumstances. Everyone's being a team player."

"Everything seems pretty shitty to me," Lizzie said. I agreed, but I didn't say anything. I looked down at my rainbow sticker instead.

At least I would be going back to the zoo, I remembered. Serengeti planned to unveil the giraffe's memorial statue at a big party on Saturday afternoon, and I was invited. Everyone was invited really, anyone who wanted to spend forty-five dollars for a ticket, with 50 percent of the proceeds going to giraffe conservation. But I got to go for free, and after that I would go back to volunteering. I could wear my orange Zoo-Teen T-shirt again, my photo ID badge looped around my neck.

Lizzie and Dad were both coming to the unveiling, had bought tickets; Dad's therapist thought it would be a good opportunity for family bonding. I warned them both in advance not to embarrass me in front of my colleagues. Dad laughed when I said that, but Lizzie crossed-her-heart-and-hoped-to-die that she wouldn't. It was one of her good-sister moments.

The morning of the unveiling, I went downstairs for breakfast. I could see Dad from the window, gardening out back, wearing Mom's straw sun hat.

"I need a ride to the zoo," I yelled out the door, and Dad sprayed the hose in my direction.

"Are you wearing sunscreen?" he yelled back, and I knew a year ago he wouldn't have thought to ask.

Dad dropped me off an hour before Harrison's party started, because I wanted to walk around the park first. I had been worried that some of the animals would forget me. Susie the bobcat was very particular about who she would accept her dead mouse and bowl of kitty chow from, but she rubbed against the bars when she saw me, pressing her forehead against the cage so I could scratch between her ears.

Lizzie and Dad met me at the front gate at two o'clock, and we walked to the unveiling together. The bronze Harrison was life-sized, seventeen feet tall. He had a round belly; there was nothing starved-looking about him. He gazed down at us with an amused expression on his face.

The zoo had ordered another smaller statue too, one for the prehensile-tailed porcupine who had passed away in March. Snuffles was only a minor attraction at the zoo, but the staff was attached to him.

As everyone crowded around Harrison's seventeen-foot statue, Lizzie and I ended up over by the bronze porcupine that no one else seemed to notice.

Dad had gone off with Pamela; she was giving him a full tour of the zoo. I wondered what Pamela would be like as a stepmother. Strict, I thought, but fair.

Lizzie stole a bottle of champagne from the refreshments table and poured splashes from the green glass bottle into our cups of punch. She sat on top of the stout porcupine, as if the memorial statue were a stool. She fingered the grooves of Snuffles's nostrils. "It's not a very good sculpture," she said, looking between her legs at its spiny face. "Looks like a pig with quills. They should have commissioned Soda."

"The statue looks weird because it's not a North American porcupine," I explained. "Snuffles was a prehensile-tailed porcupine, native to Central and South America. You've probably never seen one."

"Oh," Lizzie said. "So like a hedgehog."

"Hedgehogs aren't actually related to porcupines," I said, delighted that Lizzie seemed to be listening. "Hedgehogs are insectivores, and porcupines are herbivores. Porcupines belong to an order of rodent that includes guinea pigs, chinchillas, the naked mole rat. Those are their cousins."

"Cool," Lizzie said. She was starting to have trouble sitting on Snuffles's head.

"Naked mole rats *are* cool," I said. "They can't feel pain."

"Sounds like our kind of animal."

"Lizzie," I said, feeling loose after drinking half my punch. "Do you know you're sleepwalking again?"

"I had a feeling." She sighed.

"Are you going to have to go back to St. Cloud's?"

Lizzie started to cry. I'd never seen my sister cry before, and now she was crying in such a public place. "I wish there was something I could have done," she whimpered. "Something I could have done to stop it."

"Are you taking your medication?" I asked.

"Yeah." She wiped her runny nose with the back of her hand. "I don't think the pills are working anymore. I just feel so guilty."

"I feel guilty too," I told her. "It's a normal stage of grief."

"I don't think you need to feel guilty about anything," Lizzie said. She rubbed her eyes, and gulped down the last of the champagne.

On the drive home, I understood why adults liked alcohol so much, and the champagne had tasted much better than the beer I'd had that winter when we were roasting the pig. It had felt so easy to talk to Lizzie after the punch had set in; she'd listened to me about the naked mole rats, about the different species of porcupines. I was glad she had cried in front of me, it felt healthy somehow. I thought Ms. Bernstein would approve.

But when we got in the house, I passed by a rabbit cake frosted on the counter. It winked at me, and I wasn't sure what Ms. Bernstein would think of that.

Dad made stuffed shells for dinner, and by then I was feeling a little less loopy. I looked at the rabbit cake on the counter and it didn't move.

"It's what Italian mermaids eat," Dad said, spooning a pasta shell onto my plate.

"I'm worried about you," Lizzie said.

232

"Because I have an active imagination? Or because I love ricotta cheese?"

"Because there is glitter on your eyelids."

As soon as we'd gotten home from the zoo, Dad had given himself a full face of makeup.

"Oh, Lizzie-bell," Dad sighed. "It's just an experiment. Dr. Judy says I'm understanding the female perspective."

"Dr. Judy is a quack," Lizzie said. The parrot started quacking then. I had forgotten we'd taught him all the barnyard animal sounds.

"Ernest, say *moo,*" Dad squealed. "With a moo moo here. Here a moo, there a moo, everywhere a moo moo," he sang, dancing around the kitchen, and everyone laughed then.

I had just gotten into bed that night, and was listening to Lizzie in the bathroom, brushing her teeth. It seemed like forever ago that she'd been sticking the handle of her toothbrush down her throat trying to bring up what she'd eaten in her sleep the night before.

Since she'd gotten back from St. Cloud's, I'd been waiting for Lizzie to explode, but maybe it wasn't going to happen. I heard Lizzie turn off the faucet after she finished washing her face, and then she shut out her light and crawled into bed, the mattress springs creaking. The walls between our rooms seemed extra thin that night, like I could punch right through them if I tried.

"Good night, Jesus," Lizzie said. She had started keeping Ocean Jesus right by her bed, had decorated him, draped gold necklaces around his neck. He really glittered now, between the fish scales and Lizzie's costume jewelry, plus the glint of a few real gems from Mom's jewelry box.

I thought about knocking on the wall, getting up to tell Lizzie that she didn't need to worry about sleepwalking, that we would figure it out. I wanted to tell her that I was crazy too; I could tell her that I'd seen a rabbit cake move again. I meant to get up, but my eyelids were much too heavy.

"Have you seen your sister?" Dad said, first thing in the morning. "She's not in her room."

Mom's Honda wasn't in the driveway, the keys taken from the hook in the hallway. Lizzie's rolling suitcase was missing, her drawers empty, most of her dresses ripped from the clothing hangers. Ocean Jesus was gone too, leaving only a few stray silver fish scales stuck to the wood floor.

I'm sorry El, she'd written on the bathroom mirror using one of Mom's lipsticks, the shade Dad loved the most, Showgirl Red.

■ ■ ■ ■

PART III
MONTHS 13 TO 17

■ ■ ■ ■

29.
J̶U̶N̶E̶, July

Lizzie wouldn't answer her cell phone, but we put it together pretty quickly that Soda had been released from jail, once I told Dad about the letters Lizzie kept in a shoe box underneath her bed. Lizzie had taken the shoe box with her, so I never found out how long they'd been planning it, but she must have picked Soda up from jail in the Honda. She'd just passed her driver's test.

Dad went out in the truck to look for Lizzie. As soon as he drove off, I dialed Miss Ida.

"Hello, Elvis," she said, after I'd put Dad's credit card information in.

"Lizzie is missing."

"Ah," Miss Ida said. "She's probably with that boyfriend she told me about. She wanted to know if he loved her."

"Yeah, we're pretty sure she's with Soda. What should we do?"

"She'll be home by September."

It was only July; I didn't think we should wait until September. "That's what you're seeing with your psychic powers?"

"Oh no," Miss Ida said. "The cards aren't showing me much today. But Lizzie is a teenager. Flames burn hot, but burn out fast. She'll come home brokenhearted."

"So what do we do?"

"Give it the summer. She's not in any danger. Phillip is a nice boy."

I hadn't told Miss Ida that Soda's real name was Phillip, but maybe Lizzie had.

Dad came home empty-handed after driving around for hours. Lizzie wasn't at the Silver Sand Motel, at least not yet, and she wasn't at any of her old hangouts, places she used to go with Megan Sax. Dad was about to call the police to report Lizzie as a runaway, until he saw online that if the state police found her, she could be held in a "secure detention facility" for an indefinite amount of time.

"She could go to *jail* for running away." Dad put his head in his hands, and when he looked up, his expression had changed. "Elvis, don't tell anyone. She'll come home soon, on her own."

Miss Ida had said to wait until September, but I was worried about what could happen between now and then. "Did you know she's sleepwalking again?" I asked.

"No." He sighed. "I didn't know that either."

Two days after Lizzie left, a postcard arrived with a laughing cartoon dolphin on the front. *Greetings from the Silver Sand Motel and Marina,* it read. On the blank side of the card, Lizzie had written *I'm in love!* in purple pen.

After he read that, Dad went out into the garage and went at the punching bag, which I hadn't seen him use since Mom bought it for him for Christmas years before.

"At least we know where she is," I pointed out, when Dad came back in, sweat all through his T-shirt, his knuckles bleeding because he hadn't worn boxing gloves. The motel was a forty-five-minute drive away, too far to bike. Dad said he wasn't driving to get her, he was too mad at her.

"Mad at her for being in love?" I asked.

"Mad at her for being stupid."

"Stupid," the parrot repeated.

I left long voice mails on Lizzie's cell phone, most of them begging her to come home. She didn't call back, but she sent another postcard that said she was happy with Soda, and that he was helping with her sleepwalking episodes. She said I should leave her alone.

I remembered Lizzie on the boat, laughing with Soda. She had looked happy. He had told her she was pretty when she laughed, and she didn't have eyebrows that week. But even if she was happy with Soda, she should be at home with us, with her family.

"Dad, why don't we go get her?" I asked. "We know where she is."

"She'd run again."

"So we'd go back and get her again."

"Some Alabama teenagers run a lot farther than Guntersville. If she ran to New York or California, we'd never get her back. I know she'd run. She has to come home on her own. She will."

"Okay," I said. "I still think we should go get her." I didn't want to give it the summer, no matter what Miss Ida had said.

"Your opinion is noted," Dad said, which meant the conversation was over.

Later that night, I read online that the families of runaway teenagers have *feelings of indescribable grief and confusion*. I wondered if I should start another grieving chart, but I didn't know how many months

I should put down. If Lizzie was gone, but alive, I didn't know how long it would take to stop missing her, if that would take more or less months than a death.

I was volunteering at the zoo as often as I could, because Dad kept saying there was nothing I could do about Lizzie. He said maybe I should work on Mom's book, so I checked out a few books from the zoo's reference section. I learned that giraffes can go weeks without sleep, and birds slept with only half their brain, leaving them half-awake and able to fly. I wondered if sleep-walkers sleep with half their brain too.

There had been a few new additions to Serengeti in the weeks of my suspension; zoos are always swapping animals. We had a new giant anteater with a huge plumed tail and a trunked snout. A dozen northern red-bellied cooters had been born as part of the turtle conservation program and were to be released into the wild at eight months. The musk ox was pregnant, and we had a new Amur leopard; only thirty were left in the wild. He panted in his cage like a dog.

Pamela introduced me to the new three-legged meerkat, Cletus, whose mob had turned on him in a zoo in Cincinnati. Meer-kats are social animals, but Cletus would have to live alone from now on; it's too hard to introduce a meerkat to a new mob. It made me sad for him, but Pamela said we'd be sure he got a lot of stimulation: chew toys and cardboard jungle gyms. I fed Cletus six live mealworms with a pair of tweezers. He barked after me when I walked away.

Even though I was happy to be at the zoo, there was always the pit in my stomach because I knew Lizzie wasn't at home watching TV on the couch. I tried to figure out what Mom would do if she were around. Mom would have probably driven to Lake Guntersville straightaway and dragged Lizzie to the car.

When I finished my shift, Dad would pick me up in his truck, and when I'd get in the cab he and the parrot were usually both silent. Dad had become morose again since Lizzie had left, and Ernest seemed to take it personally. I knew if Lizzie had been around she would have joked that the honeymoon was over, but Lizzie wasn't around. She hadn't even called.

After Lizzie had been living with Soda for two weeks, I was assigned to work with Cleopatra, the pygmy hippo. She had turned against many of the other volunteers.

"Cleo's a diva," Pamela said. "She wants things her way. She only likes women, and no gray hair, no jewelry, no perfume. She must be kept in her own pen at night."

As I raked up Cleopatra's old hay, visitors would ask me questions about her over the fence. Many visitors hadn't known pygmy hippos existed, and they thought Cleopatra was a baby hippopotamus. At six years old and fully grown, she was only the size of a pig. Except for her occasional temper tantrum and her dislike of perfume and silver jewelry, Cleopatra was pretty docile during the day, asleep most of the time. She had to be housed alone after the night of *the incident,* when she'd killed the African spoonbill who'd shared her enclosure.

I read up on pygmy hippos during my lunch break. In my research, I found that pygmy hippos are nocturnal, solitary animals. Like their larger cousin, they close up their ears and nose underneath the water. They don't have sweat glands. To keep cool in the jungle, they secrete something called blood sweat. It's not blood and it's not sweat, but a red foam that keeps them damp. There was an old legend that said that the blood sweat made the hippos impossible to pierce with arrows or bullets, but people insisted it was good luck to kill one, if you could find a way to do it. That was how pygmy hippos had become endangered, with very few left in the wild.

There was another folktale too, one that always excited the zoo visitors, which claimed that pygmy hippos lit fire to the West African forest at night, and in the morning they'd eat the charcoal dust left behind. It was hard not to think of Lizzie's nighttime habits when I read that, but I knew she would have hated it if I compared her to a hippopotamus, even a pygmy.

On the walk out of the zoo, I wondered what nocturnal animals knew about the nighttime that I didn't. I had never really thought my mom would kill herself — no matter what Miss Ida had predicted — until she was found in the river. And until Pamela told me, I never would have thought Cleopatra was capable of murder.

"Any word from Lizzie?" I asked Dad when I climbed into the truck.

"None," he said. "She looks good though."

"What do you mean?"

"I park at the public beach." When we got home, he showed me a pair of binoculars tucked in his briefcase.

The next week, three weeks without Lizzie, Pamela told me that Dr. Rotherwood said he could use me in the exotic animal clinic for the next few days, since so much of his volunteer staff had gone on vacation. "He wants to make amends," she said. "That means you should say you're sorry."

"I know what it means," I grumbled.

When I got to the clinic, Dr. Rotherwood was rehabbing a coyote with a broken leg. The coyote had been hit by a car, and brought in by the driver, an animal lover. Dr. Rotherwood said that he had named the coyote Simon, and explained that if he healed well enough, Simon would be let go in six to ten weeks.

I hadn't realized how many animals Dr. Rotherwood treated at the zoo and then released back into the wild, but he said that was his favorite part of the job. He rehabbed tons of gray squirrels, and Alabama had plenty of those. Dr. Rotherwood said all animals were precious, people included. I really felt bad I'd ever spat on him.

"Water under the bridge," he said.

As we set Simon's back leg into a cast, Dr. Rotherwood said that everyone in the clinic would have to be careful not to pay too much attention to Simon as he healed. Sometimes animals could not be reintroduced into the wild because they'd lost their ability to hunt, had come to rely on humans for food. "A tame coyote is a dead coyote," he explained. A tame coyote would go into a person's backyard, and more than likely get shot. "It's best if coyotes remain afraid of humans."

Dr. Rotherwood said that rehabbing wild animals could get depressing sometimes. He said every May, the clinic was overrun with white-tailed deer fawns. People would bring the fawns in thinking they'd been abandoned or orphaned, not knowing that mama deer often leave their babies during the day. That is why fawns have those dappled white spots, so they can better camouflage, remain hidden when they are left alone.

"It's a well-intentioned kidnapping," Dr. Rotherwood explained. "People name most of the fawns Bambi."

Lizzie still hadn't come home, and she hadn't sent any more postcards, but Dad had reported that she looked good at the Silver Sand, tan and healthy. Maybe Soda really was helping with her sleepwalking. She'd taken the rabbit cake pan with her when she ran away, and Dad planned to continue renting the walk-in freezer at the butcher. Lizzie could still work on being a world record holder if she wanted to, and maybe Soda would even help out with her baking.

Maybe it was kind of like a well-intentioned kidnapping. I liked the sound of that.

30.

Dad and I were getting used to being alone again, the way it had been in the months when Lizzie was at St. Cloud's. I remembered what Lizzie's friend Vanessa had said once, that it was okay to be glad that Lizzie was gone for a while. Dad and I had our summer morning routine down: I'd walk the dog while he packed our lunches, and then he'd drop me off at the zoo on the way to work.

Dad wasn't morose anymore; he whistled as he got dressed in the morning. He still wore Mom's lipstick and robe around the house sometimes, but he also was ironing his flannel button-downs before he left for work. He'd grown a beard, but he was keeping it neatly trimmed.

"Are you dating someone?" I asked, when Dad came downstairs smelling of cologne, the kind he used to wear on his anniversary dinners with Mom.

"I said I'd let you know if it's serious," he said. "Nothing serious."

"Your risk for a heart attack goes down if you marry again. Remember what happened to your friend Bernie?"

"I remember," Dad said. "I read the pamphlet my doctor gave me, too." The pamphlet said that if Dad married again, he would tack an average of seven years onto his expected lifespan. I didn't think that was a statistic to be ignored.

"I've always wondered about the animals at the zoo," Dad said one morning on the ride in to work. "Do you think they're happy?"

When zoo visitors asked that same question, we were required to say: *Yes, the animals are very happy. We feed them nutritious diets and we make sure they get plenty of exercise. You can make a donation at the front office to ensure the animals continue to get the care they need. You can also help by visiting our gift shop!*

But how did you know if an animal was happy? Some of them probably didn't mind the cages, didn't know the difference. I didn't think the frogs and the turtles were unhappy, or any of the inhabitants of the reptile house. The mice in Rodent Tunnel were probably happy enough, but then we had to kill them in that terrible way. And the bigger mammals? They didn't have enough room to run, not really, and those were the ones whose happiness I was worried about. Most everyone had read that the orcas in SeaWorld were depressed. I was thankful we didn't have any whales or dolphins at Serengeti Park.

Our lion, Seymour, was on large doses of Prozac ever since his mate died. He was the one who killed her; he broke the lioness's neck. It was during visiting hours; Pamela called it a "media nightmare."

"I don't know if they're happy," I said.

"I bet they are," Dad said, because he was uncomfortable with my answer. "You take such good care of them."

"Yeah," I said, and I leaned against the window and held my breath. It had been a while since I'd pretended to drown in the car.

When Dad dropped me off, I went straight to visit the sea otters. Clayton and Bernadette were the happiest animals I could think of. When I got to their enclosure, the otters were floating around in the water, holding hands. Last year, the zoo had held a wedding for Clayton and Bernadette, since they were visitor favorites. The otters each got a bucket of clams for the occasion, and there was cake and wine for all the guests who had made a donation. The wedding made almost $40,000, which went toward saving sea otters from oil spills.

Pamela had warned me I shouldn't think that the zoo animals had human feelings, and I should remember that they were wild at heart. But I thought most people believed that animals had all the same emotions people did. Why else would everyone have given so much money to that wedding, unless they believed that Clayton and Bernadette really loved each other?

If the zoo animals were happy, and Dad was whistling in the morning, and Lizzie's postcards said she was in love, what was I missing? Maybe my grief had turned abnormal, before the eighteen months were even up. I always felt as if I had swallowed something sharp, like a house key or a thumbtack, something causing a deep pain down in the pit of my stomach.

31.
~~JULY~~, AUGUST

On the first Friday in August, Dad had an early meeting with a carpet vendor all the way in Birmingham, so he couldn't give me a ride to the zoo. When I called in, Dr. Rotherwood said he'd pick me up at home, he really needed the extra hands. I said thank you so much, and then I waited by the door, since I didn't want Dr. Rotherwood to see what a mess our house was.

"Sweet cheeks," Ernest said as I waited. "Gimme kiss." Dad had left the parrot in his cage, had apologized to the bird, explaining that it was a no-parrots-allowed meeting.

I remembered once when Mom and I had been shopping for Boomer, looking for something to help with his arthritis. "Sweet cheeks," she'd called across the store, "do you have any supplements for dogs with joint pain?"

"Did you just call Mr. Debbie *sweet*

cheeks?"

"It's an old joke."

"Weird joke, Mom," was all I'd said then, but now I began to wonder.

When Dr. Rotherwood pulled up in his Prius, I asked him if he could take me to Debbie's Petland. "Our dog is running low on food."

"Sure," he said. "I don't mind waiting in the car while you run in."

"Did you have an affair with my mother?" I asked as I swung the glass door of the pet shop open.

Mr. Debbie sighed, wiping his forehead. "Hi Elvis."

"Did you?"

He asked me to come to the aquarium room in the back. He said he didn't want to bother the other customers. There was no one else in the pet shop, but I went with him anyway to the dark part of the store, our faces lit up by black lights. He spoke just loud enough so I could hear him over the sound of the aquarium filters bubbling.

"You're probably too young to hear this," he said, putting his hands on the back of his neck like his head might fall off. "But you've got me on the spot." He said he'd been having an affair with my mom for two years

255

before she died. That was why Ernest imitated her voice. It was a trick Mom had taught him. "Please don't tell Mrs. Debbie," he begged.

"Oh my God," I said, backing into a tank full of clownfish, sloshing their water a bit. Mom used to say: *Do it once, it's a mistake; do it twice, it's a habit.*

Did my mom have affairs as a habit?

"You'll understand when you're older." He turned around to skim a layer of algae off one of the tanks with a tiny green net.

I rolled my eyes, just like Lizzie would've, and turned to walk out of the store. As I walked through the aisles, I grabbed a bag of dog food, plus a squeaky bone for Boomer. I stopped just before the exit.

"You didn't kill her, did you?" I asked.

"Who? Eva?" Mr. Debbie said. "God, no."

"Did she ever mention any health problems? It's very important that you tell me everything you know, Mr. Debbie, or I'll have to ask your wife."

"She did have awful headaches," he said. "I sent her to my brother. He's a doctor in New York."

I remembered the trip Mom had taken to New York alone. She'd said it was for a conference.

"Do you have his number?"

"Look him up," Mr. Debbie said. "*Dr. Paul Debbie.*"

"I will," I said, and walked out without paying for the dog food. I thought Mr. Debbie deserved to be punished a little, since I wasn't going to tell Dad about the affair. I knew it would really break Dad's heart about Ernest if he knew the way the parrot had learned Mom's voice.

In Mom's life before, not in her past lives, but in her life before Dad-and-Lizzie-and-me, she had eaten a special kind of cactus at a music festival, a huge concert in Sedona, Arizona. Dad hated when she told this story to us, because he said it glorified drug use.

"They don't know what peyote is, Frank. I never said anything about drugs." The cactus made Mom hallucinate, she said, and she had walked down what she thought was a tunnel made of glass for miles and miles.

When she awoke, Mom was in the storage room of a crystal shop. The store was owned by Miss Ida, and there was a red-and-white *Now Hiring* sign in the window. Mom had run out of money, so she took the salesclerk job. She had six months before she'd be starting her PhD program, and she wasn't about to move back in with her mother, not at twenty-four years old. Mom used to tell Lizzie and me stories about Miss Ida before bed.

Miss Ida liked to tell everyone she was from the Amazon, but she was really from Chicago. She was a psychic and a witch doctor; her customers didn't expect her to be from Hyde Park. Mom told me that people often came to Miss Ida with tapeworms. So many people were eating bad meat from fast food restaurants, it was like an epidemic. The regular doctors would have no idea what was wrong, just prescribe Tums for heartburn.

Miss Ida would tell the person to fast for a week, to drink only water, and then come back. When her patient returned several pounds skinnier, she'd have him lie on his back, would place a bowl of warm milk on his chest. The starved tapeworm would smell the milk and crawl out from the mouth, or the nose, and inch toward the milk. Once the worm had reached the bowl, Ida would pinch it around the head and pull. Sometimes the tapeworms were several feet long.

"Ew." I'd squirmed at that part.

"There's billions of organisms inside you right now," Mom had said. "There's no telling the secrets the body holds."

Mom might have held a secret tumor in her brain that would explain everything, her multiple affairs and her mysterious death, but I knew we couldn't dig up her body for a second autopsy. Nothing could recover the truth; her body was scattered across the twelve miles between our home and the dam at Goat Rock. Mom was gone for good; we hadn't even kept the dust she'd left behind. I wished we'd put her ashes into a jar instead, so I could ask questions to her remains.

When Dr. Rotherwood dropped me off that evening, our driveway was empty. Ernest had been stuck in his cage all day.

"Traitor," I snarled at the yellow-and-blue bird, angry at his clownish face.

Ernest continued cracking macadamia nuts with his beak. "It's what macaws eat in the wild," Dad had insisted. The nuts were ten dollars a pound, and couldn't be cracked with a regular nutcracker, but Ernest's beak was built for it. Parrots have a bone in their tongue. Whenever another nut split open, Ernest would spit the shell onto the floor, letting out Mom's long happy laugh.

32.

It was easy enough to find Dr. Paul Debbie online, and I called his office when it opened on Monday.

"Oh right, the one with the headaches," Dr. Debbie said. "She never came to see me. She missed her appointment and she never rescheduled. How is she doing?"

"She's dead."

"Oh my God," he said.

"Thanks for the help," I said, and hung up. I guess it was rude, but I was frustrated. I dialed Lizzie's cell phone; I wanted to tell her about Mr. Debbie, but of course she didn't pick up, she never did. Her mailbox was full, so I couldn't leave a message.

I went online to research articles about women who cheat on their husbands. One website said *as their children grow older, women turn more vulnerable to affairs, as they have more time on their hands.* The article suggested that women with older children should *work to develop hobbies and get more involved in their church.*

It was hard to picture Mom going to church, even though she'd ordered a Jesus statue, since she used to say it was nothing more than a fashion show. But when I looked up reasons to go to church, it seemed like many people thought church was a helpful place to deal with their problems. The church near us, Our Lady of the Valley, had a bunch of support groups; there was one for people with diabetes and one called Widows Supporting Widows. I wasn't sure I really wanted a support group, but I wanted to know what a holy place was like. I wanted somewhere I could go to think.

"Will you drive me to church?" I asked Dad the next morning when I went downstairs.

"Why?" he asked.

"I'd like to try it."

"On Sunday?"

"Today's fine."

"It'll be empty, you know," he said. "I guess God will be there."

I didn't laugh.

He said he respected that, and that he'd drop me off there before he did a home carpet fitting, but he couldn't come into the church with me. Churches gave him the heebie-jeebies. "The smell weirds me out." He shuddered. "That strange incense." Dad wasn't religious. He had been raised Catholic by his parents, had been an altar boy, but he'd fallen out with the church sometime since. If anyone asked, he called himself an "atheist with a capital *A*." Before Mom died, I'd heard Dad say he believed we rotted in the ground when we died, food for worms — *nothing mystical about it.* But sometimes I heard him calling the parrot Eva, so maybe he'd changed his thoughts on reincarnation, or maybe that was just old habits dying hard.

Dad dropped me off at Our Lady of the Valley, said he'd be back to pick me up in an hour, asked if that was enough time. I walked up the stone steps and opened the heavy door. The church was empty. There were two rows of wooden benches below a Jesus hanging off the cross, several of his wounds bleeding. It made me sick to think they really used to nail people up like that, and it wasn't only Jesus who had died that way either.

I didn't know what I believed about God or the afterlife. I didn't believe Mom could be gone completely when there was so much of her left everywhere. There was her voice in the parrot, her sleepwalking in Lizzie, and now Dad asked me questions like if I was wearing sunscreen or if I'd had enough to eat. Mom showed up in parts of me too: I had her scientific mind, and now, without her, I was Boomer's favorite person in the family.

There was a sign over the church door that said: *Jesus Is in Us All.* Maybe we do breathe in a dead person's leftover spirit, like Soda had said. That's why there were parts of Mom still in the house, and parts of her in the river, parts left in Lizzie and in me. Maybe a spirit evaporates like vapor off the bag of frozen peas you steam in the microwave: the droplets go everywhere, settle wherever they land.

I was by myself in the church for about ten minutes when someone walked in to sweep the floors. She looked familiar somehow, but I didn't really recognize her until I saw the rattlesnake tattoo wrapped around her neck. Her brown dreadlocks were gone, a short bleached-blonde pixie cut in its place. She had a new tattoo of a sailboat on her forearm, the black outline of one, not colored in yet.

"Vanessa," I said. She blinked a few times, hard and slow, and rubbed her temple, like she was trying to remember who I was.

"Elvis," she said. "What are you doing here?"

"Talking to God," I said, which wasn't really true. I had just been sitting there thinking.

"Ah," she said. "Cool."

"What are *you* doing here?"

She looked at the ground. I think she thought she had a lot of explaining to do. She apologized profusely for hitting on Dad; she said she had only wanted to stay at our house. She said Lizzie was like a sister to her.

"He said you could stay as long as you wanted," I said, because we'd both heard my dad say that. A mean part of me wanted to say that Lizzie wasn't her sister; Lizzie was mine.

Vanessa said it was her stepfather's fault, and that I really didn't get. She said her real dad died when she was a kid and her mother remarried, only to also die soon after, leaving thirteen-year-old Vanessa behind with a stepfather who had never legally adopted her.

"He was a total creep," she said.

She said the next morning, my dad had dropped her off at the bus station and bought her a ticket to Charleston, where she'd said her aunt lived. The only problem was, she didn't have an aunt to stay with. She had lied because she didn't want Dad to call her stepfather. Vanessa had intended to board the bus, but there were too many choices, too many stops between here and South Carolina. It was overwhelming. So instead, she went across the street to the homeless shelter. Lizzie knew where she'd gone; they talked on the phone.

"You pulled your hair out?" I asked, remembering Vanessa's hair-plucking disease.

"Nah." Her hand rose to touch her short hair. "Father Tillman made me shave the dreads. I bleached it so I wouldn't look too boring."

Father Tillman ran the homeless shelter. He liked Vanessa and had hired her to help with running the church. Vanessa was in charge of ordering and maintaining flower arrangements and cleaning, and she also ran a support group for troubled teens. She lived in one of the vacant nun apartments. It wasn't easy to find nuns, and Father Tillman hoped Vanessa would consider the profession.

"Enough about me," Vanessa said. "What's going on with you?"

For some reason I trusted Vanessa. I don't know if it was because she was Lizzie's friend, or because we were in a church, or because I'd always liked her, but I spilled everything. I told her that Lizzie had run away and she nodded, that was something she already knew. I told her about my mom's affair with Mr. Debbie, and about the parrot, and about sixth grade starting soon. Vanessa listened with her head cocked slightly, like Boomer did when he was trying hard to understand. Vanessa was a really good listener, I realized.

"I just wish Lizzie was around to help me figure it out."

"Figure what out?"

"If my mother killed herself. If she did it on purpose."

"What do you mean? Did you find a note?" Vanessa asked.

"No, but I've been looking for something like that, proof of some kind. I think she may have had a brain tumor, so she killed herself."

"Where did you get this idea?" Vanessa said slowly, carefully.

"It's a feeling I have." I wished I had more proof, but Dr. Paul Debbie had been a dead end.

"I think it's a feeling you *want* to have," Vanessa said. "You want someone or something to blame for your mother's absence in your life."

"How do you know that?" My mouth felt dry. I swallowed.

"My mother died when I was about your age," she said. "I remember what it was like."

"No one knows what it's like," I said. "No one knows what it's like but me and Lizzie." I started to cry then, and I couldn't stop. I crumpled off the wooden bench and onto the floor, sitting on the red carpet in the aisle. I gulped for air between sobs. I tried to think of Mom telling me how we weren't a family of criers, but I couldn't stop even then. "I need to get Lizzie back."

"We'll think of something," Vanessa agreed, and pulled a pack of tissues from her purse.

When Dad pulled up in the Dodge and honked his horn, Vanessa didn't duck back into the church like I thought she might.

"Hi Frank," she said, when Dad opened his door. Ernest was perched on the steering wheel.

"It's Vanessa," I said, because Dad looked confused. "Lizzie's friend. She stayed with us, remember? She likes Tom Cruise."

"I know," Dad said. I wondered if he could tell I had been crying.

Vanessa said Lizzie would be home soon, she was sure of it. She was talking to Dad like nothing weird had ever happened, like he'd never seen her pull down those SpongeBob boxer shorts to her ankles.

"Okay," Dad said. He was staring at Vanessa as if he'd seen a ghost.

I got in the truck, and Dad started the engine. "Jesus Christ," he said, as we pulled out of the church parking lot. "Why is Vanessa at the church? She looks terrible."

"She's working for Father Tillman," I said, and that seemed to make Dad feel better. "Dad, why don't we go get Lizzie?"

He was keeping his binoculars hung around his neck at all times.

"She's not a little kid anymore," Dad said. "She has to *want* to come home. I can't make her."

"Maybe she'll come home dead like Mom did," I said.

"Elvis," Dad snapped.

I wished for the thousandth time that I could talk to Mom about all this. I bicycled down to the Chattahoochee River, down the road to the bank where Mom used to wade in. I hopped off my bike and squatted where we had once found a pair of abandoned swim goggles.

"This is the place my mother drowned," I said to no one, pointing out at the water, although it could have been miles from that spot. She could have swum a long way before she drowned.

The river didn't look so dangerous now. When Mom drowned, the Chattahoochee had overflowed the banks and risen onto the street from all the rain we'd had that spring. It was why Mom's body had floated so far away, why she hadn't gotten tangled up in the rocks sooner. White-water rafting companies usually gave the Chattahoochee River a Class II difficulty level, but that June they'd upgraded it to a Class V, which meant expert only, rafters beware.

I don't know when I started crying sitting there on the riverbank, but I sobbed and sobbed. I didn't worry about my face looking ugly, and my chest filled with fresh air as I gasped. I'd turned into a little crybaby, but so what? Who was there to see?

When my tears finally slowed, I blew my nose with a leaf. I stood up and mounted my bike. It was Lizzie who had taught me to ride it, years ago. Mom had given her twenty dollars to teach me; it was one of her tricks to get us to spend time together. Lizzie hadn't let me use training wheels, had held the back of the seat to help me balance as I pedaled. I had trusted her not to let me fall. One day she had let go and I went straight into the trash cans, but Lizzie had said that was part of learning.

When the phone rang later that afternoon, I hoped it would be Lizzie, but it was Vanessa on the other end.

"Can I come to the zoo with you tomorrow?" she asked. "I've never been and I have the church van all day, I can drive us."

I told Vanessa that the zoo was closed to visitors for the week. I didn't feel like seeing anyone. I wanted to be alone, or I wanted to talk to Lizzie.

"It's open every day except Christmas," Vanessa said. "It says on the website."

Even on Christmas, the zoo wasn't really closed. Someone had to come in and feed the animals every single day of the year, so it wasn't too much to have someone in to man the ticket booth as well. Still, no one ever visited the zoo on Christmas. Everyone always had someplace else to be, a family to spend the day with.

"I have a plan to get Lizzie to come home," Vanessa said.

"Fine," I said. "Pick me up at eleven. Wear closed-toed shoes."

33.

As Vanessa and I walked toward the part of the zoo called Australian Outback Adventure, she explained about statutory rape. In most states, she said, the age of consent was eighteen. That meant: the age a person could legally have sex. People got into trouble when they had sex with people younger than themselves; it was something you could go to jail for. I remembered a case like that, a teacher in Florida in love with her student.

Vanessa asked if I knew how old Soda was.

"Nineteen," I said, or maybe he had turned twenty, I'd never asked when his birthday was. "That's not that much older than sixteen."

"It's too old," Vanessa clucked. "It's the law."

"But how do you know they're having sex?" I asked. "He said he was a virgin."

Vanessa looked at me with a sly smile.

"Because," she said, "of course they are."

So what Soda was doing to Lizzie was illegal, maybe worse than the drug use.

"Very interesting," I said, as we watched Kangaroo Bill bound across the grass. "Do you think it will work?"

"I'm not sure," she said. "But I don't think she'll come home on her own. She's stubborn."

We walked to the African animals next, and I showed Vanessa the male lion, asleep on his side. Because of the Prozac he was on, Seymour had gained weight. An extra forty pounds doesn't look like much on a lion. You could still see his ribs.

"A male lion copulates over six hundred times a week during mating season, and with multiple lionesses," I told Vanessa. "A male lion will kill all the cubs fathered by any other lion."

"Sounds something like my stepfather," she said. "Did you know your dad sent Lizzie a letter every day when we were at St. Cloud's? I always wished and wished I had a dad like that. My stepdad didn't write me once, not that I'd read any letter he sent."

I knew Dad had written Lizzie, but I didn't know it had been every day. Dad wasn't much of a writer; he used to make

Mom sign our Christmas cards. I wondered if he'd written to the Silver Sand Motel, if he'd told Lizzie he was watching her with Mom's bird-watching binoculars.

"I talked to Lizzie again yesterday and —"

"You've talked to her? She won't talk to me. How is she? What's going on?"

"She's fine, Elvis. Well, she's okay. The sleepwalking is getting worse, and I'm starting to worry. She thinks she's doing your family a favor by staying away."

"A favor?"

"She's worried she's dangerous."

"Is she suicidal?"

"I don't know."

"What *do* you know?"

"She thinks she's going to hurt someone else while she's asleep. She knows Soda can handle himself; his bunkmate in prison was a murderer."

I knew that wasn't true; before Lizzie had left, I'd read one of Soda's letters about his roommate who was in jail for not paying his taxes. I ignored Vanessa's lie, because something more important was bothering me. "Why will she talk to you and not to me?"

"I think there's something Lizzie doesn't want you to know," Vanessa said. "I think she has a secret."

"About what?"

"There was something that happened at St. Cloud's."

"I don't understand what happened at St. Cloud's," I snarled. "They don't allow visitors."

"That's right," Vanessa said. She put her hands on my shoulders. "I'll tell you everything."

She steered me to a bench outside the zebra pen where we sat while she told me about St. Cloud's. Lizzie and Vanessa were second-floorers — the floor where they kept patients with impulse-control problems: explosive anger disorder, kleptomaniacs, pyromaniacs, sex addicts. On that floor, violent video games, R-rated movies, pornography, those were all banned. They watched a lot of Disney movies, except for *Mulan* because there was swordplay in that.

The first floor was for the jumpers, which was what St. Cloud's patients called the girls who were suicidal, and also for any patients who used a wheelchair. The third-floorers were girls with eating disorders. That floor always smelled from vomit and the smuggled-in laxatives. Fashion magazines were banned on the third floor, as well as any movies with nudity, anything that promoted an unrealistic body ideal. The fourth floor was home to girls with anxiety disorders, those prone to panic attacks. And on the fifth floor, the girls who heard voices or saw hallucinations were kept.

"Those girls are the spookiest," Vanessa said. I thought of the rabbit cakes coming alive, the hallucinations of loss, and I worried about going crazy.

"Most of us were candidates for more than one floor," Vanessa went on. "Some of our floor placement was simply which rooms were available. It's not so easy to label people one illness or another. We're all different combinations of crazy."

Lizzie and Vanessa were roommates, assigned not picked. Lizzie had impulse-control problems with complicated sleep-walking issues, and Vanessa was a hair plucker and a compulsive liar. They'd gotten along immediately.

"We'd stay up talking," Vanessa said. "She talked about you a lot. She had this stuffed animal, this cat, that she said was yours. She said you'd told her it warded off evil spirits, and she used to wiggle it at every nurse who came in for night checks." So that was where Mr. Tequila had gone, I thought, my favorite stuffed toy, the orange tabby.

In the mornings, the St. Cloud's girls had

group therapy. The therapist would ask: "What's your safety level today?" which meant how likely it was that you were going to hurt yourself or those around you. The safety level was measured on a scale of blue to red, with shades of purple in the middle. Blue was safe, red was murder or self-harm. When it was her turn, Lizzie always said she was feeling as purple as a bruise, which won her no points with the therapists, but it didn't get her put in solitary confinement either.

Vanessa said she and Lizzie both signed up for TV time during the same shows; they both liked reruns of *Friends*. Lizzie liked to play poker before dinner, and after dinner there was letter-writing and journal time, which had to be done with crayons since pencils and pens were too easily used as weapons. A crayon couldn't puncture an artery.

"Things were mostly going well," Vanessa said. "I wouldn't say Lizzie was getting better, but she wasn't getting worse. And then, it happened." Lizzie was four weeks into her treatment when she had a breakdown in her private therapy session. "She really flipped out, I guess. She wouldn't tell me what happened, she still won't. It was right after the girl died from the seizure. I heard from one of the orderlies that the therapist was asking Lizzie questions about her mother's death, and Lizzie just lost it."

Then Lizzie was taken to the sixth floor, which everyone called heaven because most of the girls who went up there never came back. Vanessa said she was miserable without Lizzie, and they didn't even get to see each other in the dining hall. The girls in heaven ate at a different time.

When Lizzie did come back down from the sixth floor, Vanessa said, they had her on way too many meds. "She was loopy," Vanessa said. "She wasn't herself. She was like that for a while after, you remember."

I'd already read in the *DSM for Kids!* that there were lots of reasons for breakdowns, including stress and grief. Hallucinations were symptoms of a breakdown too. "I don't know," I said. "Maybe we already know the reason she had a breakdown. Our mom died."

"Okay," Vanessa said. "I just thought you should know."

I really didn't think Lizzie had a secret, or at least not the kind of bad secret Vanessa seemed to think it was. Besides, I didn't even know if Vanessa was telling me the truth; she was a proven liar.

Vanessa and I stopped talking as I led her

through the huge greenhouse called Bird Paradise. The birds could fly free in here, so you had to be careful when you opened the doors. Powerful fans kept the birds away from the exits, although occasionally a budgie would get loose. Inside the temperature-controlled garden, the female Costa's hummingbird had built a nest, using plant fibers, animal hairs, and spiderwebs to weave it together. The male hadn't helped with the nest, as hummingbirds don't form pair bonds.

"It's so small," Vanessa marveled, leaning forward toward the nest.

"Second-smallest hummingbird," I said. "Both eggs could fit on a dime."

"Wow," Vanessa said, looking down at her thumb. "The thing was," she continued, "St. Cloud's was the happiest I've ever been and I really mean it. It was safe there, just Lizzie and me. What can go wrong when the world is that small? Like a hummingbird's nest."

I didn't tell her that a lot could go wrong in a hummingbird's nest. It is hard to breed hummingbirds in captivity; the female Costa's had been laying eggs for the past two years, but none of them had hatched. The zoo would let her sit on them for long after they'd determined they wouldn't hatch, the bird waiting and waiting, because the visitors liked to see the hummingbirds when they were still, when they weren't flitting about. Eventually a zookeeper would take the tiny eggs away, toss them into the compost, where they were dwarfed by other eggshells, the speckled ones we threw out from the nest in the waterfowl enclosure.

We walked through Asia Quest next. I showed Vanessa the Amur leopard, and then we walked by the red pandas. I waited for her to say that with their ringed tails and bandit masks they looked like red raccoons, not pandas, but she didn't say that. I told her that the red panda's taxonomic name means shining cat.

"Why can't they just be their own animal?" she asked. "They aren't pandas *or* cats."

I wanted to tell her that I'd touched the male red panda once when I'd cleaned his cage and his fur felt softer than any housecat but instead I ushered her along toward the prairie dog exhibit. "They aren't dogs either," I said, trying to let her know I understood what she meant exactly.

I knew once school started up again the next week, everyone would call me Lizzie Babbitt's little sister. All the Three Rivers teachers would definitely remember her. I would never be my own animal, whether my sister ever came home or not. She had already made her mark.

Vanessa drove me home, but she got out of the van when we got to the house. "I have something for you," she said. She pulled an envelope out of her backpack. "If I had a good dad like yours, I'd want to live at home, whether I realized it or not."

I opened the envelope and pulled out a stack of paper. I only had to read the first few lines of legal jargon before I stuffed the document back into its pouch.

"Thanks Vanessa," I said, and she gave me a thumbs-up.

I ran upstairs and called the Silver Sand. The call went to voice mail, asking me to leave my name and number and the dates I'd like to book a room. "Thanks for calling the Silver Sand Motel and Marina," the recording said. "We look forward to having you stay with us."

I didn't leave my name or my number. Instead, I read out loud from the pages of *Statutory Rape: A Guide to the Law and Reporting Requirements.* I was glad when the system cut me off because the specifics of the law were getting pretty graphic. I was sure I'd made my point.

■ ■ ■ ■

When Dad got home from work, he called me into the living room and showed me his phone. *The age of consent in Alabama is sixteen,* the first text message read, followed by: *Pass that along to my little sister.*

So Lizzie was old enough to have sex, I guess, at least in Alabama.

"Sorry," I said. "I just wanted her to come home."

"Me too," Dad said. "Me too."

34.

After a long hot summer, the school year started up again. At Three Rivers, I had a different teacher for each subject, so I didn't get to know my teachers that well, not like I'd known Ms. Powell. But school really wasn't that bad. We were reading *Island of the Blue Dolphins* in English class, which is about a girl surviving on an island by herself and the girl's only friend is her dog. We were learning about the structure of cells in science class and the teacher didn't seem to notice when I doodled in my notebook during math.

The cafeteria tables at Three Rivers were divided exactly like cafeteria tables in the movies: a table for the popular kids and one for the geeks and one for the jocks and another for the kids in marching band. Everyone was always ready for a fight in the cafeteria. The first week of school, there were punches thrown between two girls.

Since I didn't have any friends at all, I sat in the No Bully Zone, the designated part of the cafeteria where anyone could sit alone, guarded by a security guard in a blue suit with a gold pin-on badge. The security guard was paid for by the parents of Matthias Matthews, also known as Matt-Matt. Matt-Matt was a legend at Three Rivers. He'd hung himself days after he was beaten up in the Three Rivers lunchroom. This was years ago, and I never knew Matt-Matt, but I thought of him every day when lunch began.

The second week of school, the gym teacher told me in the middle of a volleyball game that she thought I had scoliosis. The school nurse gave me a plastic back brace that strapped around my middle. She said I'd have to wear it day and night for at least nine months. Scoliosis meant that I didn't have to go to gym class; I had an extra study hall now instead.

We'd watched a video about the condition in health class. The class had been transfixed as a series of X-rays first showed a slight curve in a spine that then grew into a gnarled, twisted root. It looked like the carrots that I'd grown in the garden two years ago, which turned out nothing like the simple straight ones we could buy in the grocery store. "Probably too many rocks in the yard," Mom had said, and I imagined rocks in my body too.

Scoliosis also meant I couldn't clean cages at Serengeti Park; it was too difficult to bend at the middle while wearing my brace. Dr. Rotherwood offered me a permanent space as the volunteer afternoon-and-weekend receptionist at the exotic animal veterinary clinic. He gave me a vet clinic sweatshirt with my name stitched in yellow thread on the sleeve. He had even ordered it a size up so I could wear it over my spine-correcting brace.

Lizzie still hadn't come back, so I called Ms. Bernstein's home phone. I needed to talk to a guidance counselor and didn't want to start all over with a new one at Three Rivers. She said it was good to hear from me, and she asked about my sister, like she always did. I told her Lizzie had run away with my mom's old boyfriend.

"Well, he's her old student, really," I said, correcting myself. "It sounds worse than it is."

"Wow," she said. "No impulse control."

"Yeah," I said, and I wrote that down so I could look up what it meant later. I remembered Vanessa had also mentioned impulse-control problems.

"How are you liking middle school?" she asked.

I told her about my promotion at the zoo.

"What about the other kids in school? Made any new friends?"

"The pygmy hippo is pregnant," I said. "We gave her an ultrasound today. She's due the end of January, it's a six-month gestation period for pygmy hippos, and Cleopatra is already a month along. She's part of the worldwide captive breeding program. They're endangered."

"That's nice, Elvis," she said. "But I'd like you to focus on working on your social skills. Maybe you could join a club. I know they have a Middle Earth club."

"I didn't like *The Lord of the Rings* that much," I said. "Not even the movies."

"Science club?" she offered.

"You're not my guidance counselor anymore," I reminded her, even though I had been the one to call.

"I know, Elvis," Ms. Bernstein said. "But I really care about you."

"Do you have any ideas on how to get my sister to come home?"

"Call the police," Ms. Bernstein said. "Lizzie is a minor."

"Okay," I said. "Thanks." I couldn't call the police; they might put her in jail. Dad had been crystal clear about that.

Ms. Bernstein said I could call back anytime, but not too often because she had a new boyfriend, and he didn't like it when she brought her work home with her, whatever that meant.

"I heard hippos are mean bastards," Dad said when I went into the kitchen to give him back the phone. I guess he'd been eavesdropping. "How'd you give the ultrasound?" he asked.

"Cleopatra is sweet," I said. "She'll do anything for a carrot." Dr. Rotherwood had said we were never to speak poorly about the animals. He said Cleopatra was "a radiant spirit," even after she'd charged at him.

"Sweetie," Ernest whistled.

"You're a sweetie," Dad cooed. He was paying more attention to the parrot again; maybe he was getting used to Lizzie being gone.

When I looked later, the *DSM for Kids!* said an impulse-control disorder was a failure to resist certain urges or temptations. One suggested way for parents to help cure impulsive tendencies in their children was to *provide a stable home environment, and a regular routine.* I realized that was what

Vanessa had liked about St. Cloud's, why she thought it was so safe there, like a hummingbird's nest. She liked how predictable her day was.

A regular routine would never happen at the Silver Sand. People were always checking in and out at a motel. It wasn't a real home for anyone.

35.
~~August,~~ September

The second week of September, I came home from school to find Ocean Jesus sitting cross-legged on the living room couch and my sister lying on the carpet. She'd called Dad to pick her up at the motel that morning. She'd come home on her own in September, just like Miss Ida said she would.

But once she was home, she couldn't stop crying. "I can't believe *he* broke up with *me*," she kept repeating. "He promised he'd help me. He promised we'd be happy. He said he understood."

"So, what happened?"

"He was freaked out by the sleepwalking," she sniffed. Soda had known from the beginning that she was a sleepwalker, he had promised her he would help her with it. But Lizzie said that Soda got upset with her after the motel guests started complaining about the strange noises they heard at night.

288

"Coyotes, maybe," Soda told them. "Wild-life."

But the guests insisted that the noises were *distinctly human in nature.* It was deer-hunting season in Alabama, and the Silver Sand rooms were packed with hunters, people who should know the sounds of an approaching wild animal.

"He asked me if I could stop," she said. "He said I was ruining his business." Lizzie broke into a fit of hiccups then, so I brought her a glass of water. "It wasn't my fault that he was losing guests to the new Motel 6."

Apparently a lot of the guests thought that the Silver Sand was haunted, and that explained the nighttime noise. She said it was amazing how many people believed in ghosts. It didn't help that the deer popula-tion was down this year and the hunting was not very good. Many people left early, packing up their rifles.

Things got even worse when Soda tried to wake Lizzie up one night when she was in the middle of a sleepwalking episode. She hit him so hard in the face that she broke one of his molars.

"That's when he said he'd had it," she said. "He said I meant to do it. He said I was a devil woman."

"We're glad you're home," Dad said, poking his head in from the kitchen.

"I'm not," she sniffed. "Daddy, I can't stop sleepwalking. What if I hurt you or Elvis?" I was surprised that Lizzie was talking like a baby. It was unlike her.

"We'll get locks on our doors," he said. "I'll go out and buy them today." Dad had heard about Soda's broken molar.

While Dad was out at the hardware store, Vanessa came over to hang out with Lizzie. Vanessa gave me a warm wink, but she closed the door to Lizzie's room behind her.

I decided to get a routine planned out, something that would really help Lizzie. That week, I made the same thing for dinner every night, mac and cheese from a box, and for breakfast we had brown sugar Pop-Tarts. I woke her up at the same time every morning, handed her a toothbrush, and pushed her into the shower. She let me do it, and she even let me put her to bed at night, dragging her off the couch by her hand. She was pretty tame during the daytime, now that she had a broken heart.

When Mom was alive, dinner was always at seven, unless she had a headache. Mom had done laundry on Wednesdays and Sundays; we'd always had clean underwear. We'd never run out of toilet paper or toothpaste or cereal. Mom wouldn't have let this all happen with Lizzie and Soda, none of it. She would have yanked Lizzie home by the ponytail.

At night, I lay in bed listening to Lizzie howl, woofing and writhing, stomping and clawing as she sleepwalked. I tried to understand how those noises were *distinctly human.* Boomer pawed at me, begging me to make her be quiet, but I was doing all I could. The routine would take time to work, that was what the *DSM for Kids!* said. Dad had called the doctors at St. Cloud's to refill her prescription, but the pills were no use.

36.
September, October

Dad announced that we would be going to the annual Carpet Bazaar that year. We'd skipped last year's because Dad had been too sad about Mom. The Carpet Bazaar was held every October in a different city and it was a big deal in our family. At the bazaar, Dad's carpet store always had its own booth, and he loved going to the antique carpet auctions while the rest of us went sightseeing. This year the fair was in South Carolina, in a fancy hotel on the ocean.

I didn't want Lizzie to break her new routine of proper bedtimes and bland foods, all my progress would be undone, but I was excited to go to the bazaar. It seemed like a long time since we'd done something fun.

Dad said he planned on smuggling the parrot into the hotel, but Boomer would have to stay home. Vanessa agreed to take care of him. Mom always said Boomer couldn't stay in a kennel because it would be too traumatic for a dog who had been in the pound. "He's so sensitive," she'd say, stroking the fur between his ears. "He'd think that we'd abandoned him."

I wondered if Boomer remembered my mom, if he thought about her ever. Border collies are supposed to be exceptionally smart, but Boomer was getting older. One of his eyes had gone milky and maybe his memory was going too.

I thought Lizzie would be feeling better by the time of the bazaar, but I guess a broken heart takes longer than a few weeks to heal. I'd never been in love before, so what did I know? Lizzie said it was definitely love when I asked, and then she put her face back down into the pillows of the couch.

Lizzie moped all around the house before we left; she wasn't at all excited about the trip. When we got to the hotel, Lizzie waited in the truck while we checked in; she said she was too tired to move.

"One room?" I asked, after we walked away from the front desk.

"Two hundred and fifty dollars a night," Dad said. "Of course I only got one room."

"What if she sleepwalks?" I asked. "She might knock your teeth out."

He shrugged. "We won't try to wake her up."

After we fetched Lizzie from the truck, we took the elevator to the twelfth floor.

"One room?" Lizzie asked.

"One room." He nodded. Dad said he had to get to work immediately. He had an antique carpet he wanted to auction, and he was looking for some more contemporary stuff for the store. He left us some cash and permission for reasonable room service privileges. He left Ernest in his cage in the corner, and put the *Do Not Disturb* sign on the door so that housekeeping wouldn't come in.

There was an art museum and a planetarium near the hotel, but Lizzie said those were the worst ideas she'd ever heard. She was sprawled on the bed like a starfish.

"We could walk to the ocean," I suggested.

"Okay," Lizzie said. "I guess." She grabbed her jean jacket off the desk chair.

It wasn't a long walk to the water. No one else was on the beach except for a bunch of seagulls. I bent down to pick up a dead crab, missing its claws, the meat picked clean from the shell.

"What do crabs eat?" Lizzie asked.

"Dead things," I said. "Which is called carrion in the nature world. They'll eat fish, worms, anything dead. They'll eat their own species."

"Oh." She bent down to trace her name in the sand. I dropped the reddish-white crab shell into my pocket.

"There's one crab species, I forget which one," I said. "The female crab only mates once, but she'll produce millions of eggs during her lifetime, from that single mating."

"Phillip loved the ocean," Lizzie sniffed.

"His motel wasn't even on the ocean," I said. "You can do better, Lizzie. You'll do better next time. Mom had lots of boyfriends before she found Dad, and a few even after that."

She must have thought I was talking about Soda, because Lizzie let out a yelp. She started running away from me, leaving a sneaker imprint in the sand over her name. She ran down to the water, but she didn't stop there. She splashed right in, all her clothes still on, lifting her knees high, frothing up the waves. She didn't stop running until she was swimming.

I thought about going in after Lizzie, but I wasn't supposed to take my back brace off, and I was worried it would be hard to swim with it on. I hadn't been swimming since before Mom died, even though the heat had been unbearable in the summer.

I threw pebbles off the beach in Lizzie's direction. Some of them plunked near her, but three or four of them hit straight on. First she moved farther out, then she went underwater completely. I couldn't see where I should aim. I took my shoes off and rushed into the water up to my waist. "Lizzie!" I yelled. I scanned the waves, but I couldn't see her.

She finally bobbed up, and I exhaled in relief. She swam in, emerging from the water like a sea creature, a string of seaweed wrapped around her neck. You could see straight through her T-shirt and her sneakers were probably ruined. I slapped her on the arm, as hard as I could.

"Ouch," she said.

"You scared me." My stomach was still in a knot.

"I was just swimming."

"Okay," I said. "But you scared me."

Back at the hotel, Lizzie took one of the white terry cloth robes hanging in the bathroom closet and wrapped herself in it.

"Do you ever wonder what it's like to drown?" Lizzie asked.

I had, of course, but I was worried that Lizzie was serious about trying it. "No," I lied. "Never."

"I read the last few minutes are peaceful, like going to sleep. Do you think that's true?"

"I know you miss Soda." I gulped. "But that's not a good reason to drown yourself."

"It was just a question."

"What did you see in him anyway?" I asked. "Even Vanessa thought he was a loser."

"He helped me."

"With your sleepwalking?"

"Yeah," she said, looking out the window to the parking lot below. "And with other things. He said we just needed to keep talking, that talking would eventually help."

"What did you talk about?"

"Everything."

"Like what?"

"He understood why I feel so guilty about Mom's death."

"It's a normal stage of grief."

"Elvis," Lizzie said. "There's nothing normal about this family."

Ms. Bernstein had explained that abnormal grieving means that nothing changes in the patient, nothing improves. If what Lizzie said was true, if we were all abnormal, we would be trapped here forever, stuck to grief like it was flypaper.

That night, Lizzie had one of her worst night fits I'd ever seen. She was biting, tearing at Dad, trying to rip his hair clean from his scalp. She was screeching and growling.

I don't know how he managed it, but Dad got Lizzie into the hotel bathroom and held the door shut. We heard her tear the shower curtain right off its rings. She flushed the toilet again and again.

"There's nothing in there she could hurt herself with," Dad said. "I didn't bring my shaving kit."

"What about the shampoos?" I asked. "What if Lizzie drinks those?" I'd seen a news segment once on people who ate bath salts, and I guess all that soap made them crazy.

"She'll be fine in the morning," Dad said. "Help me use the bed to blockade the door."

In the morning, we found Lizzie in the bathtub. The sight of her there reminded me of Mom when she was mourning Nana. We drove back from Charleston in silence, a whole stack of new carpet rolls in the back of the truck.

At the house, there was a voice mail waiting for Lizzie. The Guinness World Records office was asking for an update on Lizzie's project. A lot of people start world records, but not a lot of people finish them, and they wanted to know whether they should keep her on their list. They wondered if she could be done by the end of the year, they really wanted to include her in this year's book.

"I'm almost done," she said, when she called them back. "I have seven hundred and fifty-seven cakes, but I'll get to a thousand." I guess she was ready to start baking again, even if she was heartbroken. "I'm not going to be one of those people who *almost* has a world record," she said. I was surprised to hear she was already in the seven hundreds, but Lizzie said she had baked quite a few cakes at the Silver Sand Motel and Marina, and Soda had taken them to the butcher's freezer for her. Those months hadn't been completely lost.

"What about school?" I asked. She wasn't cleared to be homeschooled this year.

"Let Lizzie finish her cakes," Dad said. "Then we'll talk about school." Dad was still rattled by how bad Lizzie's sleepwalking fit had been. At least she wasn't eating in her sleep this time around, which was a good thing. We had rabbit cakes spread all over the house, and if she had eaten those, it would have been a major setback.

I didn't know where Lizzie had read that drowning was a peaceful death. I had searched *what is it like to drown,* and I'd found a story on a message board about near-death experiences: a boy who had almost drowned in a pool in his backyard. As the water filled his lungs, all he had seen was the color purple. No tunnel of light, just purple everywhere, like he was swimming in grape juice. He had wanted to scream, but he couldn't make a noise.

He didn't say drowning felt like going to sleep, but it didn't sound that bad either, as far as dying went. I had looked up brain tumors, and deaths by kidney failure, the way Soda's mother had died, and those kinds of deaths sounded much more horrible. I would rather drown, given the choice, based on the information I had.

Of course, the boy in the story didn't drown all the way; he had only started the process. His mom had been there to pull him out, had given him puffs of air through CPR. But if Mom had drowned because of a brain tumor, I reminded myself, nothing could have been done to save her. CPR wouldn't have mattered; not even a doctor could have helped.

37.
~~OCTOBER,~~ NOVEMBER

Lizzie baked through October, and by November, seventeen months since Mom's death, she was doing better. She was back to showering first thing in the morning, and I didn't even have to turn the faucet on for her. She wasn't crying. She was baking all day and making our dinners at night, no more boxed macaroni shells. Lizzie had started her own routine, and it seemed healthy. I thought we were moving in the right direction, even if she was still sleepwalking.

One morning before school, there was a pan of brownies on the counter. Lizzie had left them out uncovered, and I wondered if she'd been eating them in her sleep. I cut a large brownie to eat for breakfast, since we were out of Pop-Tarts.

In the middle of second period, my math teacher, Mr. Reed, carried me to the principal's office after I told him I couldn't work my legs. Both limbs had gone tingly. Mr. Reed left me on the floor of the office until my dad could get there. The carpet was such nice quality, I bet it had come from Carpet World. I stroked all the carpet's little red hairs.

"Elvis," Principal Stuart said to my father, "is noticeably impaired."

"She's always been a little different," Dad said. The whole room was fuzzy, not just the carpet.

"Mr. Babbitt," Principal Stuart said, "your daughter is very, very stoned."

"Am I going to die?" I asked. Dad picked me up off the floor.

I was suspended from school for a whole two weeks for drug use. That was a longer suspension than Lizzie had ever received. I was trying to be mad, but everything seemed too funny and I was starving.

"I didn't mean to leave them out," Lizzie swore. "I didn't know Elvis would eat them."

"Where did you get the dope?" Dad asked. "Where's the rest of it?"

"No one calls it *dope*, Dad," she said, and he gave her the worst look I'd ever seen from him. She said she didn't have any more, but Dad found the rest of the marijuana when he ransacked her room.

Dad asked her if she had gotten it from Soda, but she wouldn't say. "I'm in over my head," he said, as if this was the first time he'd noticed. He went upstairs to his room with the baggie of leafy marijuana and his laptop. Ernest hurried after him, flying for a few feet.

I shoveled my hand into an open bag of potato chips, but Lizzie snatched the bag away.

"This isn't a vacation," Lizzie said. "I need help with the rabbit cakes. We're on a deadline."

I told Lizzie I would assist with the cakes every day except for the days when I was on the volunteer schedule at the zoo. Dad said I could still go to Serengeti Park, I wasn't being punished since I hadn't meant to take drugs; it had been all Lizzie's fault. Lizzie was grounded, but she never left the house anyway.

On Wednesday at the clinic, Dr. Rotherwood looked tired, and I knew there was a lot he was stressed about. The scheduled building of the orangutan exhibit had been delayed due to budget cuts, which left all the employees nervous about their next paycheck. As a volunteer employee, I had nothing to worry about, but I didn't like to see the rest of the staff on edge. The animals could sense fear, and it made many of them harder to handle.

Then there was the sad day that Nacho, our California black bear, had to be euthanatized. Nacho had emphysema caused by his years of smoking cigarettes in the circus, and he was having too much trouble breathing. I was worried about Yoyo, the female. The bears had been together for most of their lives. On the other hand, now Yoyo had the waterfall in the exhibit all to herself.

Vanessa knocked on our door while we were on our 889th rabbit cake. Her eye makeup was smeared all over her face, and her lip was split.

"I had a fight with Father Tillman," she said.

"He hit you?" Lizzie asked.

"No. I crashed the church van."

"Is that what you fought about?" Lizzie asked. "The van was a piece of junk anyway."

"No, the fight was before the crash. The crash happened a minute ago, the big tree at the end of your driveway. I was crying so hard, I guess I shouldn't have been driving."

We went out to see the tree. It was missing a big chunk of bark. Glass from the windshield was sprinkled all over the ground.

"We'll have to sweep this up," I said. "I don't want Boomer stepping on glass." Vanessa nodded.

"So what happened?" Lizzie asked.

Vanessa said Father Tillman had kicked her out of the nuns' apartments after he'd found out that she had been telling children in the Sunday school that the rapture was coming, and that only the good kids would get zapped up to heaven.

"Vanessa, that's so messed up," Lizzie said.

"I was trying to make them all behave. I'm sorry I said it, but it's too late to take it back. What am I going to do now?"

"You'll live here," Lizzie and I said at once.

It wasn't hard to convince Dad. He felt bad he'd kicked Vanessa out in the first place when she had nowhere else to go, and I'm sure he remembered how good Vanessa had been with Lizzie before.

This time around, Vanessa kept her distance from Dad, and got undressed in the bathroom. She didn't complain about the lumpy couch. That week, we were baking more than a dozen cakes a day and Vanessa made the baking more fun, somehow. I think we were all glad to have Vanessa around.

While rabbit number one thousand was baking in the oven, Lizzie stood up on the couch to give her acceptance speech. Vanessa, Dad, and I applauded and the parrot yelled, "Encore, encore," which he always did when people clapped their hands. The Guinness World Records office called to congratulate Lizzie on completing her goal, and said they'd send out the world record adjudicator in a few weeks to verify the existence of the cakes and take a few photos.

"I'll be ready," she said.

"We'll be ready," we chorused.

"I think this is as good a time as any," Dad said at the end of our celebratory toast, sparkling cider for everyone. "I wanted to tell you kids some news of my own. I've met someone."

"That's wonderful," Vanessa said. "Way to go, Mr. Babbitt."

"I met her online," Dad said. "We've been talking for a while, and she lives in Texas. She wants to come visit in a few weeks, the first week of December."

I wasn't sure what someone from Texas would be like. I pictured a woman who rode

sidesaddle, smoked a pipe, someone who
sauntered instead of walked regular.

"What would Mom say?" Lizzie snarled.

"If you really want to know, your mother
would say, 'Go for it, you old dog.' Your
mother always thought I should get out
more."

"Get out more?" Lizzie asked.

"We had a nontraditional sexual relation-
ship. An open marriage, if you want a word
for it. Your mother took more advantage of
our arrangement than I ever did, but she
had more free time."

So the secret I'd been keeping for over a
year wasn't even a secret. Dad wouldn't care
about Mr. Oakes and the trailer; maybe he
already knew. But after I thought about it
for a second, I believed it would hurt Dad if
he knew about Mr. Debbie, about how
Ernest got Mom's voice. I'd keep that secret.

"Your dead mother had other lovers,"
Lizzie repeated. "Just what you want your
dad to say on the best day of your life, the
first day you're a world record holder."

"It's happy news," Vanessa said. "I'm glad
Frank shared."

"Shut up, Vanessa," Lizzie snapped.

"She's coming to visit soon," Dad said.
"And you're going to be nice."

"We'll be nice," I promised.

"If you don't like her . . ." Dad trailed off. If we didn't like her, then what, I wanted to know.

That night, Lizzie didn't sleepwalk, but she screamed and screamed like her bed was on fire. She had started sleepscreaming as she walked around the house, but she also screamed on nights when she wasn't sleep-walking. She'd lie on her back, stiff as a board, shrieking at the top of her lungs. You could turn on the light in her room and watch her face turn red, then purple, then white. I worried she would choke on her tongue, but Vanessa said that never happened to people.

"Let her scream," Vanessa said. "Maybe it's therapeutic for her." Vanessa was reading lots of books on child therapy; she had decided she wanted to go back to school.

Dad and I were keeping our doors locked, but I would get up in the night to pee. Vanessa was sleeping defenseless on the couch, and nothing bad had happened. We were standing in Lizzie's room now, and she didn't even know we were there.

I looked down at Lizzie's sleeping expression, her face frozen in a look of horror. Maybe she was only a danger to herself.

■ ■ ■ ■

In the morning, it was obvious that no one but Lizzie had slept. Even Boomer was tired. I didn't know if it was really possible for a dog to have circles under his eyes, but I could have sworn Boomer did, underneath his black-and-white fur.

I was exhausted, but I had to go back to school; my suspension was up. We were reading a new book in English class, and everyone had heard I'd been stoned in math. Suzanna Zebb asked me to sit at her table at lunch. Suzanna's friends were known as the druggies, although I discovered when I sat with them that they'd never done any drugs, not real ones anyway. They said they'd huffed paint in Suzanna's garage.

"Is it medical marijuana?" they asked. "For your scoliosis?"

"Yeah," I said, although my crooked spine had never hurt me.

"I've heard that shit is crazy," said Glenn Lego, a scrawny friend of Suzanna's. Some kids just called him Lego, but I didn't know him that well. "Can you get us some?"

"Sure," I said, but I wasn't paying much attention to Suzanna or Glenn Lego. I scanned the lunchroom. I looked for the security guard in the No Bully Zone, wondering who he would talk to about his two shih tzus now. I was surprised to see that Jackie Friskey, the former fifth-grade class president, was sitting with him. Jackie had always had a ton of friends; she didn't belong in the No Bully Zone.

"You didn't hear?" Suzanna said, when she saw me staring. "Jackie Friskey has an STD. I bet she got it from someone old and totally gross."

"I wouldn't touch her. Not with a ten-foot pole," Glenn Lego said.

I got up and walked toward the No Bully Zone, stepping over backpacks and weaving through lunch tables to get there. Jackie had given me a flower once, a rose, and she had waved when I saw her that time at the river, hadn't looked the other way. She was the nicest person in the middle school. She didn't deserve to be gossiped about.

"I've never even been kissed," Jackie sniffed as we talked. "I had a urinary tract infection, which my mom said anyone can get."

We had learned about chlamydia, gonorrhea, and AIDS from our sixth-grade health teacher, shortly before we'd learned about scoliosis. We hadn't covered urinary tract infections, but I knew what a UTI was from my work with Dr. Rotherwood; our camel had gotten one, and it had spread to her kidneys, turned very serious.

"What am I going to do?" Jackie asked me, and I guess she was asking the security guard too, but he looked pale in the face, pretending not to listen.

"Fuck everyone." It was something Lizzie would say, but it seemed like the right thing. "Let's get chocolate milks. Come on."

"You're the bravest girl I've ever met," Jackie said, her eyes big and sweet like a sheep's.

38.

I worried about Lizzie's routine changing, with nothing left to bake. Lizzie couldn't go on baking cakes forever, we didn't have room for them, not even with the rented walk-in freezer. She would have to stop.

I asked Vanessa about it, and she said that the rabbit cakes were a coping mechanism, which meant they were something to make Lizzie feel better.

"I thought it was about a world record," I said.

"Well, that too," Vanessa said. "But it's more complicated than that."

Vanessa said my investigation into Mom's death was another coping mechanism. "You are both trying to keep your mother alive somehow."

"I know she's dead," I told Vanessa. "I just want to know how it happened."

"Why does it matter?"

"Well, how did your mother die?" I realized I'd never asked Vanessa that before.

"Heroin," she said. "She killed herself, by accident. An overdose."

"She killed herself by accident," I repeated, letting the idea sink in.

At Thanksgiving, Lizzie made the turkey and Vanessa made the sides: yams with marshmallows and a green bean casserole. I made the sticky buns, which just meant I had to take the buns out of the can and put them on the baking sheet. Dad set the table and put the cornucopia figurine in the middle.

"I'm thankful for all of you," Vanessa said when we went around the table, and I didn't think she was lying. I'd said I was thankful for the zoo and for Boomer, but after Vanessa spoke I wished I'd said something nice about Lizzie, Vanessa, or Dad.

Vanessa was starting to feel like part of the family, so I was surprised when she announced at the end of dinner that she had to go down to New Orleans for a while. She said she'd be gone only two weeks, three at the most. She promised she'd be back by Christmas. She had a friend who had finally been released from St. Cloud's and needed help moving into her new apartment. The girl's family had offered Vanessa a thousand bucks to make sure there were no mirrors in the house, that the windows were tinted, that the bathroom faucets were not chrome, the surface of the coffee table not reflective. The girl had a narcissistic personality disorder. Vanessa said her friend had once caused a five-car pileup when she caught her own image while adjusting the rearview mirror and braked right there. It was only a little sliver of her forehead, but it was the most beautiful forehead the girl had ever seen.

The first night without Vanessa, Dad forced us to have a game night, said we could use some concentrated family time. Ernest kept pecking at the board, knocking our hotels over. Lizzie made me count her pastel money for her, since she was painting her fingernails.

"Did you ask Vanessa to leave?" Lizzie asked as Dad rolled the dice. She didn't look up at him, admiring her slick red nails instead.

"What?" Dad said. "No, I didn't. You know I like having her here."

"But isn't your internet girlfriend coming to visit next week?"

"She is. So?"

"Wouldn't it be confusing for your girlfriend?" Lizzie said. "I assume you told her you have two daughters, not three."

"Lizzie," Dad said. "It's a coincidence."

I chose to believe Dad. Lizzie was probably just looking for something else to be angry about, now that she was getting over Soda.

The next morning, we got a package from Guinness World Records. The scrolled certificate read: *Elizabeth G. Babbitt: Creator of the World's Largest Collection of Rabbit-Shaped Cakes.* They also sent a bunch of pencils with *Certified Guinness World Record Holder* stamped on the side. The world record adjudicator had to come sign the certificate, the note said, before it was official.

"We'll have to frame this," Dad said, unrolling the scroll. "This is really something."

"I wish it said Lizzie," Lizzie said. "No one calls me Elizabeth."

The only thing I had framed on the wall in my room was the grieving chart. I was only three *X*s away from the end, where Ms. Bernstein had written *FIND CLOSURE* in all caps.

After Nacho the bear had been put to sleep, Dr. Rotherwood decided that Yoyo, his mate, needed closure. The zookeepers brought Nacho's body into Yoyo's cage with a forklift, placed him on a flat rock by the swimming hole. They left his huge limp body there for five hours, let zoo visitors come by with flowers to pay their respects. But Yoyo wouldn't come out of the sleeping cave. Dr. Rotherwood turned up the thermostat in there to make the cave uncomfortable, hoping to drive her to the water, but she stayed put, even after her nose had gone dry from dehydration.

Yoyo still wouldn't go near that one rock, so the zoo was thinking of dividing her enclosure into two, in order to make room for a pair of red-crowned cranes.

I wasn't sure I wanted closure, because Yoyo hadn't been the same since. She wouldn't wave her paw in the air anymore when you called out her name. She wouldn't even lift her big black head in response.

■ ■ ■ ■

Part IV
Months 18 to 20

■ ■ ■ ■

39.
~~November,~~ December

It was December, the eighteenth month on the grieving chart, and I came home from school on Friday to find that Lizzie was in the bathroom dyeing her hair. There was L'Oréal Superior Preference Intense Red Copper all over the sink and on the towels. Dad's new girlfriend was coming for dinner that night.

"Mom would hate it that you're dyeing your hair," I said. Mom had claimed she'd never dye her hair, not even to color the gray. She hadn't lived long enough to go gray, other than a strand here and there.

"Mom would hate a lot of things around here."

"What are you making for dinner tonight?" I asked, changing the subject. "For Dad's friend?"

"Nothing," Lizzie said, squirting more goo from the nozzle into her scalp. "That's Dad's problem."

I went downstairs and started on dinner, since Dad wouldn't be home in time; he was driving to the Birmingham airport and back. I boiled water for mac and cheese. I made miniature cucumber sandwiches, because those were supposed to be sophisticated, but we didn't have cucumbers in the house so I used a jar of dill pickles we had left in the fridge.

Ernest had been trapped in his cage all day, because Dad said he didn't know how the bird would react to the girlfriend. Parrots are very jealous animals, possessive and temperamental. I gave Ernest a dried ear of corn to keep him busy.

I heard the truck pull up, and I watched from the kitchen window. Dad helped her out of the truck, and they held hands as they walked to the front door. She was wearing a tight pink dress, and she didn't look that much older than Lizzie. As soon as she walked into the house, Boomer stuck his nose right in her crotch, like he was trying to lift her off the ground with his head. "No no no," she said, and swatted at him. Boomer slinked off, ashamed.

"This is Samantha," he said, gesturing to Lizzie and me.

We both already knew that. Lizzie and I had looked at her dating profile when Dad was at work, so we knew she was twenty-nine, many years younger than Dad. She was interested in men between the ages of twenty-five and fifty-five, she liked white wine and beach vacations, she had a nut allergy, and she wanted kids someday, with the right person.

"Nice to meet you," she said, making eye contact with me. "Elvis, I presume." I felt butterflies in my stomach. We'd learned in school about kissing the ring of the pope or the king as a sign of respect, so I grabbed her hand and pulled her turquoise ring to my lips. She looked surprised but she let me do it. Dad laughed. He was in a good mood.

"I like the new look," Dad said to Lizzie. "You look like Lucille Ball."

"Mom would hate it," I said. "She would say you look like a cheap hooker."

"Elvis!" Dad scolded, his eyes wide.

Lizzie laughed, not because I had called her a hooker but because I had upset Dad in front of his guest.

Samantha pulled a six-pack of beer out of a paper bag and placed the bottles on the kitchen table.

"Oh, thank you," Lizzie said. "Dad must have told you how much I love beer."

"Lizzie," Dad warned.

"It's fine," Samantha said. "I'm sure this whole thing is weird for them."

"I'm very glad to meet you," I said. "I'm happy Dad has a girlfriend."

Samantha blushed. "What about you? Do you have a boyfriend?"

"I'm eleven," I said.

"She's asexual, like a crab," Lizzie said.

"Crabs aren't asexual. You're thinking of the blue crab. The female only mates once in her life, but that doesn't make her asexual."

"I hope you enjoy that one time."

"Lizzie," Dad said. "Pick on someone your own size."

"Like Samantha?"

"No," Dad said, "not Samantha."

When Dad saw what I had made for dinner, he ordered pizza. Samantha was the kind that didn't eat her crusts. At dinner, she let me quiz her like it was a game show. She owned an art gallery in Dallas, she didn't have a dog, she had ridden a horse but only a few times. She had never been married, she loved canned tuna fish but she always tried to buy the dolphin-safe brand, she had a little brother named Steve who lived all the way in Alaska so she almost never saw him. She wanted to write a book someday about her favorite painter, someone I'd never heard of. "He's not that famous," she said. "But he will be when I'm done."

"Lizzie dated an artist," I said. "He dumped her."

"Elvis," Lizzie growled.

"You don't want to date an artist, anyway, so it's for the best. They are much too self-involved," Samantha said. "Take it from me, I've dated several."

Lizzie rolled her eyes, even though I thought it was good advice. Lizzie's hands were stained red from the hair dye, like Lady Macbeth's.

"What are your feelings on Shakespeare?" I asked.

Dad interrupted me, asked if anyone wanted apple pie for dessert. It was a store-bought one in a silver foil pan, but it wasn't bad after Dad warmed it in the oven.

After dessert, Dad suggested we take Samantha to see the rabbit cakes, and Lizzie brightened up. She was glad for a new audience, even if the new audience was Samantha. We drove down to the meat locker all together in Dad's truck, and stood back as Lizzie put the key in the padlock.

Before she opened the silver door, Lizzie explained that the collection was over a thousand, with number 1,003 cooling on the counter at home. Lizzie always wanted to go above and beyond. Most of the thousand rabbits were in the walk-in freezer at the butcher's, although fifty of them remained in the chest freezer at home. Both freezers were at capacity, the rabbits lined up shoulder to shoulder like soldiers in the army.

Lizzie took out her two best rabbits to show Samantha: one black and white like Boomer, a border collie rabbit, and the other a light brown with a real cotton ball for a tail. Lizzie let Samantha hold the black-and-white cake, making her promise to keep her hands flat on the bottom for proper support.

"Wow," Samantha said. "It's heavy." Lizzie beamed. "I like the markings on it, too," she continued. "Looks realistic."

I told Samantha about the time Lizzie shut me into the walk-in freezer, how dark it was. I didn't tell her that the rabbit cakes came alive when I was in there; I didn't want Samantha to think I was crazy.

"She shut you in the freezer?" Samantha asked, not smiling. "You could have frozen to death." She placed the black-and-white rabbit back on the shelf. The rabbit's nose twitched, and then the one next to it flicked its ear. Samantha didn't seem to see anything; she walked right out of the freezer.

Maybe the rabbits were mad about Samantha, because they thought we were replacing Mom. "She's just a girlfriend," I whispered to the rabbits.

"Elvis, we're leaving," Lizzie said, poking her head back in. "Let's go."

That night, Samantha stayed in a hotel, I think because Dad didn't want her to hear Lizzie's night screams. Boomer and I were the only ones to hear Lizzie that night, because Dad snuck out to go join Samantha at the Motel 6. They'd made a big show of saying good-bye when we dropped Samantha off at the motel, but of course Lizzie and I both heard Dad leave twenty minutes after we got home, saw the truck headlights bright in the driveway.

40.

"Your dad tells me you work at the zoo?" Samantha asked at breakfast. Dad had brought a box of donuts home, pretending he'd woken up early to pick Samantha up at the motel.

She didn't say I volunteered at the zoo, or ask if I did community service at the zoo. I loved the way she said *work,* such a simple word. She took me seriously, the same way Dr. Rotherwood did.

"I could give you a tour of the zoo, if you want," I offered, blushing.

"Great idea," Dad said. "We'll all go."

I used my ZooTeen ID badge to let us in the back entrance to the zoo, even though Dad would have paid for tickets.

"You can get in this way at any time?" Lizzie said.

"Yeah," I said, feeling important. "They trust me." Dr. Rotherwood had requested that my badge had access to the back entrance so I could come in early on weekends and file paperwork.

We went to the exotic animal clinic first; a litter of Columbia Basin pygmy rabbits had been born two weeks before, and their eyes were open now, their soft deer-brown fur had come in. Dr. Rotherwood said everyone in our party was allowed to handle them, as long as we were wearing gloves.

"A friend of Elvis," Dr. Rotherwood said, "is a great friend of mine."

"Endangered rabbits," Samantha said. "I had no idea." She offered her hands in a cup to accept one of the teacup-sized bunnies. Lizzie and Dad held one too, but I didn't take one. I wanted them to know that this was no big deal for me, I handled endangered animals almost every day.

"It looks like the babies are tired now," Dr. Rotherwood said. "Time for a nap."

We walked from the animal hospital to Asia Quest and then to the African Safari. We went through the greenhouse at Bird Paradise and we looked at the tiny hummingbird's nest, which had a new batch of blank eggs in it. We went underground to Rodent Tunnel. I didn't tell them about what happened in Rodent Tunnel on Wednesdays, because I didn't want to cry again, the way I had when I'd told Lizzie.

At the red pandas, Lizzie said, "They look like raccoons."

"No, they don't. They look like red pandas."

"No shit, Sherlock," Lizzie said, but she was being the stupid one.

We walked across the Japanese bridge over the waterfowl enclosure. Samantha didn't complain about the smell. She used four quarters in the dispenser where you could buy food pellets, and she gave me a handful. Lizzie wouldn't take any duck food, but she did lean over the bridge to watch the birds paddle with their beaks low to the water.

At the end of the day, Samantha wanted to take us to the gift shop, the only place in the zoo I never went. She bought me a snowy owl puppet, but Lizzie wouldn't let her buy anything for her.

"Not even a T-shirt?" Samantha begged.

"Nope," Lizzie said. "Not even."

On Sunday night, after we'd all gone to the bowling alley, Dad announced that Samantha had had such a good time over the weekend that she was taking the week off from work at the art gallery, and she'd be staying with us, in our house. She moved from the Motel 6 into Dad's room, dragging her black roller suitcase. Maybe Samantha would move in for good. We didn't have an art gallery in Freedom, but we could probably use one.

"It's just so disrespectful," I heard Lizzie say on the phone, probably to Vanessa. I was sure Vanessa would like Samantha when she came back home.

I thought Samantha was a good choice for a stepmother, because she was so different from Mom. Dad would always love Mom best, he'd have to, but Samantha was warm and nice and responsible. She didn't want me getting shut in the meat freezer, she didn't want me freezing to death.

And after her first night in Dad's room, Samantha said she wasn't bothered by Lizzie's sleepscreaming, insisted that she barely even heard her roaming through the hallway. She swore she'd slept just fine. "But I feel terrible that she's having such bad nightmares."

The way Samantha said it, it seemed like such a small thing: Lizzie was having nightmares. So what? Lots of people did. Maybe we'd always overreacted to this whole thing.

Maybe everything was fine now, and the storm after Mom's death had passed. The dust was settling. I sipped the glass of iced tea Samantha had poured for me. It was sweeter than the batches Mom used to make.

Things were good at home, but at school, things were still terrible for Jackie Friskey. Before we were friends, I had thought that Jackie's life was perfect: she had boobs already and she had been the best public speaker at Beaver Elementary. But now I knew that her parents fought, and that her mom sometimes commented that Jackie was looking chubby. Jackie didn't have any friends anymore, except for me, and everyone in school whispered things about her. The rumor had started after Jackie told her friend Stephanie that it burned when she peed, which I guess is a symptom of chlamydia, as well as a urinary tract infection. The words *slut, whore,* and *ho-bag* were graffitied on Jackie's locker. I told the janitor so he could paint over it.

I invited Jackie over to my house after school, and she was so excited that she hugged me. She said on the bus ride home that she couldn't wait to meet my new stepmother.

"She's not my stepmother yet," I said. "Not officially."

"My parents are fighting all the time," she

said. "They're going through with the divorce."

"Maybe you'll get a stepmother," I said, trying to sound cheerful. I didn't always know what to say when Jackie started talking about her parents. Her mom was alive.

When Jackie and I got off the bus at my house, Dad and Ernest were at work. Samantha was wearing yellow rubber gloves and cleaning our stove. She made us a quick batch of Pillsbury cookies, cutting up the cookie dough log. We did our homework at the table, and Jackie told Samantha about the STD rumor. Jackie described how I'd marched right over to her in the No Bully Zone, how I didn't care what anyone thought. "She was my friend when I had no one," she said. "She bought me a Yoo-hoo."

"You go, Elvis," Samantha said. "It's important to stand up for others, and for yourself."

"No one would ever mess with Elvis."

"Why?"

I had the same question, but Samantha was the one to ask it.

"They think she's a . . . they think she's like her sister."

I felt a weird kind of pride then.

"What do you mean, like her sister?" Samantha asked.

"They think she's crazy. Everyone is surprised they let Lizzie out of the nut house."

"Out of the what?"

I guess Dad hadn't told Samantha everything yet. I shot Jackie a look.

"Nothing," Jackie said. "Just another rumor."

"So people are afraid of me? Since when?" I remembered when Aiden Masters called me retarded in fifth-grade chorus; he wasn't scared of me then.

"I guess since you did drugs in school."

"Drugs?" Samantha asked, shocked. I told her Jackie was just joking, that she had a weird sense of humor.

It all made sense now, why no one had bullied me or scribbled on my locker. I didn't need the No Bully Zone anymore, not with a sister like mine, a reputation I hadn't earned.

It was Friday afternoon. Dad had come home early from work, and he and Samantha were playing poker at the kitchen table. The parrot was sitting on Samantha's shoulder, and I thought if Ernest could warm up to Samantha, then Lizzie could too. I sat down at the table with them.

It was then that Lizzie brought out a rabbit cake, one that was beautifully frosted, with dark brown raisin eyes and a big licorice smile.

"Who wants cake?" Lizzie asked. "I made it this morning."

"I do," I said, surprised that she said we could eat it. Maybe this cake could be the mark of a new beginning, of a new family. It wasn't even dinnertime yet, only four in the afternoon, but Dad said it didn't matter if we ruined our appetites.

Dad unlocked the knife drawer for Lizzie, and she pulled the biggest knife out, one of the pig-carving knives. When she sliced into the cake, I swear I saw the rabbit flinch in pain. I didn't feel like cake anymore.

"Looks delicious," Samantha said, taking a bite of the ear. She took six more bites before it happened. She grabbed her throat and made a choking sound, like she was dying for water. I pushed my glass toward her.

"Were there nuts in that?" Dad grabbed Lizzie by the wrist as she tried to escape from the table. "She's allergic to nuts." Dad was panicking.

"Marzipan," Lizzie said. I could tell she'd meant to do it, but I didn't think she knew how bad the reaction would be, because she was pretty shocked by what happened next.

Samantha had rooted through her purse

and was now holding an EpiPen in her hand. I knew what it was from recess two years ago, when I saw the nurse use one on a bee-allergy kid when he stepped on a yellow jacket. But I'd never seen anything like what Samantha did. She took off her jeans at the table and her face was growing redder, puffier by the second. She jammed the needle right into her thigh.

There was a knock on my door in the middle of the night. It was Dad, so I unlocked the door and let him in. Samantha was fine, Dad whispered, she had been released from the hospital and was out in the car. They were going to drive back to Birmingham tonight, where Samantha could catch the first flight out. Dad said he would be home by morning, before Lizzie would be up and out of bed. Samantha hadn't gotten out of the truck to say goodbye, or even to collect her own suitcase, because Dad had told her not to. He didn't want Lizzie to know that Samantha had been released. He wanted Lizzie to think that Samantha had to be kept at the hospital for a few days because her reaction to the nuts was so serious. "She has to learn that there are consequences for her actions," Dad argued. "Play along, Elvis, please."

So Dad took Samantha to the airport, and in the morning, he lied and told Lizzie that she was in the hospital; he claimed that the doctors said it was still touch and go. I played along, I guess, since I didn't tell Lizzie what I knew, that Samantha was already boarding a flight to Texas. I found out later that she and Dad had broken up on the way to the airport, and it didn't even sound like it was because of the allergy attack. "Fun while it lasted, but she was a little young for me," Dad explained.

"I'm so sorry," Lizzie wailed when Dad said Samantha was hooked up to a breathing machine. "I didn't know she could die." Lizzie reached for me, wanting a hug. I let her arms hang there.

41.

That night, a cop car showed up in our driveway at midnight, its lights flashing. It was the same cop who had brought Lizzie home before, back when she had beaten up Megan Sax.

"Sir," Officer Rooney said, eyes down at his combat boots. "Your daughter broke into the zoo."

"She what?" Dad asked, rubbing his eyes. "No, Elvis works there."

"Your other daughter, Lizzie. She broke in using her sister's ID badge. We have her in a holding cell."

"No," I said. "No, no, no, no. I am going to kill her."

"Can you come down to the station with me, sir?" Officer Rooney asked. "I'll need your help filing the report."

"Please stop calling me *sir,* Mike. We went to high school together."

Dad got his coat from the closet and went

off with Officer Rooney in the cop car, the red-and-blue lights back on as if they hadn't already caught the criminal. Mom's Honda was gone again.

A few hours later, the phone rang. It was still dark out, but I hadn't gone back to bed. I'd been waiting up for Dad to get back.

"They're not releasing me yet, but they said I could make a two-minute call," Lizzie said. "I wanted to explain."

"Were you sleepwalking?" I asked. She'd driven the Honda, but some sleepwalkers drive in their sleep. Lizzie had never sleep-walked that far from our house before, but if she had been asleep, it wouldn't have been her fault. She wouldn't have done it to hurt me.

She sighed, and I knew she'd been awake.

"Go to hell," I said, and hung up, long before the two minutes were up. I was going to lose my job at the zoo for this, I was pretty sure. We weren't supposed to lend out our ZooTeen badges to anyone; the scan code on the back unlocked most of the cage doors. "I hate her," I said to Boomer, and he cocked his head, trying to understand.

By lunchtime, everyone at Three Rivers was talking about the break-in. It had been on the news that morning, because one of the zebras had gotten out and was still wandering around town. "The people of Lee County are on strict instruction not to shoot this animal," the newsperson said. Lizzie's name hadn't been released to the press, so no one knew it was all her fault.

"I heard the lion killed a zookeeper," Suzanna Zebb said.

"I doubt it," I told her. The lion was heavily sedated at night in order to treat the insomnia he had, which was caused by the drugs he was given for depression.

"Who asked you?" Suzanna scoffed.

"No one. No one asked me."

"Are you okay?" Jackie asked at lunch. "You look terrible."

Jackie took me into the bathroom and braided my hair for me. She listened as I told her about my sister stealing my ID badge. I didn't think all the media attention would be good for the zoo.

"What about your sister?" Jackie asked. "Is she going to go to jail?"

"I hope so," I said.

"You don't mean that."

But Jackie didn't understand. She was an only child, no siblings, and the worst things that had ever happened to her were her parents' divorce and a silly rumor about a sexually transmitted disease.

When the bus dropped me off, the house was empty except for the dog, so I guessed Lizzie hadn't been released yet. I was pouring myself a bowl of cereal when the phone rang again. It wasn't Lizzie this time. It was my ZooTeen supervisor.

"Everyone deserves a second chance," Pamela said.

"Thank you," I exhaled. "Thank you so much."

"That *was* your second chance," she reminded me. I'd forgotten I'd ever been suspended from the zoo. Dr. Rotherwood and I had put that behind us. I pleaded and pleaded, but Pamela said it was too late.

"Your sister broke the Big Gulp slushie machine," Pamela said. "She opened many of the cages. We found the runaway zebra, thankfully, and he's unharmed."

"Which zebra was it?" I asked. Bartleby was my favorite.

"I don't know," Pamela said. "I can't tell them apart. Elvis, I hate to ask you this, but were you there? The night watchman said there might have been another girl, but he wasn't sure."

"No," I said. "It wasn't me. Honest." I knew the zoo didn't have security cameras, except in the gift shop, so they'd never catch the other girl. I thought of Vanessa, supposed to be down in New Orleans. I couldn't believe Vanessa would betray me like this, even if she was Lizzie's best friend; she knew how much the zoo meant to me. For a second, I thought about giving Pamela her name.

"I didn't think you would do that," Pamela said. "That's what I told the police."

"Okay," I said. "Thanks."

Just after eight o'clock, Lizzie came home, released from jail. Her holding period had ended. She walked in with Dad and her lawyer, a fat man named Allan from Dad's bowling league. He wore a bow tie and suspenders.

I dove for Lizzie, my fingernails ready like claws. Dad got in my way fast and scooped me into his huge arms. I'd forgotten how strong Dad was; maybe he'd gotten that way from dragging around carpets all day.

"Elvis," Dad said, because I was still thrashing in his tree-trunk arms. "Calm down. Now is not the time."

"Elvis," Lizzie said, calmly. "I wasn't sleepwalking, but I had a good reason. If you'll just let me tell you."

"Shut up, shut up, shut up, I don't care,"

340

I said, and Dad tightened his arms around me. "I hope you fall down the stairs and break all your teeth."

"That's not a nice thing to say to a sleep-walker," Dad scolded.

"She's a sleepwalker?" Allan the lawyer interrupted. "Frank, why didn't you say so?"

Allan excitedly explained about the sleep-walking defense; several people had used it to get off murder charges. The idea was, sleepwalkers cannot act with intent, cannot consider what they are about to do before they do it. Lizzie hadn't intended to eat all those raw eggs in her sleep, she'd just done it. It was only when she was awake that she was really bad, that she really tried to hurt people.

In 1987, a Canadian man named Kenneth Parks killed his mother-in-law, and his father-in-law only barely survived the at-tack. In his sleep, Parks drove fifteen miles to the house, where he beat his in-laws with a tire iron and then stabbed his mother-in-law with a kitchen knife. Then he drove himself to the police station, and he woke up there. Parks had a family history of para-somnias, came from a long line of sleepwalk-ers.

"I've read about him," Lizzie said. Where had she read about it? I wondered. And why? Was it the same place she'd read that drowning is peaceful? Why did Lizzie know things that I didn't?

"Mr. Parks was let off scot-free," Allan said. "How well is Lizzie's sleepwalking condition documented?"

"We've got doctors' records," Dad said, finally letting go of me. "And she went to a mental hospital for it. My wife was a sleep-walker too, Allan, remember? That's how Eva drowned."

"Jackpot," Allan said. "We're golden. We'll say she drove to the zoo in her sleep, that she didn't wake up until she was in the cop car. She doesn't remember a thing."

"But she wasn't sleepwalking," I said. "She was awake."

"We're the only ones who know that," Allan said. "And we're not going to repeat it. Your sister is charged with breaking and entering, and she has to go to juvenile court. This is serious stuff, okay?"

"Elvis?" Dad asked, when I said nothing.

Lizzie could get away with anything, and that made me furious. I spat at Lizzie, but I missed her, my spit landing on the blue-and-gold Oriental, the most expensive carpet in the house.

"Go to your room, young lady," Dad said.

"Who?" Lizzie and I both asked at the

same time.

Dad needed to give Allan a ride back to jail, since Allan had left his car in the parking lot of the police station. After Dad left, I took Boomer outside and I stood on the porch while Boomer sniffed around the yard, marking his territory. I leaned against the chest freezer. It looked like a big white coffin, an expensive one. "The little sister freezer," Lizzie had called it, and I missed Samantha for a moment, the way she'd worried about me. Everyone was always worried about Lizzie instead.

Some of the rabbit cakes were housed in the chest freezer, the last fifty cakes of the world record collection. These were the cakes I had helped bake. They were made in a rush, the final sprint, the finish line in sight. They were made from Betty Crocker boxed mixes, the vanilla flavor; we'd bought out the whole aisle at the Stop 'n' Save.

I opened the top of the freezer and lifted out a naked yellow rabbit, number 993. I picked it up like a baby and carried it out into the front yard, where I set it on the ground. The rabbit didn't move. I nudged it with my boot, half expecting the whiskers to twitch.

When it didn't get up and hop away, I

stepped on its face. I left a footprint in the cake, and I felt a surge of happiness. I stepped on the cake again, and again and again and again until I was jumping up and down. When the rabbit was completely flattened, I took another out of the chest freezer. I smashed it on top of the first, and went back to the freezer for another cake, then another and another. I was surprised at how easily the frozen cakes broke apart; they didn't freeze solid like ice. I took a frosted cake up to the second floor and dropped it out the window.

I hated my sister. I hated Lizzie for being the spitting image of Mom. I hated her for almost killing Samantha, for breaking into the zoo and making me lose my job, for running away for months and leaving me behind. I hated that she thought Soda could understand her better than I could, and for being so pathetic after he broke up with her. I hated my Dad too, for lying to Lizzie about how bad Samantha's allergic reaction was, and for allowing my sister to home-school herself, for letting her stay home and do nothing but bake. I hated the rabbit cakes for making me think I was crazy.

While I stomped the last cake from the freezer, I looked up and saw Lizzie in her bedroom window, her forehead pressed against the glass. If I hadn't known better, I would have thought her face was wrinkled up in tears. I stuck my tongue out at her, but she only turned away from the window, retreating into the darkness of her room.

Dad's truck pulled up; his jaw dropped open a little when he saw I was sitting in a pile of devastated rabbit cake in the front yard. Boomer was licking the ground, his fur matted with clumps of frosting.

"We're bad dogs," I growled, scooping a fistful of cake off the ground. "We're rabbit eaters."

Dad walked by me without a word. Even Ernest didn't say anything. Boomer rolled over onto his back, paws straight up in the air, an eager apology for what we had done.

42.

That night, I took Boomer out again. It was late, two in the morning; his old dog bladder couldn't always hold through the night, so sometimes he woke me up to go out, even though I know he was ashamed. Boomer was snuffling through the grass, when suddenly, his head snapped up, like he'd heard a car in the driveway. He barked once, sharply, and I looked up to see Lizzie balancing on the roof of our house, walking along the apex, teetering at every step. I dropped Boomer's leash and I started to run.

Mom had shown us how to climb to the top of the roof; we had gone up there during meteor showers. You had to climb from the top of the truck to the garage roof, and from there you could get onto the top of the house, if you were brave enough. It was too hard to climb anything with my back brace on, so I ripped it open and left it in the driveway.

"Lizzie," I said, getting my footing on the shingles. Even though I'd been up on the roof before, it had seemed much safer then. "Don't jump. Lizzie, please don't jump."

Lizzie looked at me and grinned, like she had when I'd caught her in the chicken coop.

"Wake up, wake up, wake up, wake up, Lizzie, wake up! I forgive you, I'm not that mad about the zoo. Please don't kill yourself."

Lizzie lunged for me and there was nowhere to go, I couldn't step to either side, I couldn't run. I had to meet her head on. She grabbed my hair, so I grabbed hers back. Lizzie snapped her teeth in my face but I wouldn't let go. Her breath stank of sleep.

"The zoo was the one thing that was mine," I said. "You took that."

"Mmph," she grunted. Lizzie pulled my hair harder, and I yanked on hers.

"You take everything. You hog all the attention, it's like you think Mom only died on you. She died on me too, and Dad." Maybe if we hadn't had to spend so much time on Lizzie's problems, we might be done grieving for Mom by now. These months were supposed to be about Mom, but they'd been about Lizzie instead.

Her eyes were glazed, dark. The light reflecting from the moon was bright enough that I could see her face. "You're selfish," I spat. "You ruined my grieving chart. You distracted us from Mom's death with your stupid sleepwalking, and now we're going to be in mourning forever." I pulled her hair harder.

Lizzie let go of my hair and tried to circle her hands around my throat. I pushed her away as hard as I could; we both lost our balance then. I fell onto my back, grasping at shingles. *She always wins,* I thought as I steadied myself.

But I looked around and saw Lizzie was no longer on the roof. I crawled along the ridge of the roof to the edge of our house, and Lizzie was lying like a dead bird on the ground. My heart flew into my throat. I had killed my sister. I had been awake to do it, and angry.

But no, her legs were moving. Could a person move after she was dead? I remembered what they say about headless chickens, so did the heart die before the muscles? I turned and scurried back to the other end of the roof, where I jumped down onto the garage, and then onto the truck, then to the pavement.

Lizzie was alive, and awake by the time I got to her. She asked me what happened, her eyes bleary.

"You were on the roof," I said, wiping the tears off my face.

"Did I jump?" she gasped.

I was shaking too much to answer.

"Is this blood?" She held up her wrist.

Boomer sat next to her, and licked her hand.

"It's not blood, it's frosting," I said. We were in the middle of the rabbit cake minefield. I took a deep breath. "You attacked me on the roof, and we fought and you fell."

"Right," she said. "I remember now."

"You do?"

"I know Mom died on you too," she said. "I'm sorry I ruined your chart."

"Wait, you remember?" Sleepwalkers never remember, that's what Mom always said.

She breathed loudly out of her nose. "I don't know, Elvis. Maybe I . . ."

"Maybe what?"

"Maybe I should tell you. I guess I should tell you."

"What?"

She breathed in. "My memory is not all blank like Mom said her sleepwalking was."

"Really?"

"Sometimes it's like remembering a dream, you just remember parts of the night," she said. "And I sort of remember the night Mom drowned."

"Oh my God, what?"

"I was sharing a package of hot dogs with Boomer. We were sitting on the floor and all of a sudden he started whining and scratching at the door. But I didn't let him out. I just kept eating the hot dogs. That's all I remember, and then you woke me up. I was in the bathtub and you said Mom was gone."

"Boomer tried to save her."

"Yeah," she said.

"And that's why he was so sick after Mom died."

"I gave him a lot of hot dogs," she said, and then she broke into tears.

We sat there. I didn't hug her. I started crying too, thinking of Boomer pawing the door to get out.

"Elvis, I'm sorry." She wiped at her eyes.

"You never told anyone? All this time?"

"I called Miss Ida, and I told her."

"What did she say?"

"She couldn't tell me if Boomer could have saved her, if that would have made a difference. Sometimes dogs save people from fires, you know? Boomer could have pulled her out of the water."

That must have been the reason for Lizzie's breakdown at St. Cloud's; that was why she'd sent me the drawings of Boomer. And then I realized something else about what Lizzie had just told me: "Wait, you were eating in your sleep when Mom was alive?"

"I'd done it a few times. Mom knew. She hadn't told Dad yet. She said if I ate more during the day it wouldn't be a problem."

"I always thought it was caused by Mom's death."

"I know," she said. "It did get worse after Mom was gone."

"Oh."

"I know Dad was supposed to follow Mom that night." She started up crying again. "But it's really all my fault."

"You didn't mean to lock Boomer up." Allan the lawyer called it *mens rea,* which in Latin means the intending mind. Sleepwalkers cannot have mens rea; you cannot blame them for what they do. They are just as surprised by it as anyone.

I looked up at the moon, round as a peach, more orange than yellow tonight. I remembered what the book from the library said about those who sleepwalk during the full moon. They are moonstruck, under the influence of the sky. Most of what I had learned in all my research was that we don't really understand why people sleepwalk. We only know it is something that is out of their control. It is not something that anyone chooses, nothing anyone wants.

Lizzie did not want to be a sleepwalker. She did not want to hurt anyone, especially not our mother.

"Mom wanted to die," I said. I wasn't sure I believed it had been a brain tumor, but it was the best thing I had.

"What?"

"I think Mom killed herself because she had a brain tumor." I told Lizzie about the notes I'd found in the naked mole rat book. I told her that a brain tumor could cause headaches, seizures, and changes in sexual behavior. I told her about Mom milking Mr. Oakes.

"Gross," Lizzie said.

"I know."

"But there's no proof of that, right? I mean, you never found anything? A doctor's note?"

"No," I admitted.

"She would have told us if she had a brain tumor."

"Maybe . . ." I hesitated. I wasn't sure. No one else believed the brain tumor theory, and now I didn't believe it either. "But

Lizzie, it's not your fault. She was your mother, and you loved her."

"You don't think? You really don't think it's my fault?"

Our family would never recover if we blamed Lizzie for Mom's death. I had no idea what that grieving chart would look like, how many months that would take to get over. So I shook my head. "No, it's not your fault."

She exhaled. "I really hope Samantha is okay, or then I'll really be a murderer."

I realized that no one had bothered to tell Lizzie that Samantha was out of the hospital. Dad had just wanted to teach her a lesson, but it was too complicated to explain, so instead I said: "The nurse called. Samantha's fine. She said there's no permanent damage."

Lizzie was so excited, so relieved, she reached over to grab my face and she kissed me, smack on the mouth.

"Elvis?" she said, after she released me.

"Yeah?"

"My feet are killing me."

I woke up Dad so he could drive us to the hospital. On the ride, I was in the middle of the truck's bench seat, with Ernest on my lap. I had come around on the parrot. It wasn't his fault that he'd lived in the pet store, that he'd seen what he'd seen. Dad stopped in front of the emergency entrance, and helped me load Lizzie into a wheelchair before he went to find parking.

"I'm still mad at you," I said, as I wheeled Lizzie around the hospital hallways. There were things that Lizzie had done when she was awake; things she should be blamed for. The moon hadn't been controlling her then. "I'm mad about the zoo."

"I didn't think you'd lose your job."

"That's just the point, you never think before you do something."

"I did think. I did it for you."

"What do you mean?"

"Remember how you told me about the mice at the zoo, about what happens to them?"

"Yeah," I said, surprised that Lizzie remembered that. She hadn't even glanced over at me when I'd cried right in front of her. She hadn't let me watch *Dr. Lillian Stone* that night to make me feel better.

"I wanted to repay you," Lizzie said. "You've done so much for me, trying to help me fix my sleepwalking. I wanted to do one good thing for you. I freed all the mice and all the rats from their cages, so they wouldn't be gassed."

"Whoa."

"See? I knew you'd be happy."

We were both quiet. I could hear someone's heart monitor beeping in a nearby room. Lizzie was a better sister than I'd thought she was. She had broken into the zoo for me. She had noticed when I'd been upset. She had listened.

"I'm sorry I smashed your rabbit cakes," I said.

"It's okay. You were mad. We already have the world record."

At home, after both of Lizzie's legs had been encased in casts, she took two of the pills the doctor had given her, each one a happy yellow color. They made her pretty loopy, but talkative.

"I'm so sorry, Dad," Lizzie said.

"Sorry for what? You didn't mean to break your own feet."

"I'm sorry I nearly killed Samantha. I'm glad she's okay."

"Me too." Dad gave me a look.

"Is she still your girlfriend?"

"No."

"That's too bad," she said.

"It's okay. Not meant to be."

"And I'm sorry for breaking into the zoo. They were killing animals."

"What?"

"They kill the mice in the Rodent Tunnel exhibit."

"They breed too fast," I said, and I was starting to cry again.

"I wanted to save them for Elvis."

"You're a whack job, but I love you for it," Dad said, leaning down and kissing the top of her head.

"And I'm also sorry —"

"Forgiven," Dad said, holding up his hand.

After that, Lizzie fell asleep on the couch, drooling a small frothy ocean onto the pillow. Her whole body was finally relaxed.

"You can believe whatever you want about that night," Miss Ida had said, when I'd called her a year ago. "It won't bring your mother back."

Lizzie was probably right: Mom would have told us about a brain tumor, milked it for attention. Lizzie and Dad could believe whatever they wanted, as long as Lizzie didn't blame herself, but I couldn't let it be just a simple accident. I had a new theory, a good one, one that didn't involve a brain tumor. It was what I would choose to believe.

My answer had always been in the coffee

grounds: Mom did kill herself. She didn't have a brain tumor, didn't have a good reason to do it like cancer or another disease. She didn't mean to commit suicide, didn't really want to leave us; she was suicidal only in her sleep, the same way a sleepwalker could be an unintentional murderer.

Mom must have killed herself by accident, not with intention, because I know that Mom loved being alive. That was what her rabbit cakes were about, celebrating every small good thing in your life. I know most families don't celebrate every new moon or every solstice and equinox, but maybe they should. You never know when someone you love will shoot themselves in the middle of their own birthday party, or be found dead in another state, caught in a river dam, so everyone might as well have their cake right now.

43.

When Megan Sax came to the front door with a cardboard box, I immediately knew that it was Megan, not Vanessa, who had been with Lizzie when she broke into Serengeti Park. It made much more sense that way. Before they'd fought, Megan used to go along with all of Lizzie's bad ideas.

"My mom said I can't keep them any longer." Megan put the box in Lizzie's lap. "What happened to your legs?"

"I broke them. I fell off the roof."

"What's going on?" I asked.

"Hey Elvis," Megan said. "I'm just bringing over what we got from the zoo."

"What did you steal?" I wasn't sure what the zoo had that Lizzie would want.

Lizzie opened the box and let me look for myself. Inside, there were six rats. A blonde rat stood up on her hind legs, her little pink paws held to her chest, and I swear, she smiled at me. I thought of Mom; she had a gap between her front teeth too.

"I freed the mice, but I heard that rats make good pets," Lizzie said.

"I helped." Megan puffed her chest. "I took the rats home while Lizzie let herself get arrested. We needed to wait until the coast was clear before I brought them over."

"We didn't open the lion's cage, I didn't swim in the penguin fountain, and the zebra got out by accident. I don't know why they're making it sound so much worse than it was. Megan did break the Big Gulp machine, but otherwise, we only took the rats and freed the mice."

The zoo would never miss the rodents. Rats were just snake food, a brand-new litter every week. We never gave names to the rats; there wasn't a point in getting attached.

"Wait, the zoo said you opened the lion's cage?" I asked, realizing something.

"Yeah," Lizzie said. "They want to add some sort of endangerment charge."

The zoo wasn't playing fair. They were using the lack of security cameras to hurt Lizzie. "The zoo wants you to look crazy," I told her, that was why they were exaggerating the events of the break-in. I knew the way Serengeti Park worked, how much they hated animal activists. The zoo director would never want it to get out that Lizzie had been saving zoo animals from certain death, it would be bad for business. We were supposed to lock Rodent Tunnel while we gassed the rats. The sign we put on the door said *Exhibit closed for cage cleaning.* It had a cartoon of a smiling mouse on it.

"How could you let them kill Chucky Cheese?" Lizzie held up a gray rat. If the zoo found out that Megan had been there that night, the whole sleepwalking defense would fall apart. Lizzie would be punished for what she'd done. But it was impossible to be mad at her now; she didn't want to see defenseless animals killed.

"So," I said. "What did you name the rest of them?"

"This one's Brigitte Bardot," Megan said, holding up the blonde rat that looked a little like Mom, with the big gap between the teeth.

When I asked Lizzie later about how she and Megan had made up, she told me that she'd sent Megan a box of chocolates in the mail, and that was all it took. "She likes sweets." Lizzie shrugged, but I thought there was probably more to it. I bet Lizzie had apologized too.

Over the next week, Megan Sax came over almost every day and we built huge obstacle courses with paper-towel tubes for the rats. It was the most fun I'd had in a long time. Lizzie built a rat-sized swing set out of wood and twine.

"Listen, Elvis, I've been meaning to talk to you," Megan said, while she was swinging one of the rats on the miniature tire swing. "I'm sorry for what I said about your mom. I was mad about her and my dad, but I shouldn't have said those things. You get it, right?"

I didn't know exactly what Megan had said about my mother, but it must have been why Lizzie broke Megan's jaw into three pieces and why Lizzie said what she did about the red sausage from the butcher's. I also didn't know anything about Mom and Mr. Sax, but that was another easy guess, after what I knew about Mr. Oakes and Mr. Debbie. Dad might have been fine with the affairs, but Mr. Sax had a wife and kids of his own.

"I'm glad you and my sister are friends again," I said.

Lizzie should never have hurt Megan, especially not for something that sounded like it was partly our mom's fault. But I understood why she did: you want to defend those you love, even if the ones you love aren't very good all the time, and sometimes they are even downright awful.

44.

Vanessa came home in time for Christmas, and there was so much we had to catch her up on; she'd been gone for nearly a month. On Christmas day, Vanessa made a feast, since Lizzie had a hard time cooking in her wheelchair. Dad gave everyone coal in their stocking, except for Ernest.

"Boomer's been good; he doesn't deserve coal," I protested. Dad just laughed.

"Hide and seek," Ernest whistled.

Lizzie gave me a dog-tag necklace, engraved with: *Please return to the Babbitt family,* followed by our address.

"In case you get lost while I'm gone."

"I love it," I said. "But you're not going to jail."

"Fingers crossed," Lizzie said.

I wished I'd gotten my sister something else besides a box of new playing cards. On the back of each card, I'd written *World Record Holder* in metallic Sharpie pen. I gave Vanessa a hummingbird feeder, and she gave me a stuffed cat to replace the one left behind at St. Cloud's.

It was our first Christmas as a family without Mom, I realized, since we hadn't celebrated at all last December. I knew Mom would have been happy about this year's holiday. She would have wanted everyone to have a good time, as long as we kept her picture framed on the mantel, the one where she looked like a young Goldie Hawn.

After dinner, there was no rabbit cake for dessert, but Vanessa made figgy pudding, which I'd never had before. Lizzie resumed her old familiar position on the couch, and I sat on the floor below her so she could french-braid my hair while we watched *Dr. Lillian Stone.* Dr. Lillian was in Indonesia after a tsunami with her team of vets. The people were using elephants to clear debris, but the elephants had cut their feet on glass and shards of metal. Dr. Lillian had the vets care for the elephants while she told some of the tsunami victims she was donating money to rebuild their houses.

"She's such a good person," Lizzie said. She popped another one of the painkillers that the doctor had prescribed.

The phone rang the day after Christmas. It was Dr. Rotherwood.

"The animals are asking about you," he said. "Where have you been? I'm up a creek without you."

"Pamela fired me," I said.

"What? Why?"

"I thought you knew. My sister broke into the zoo."

"But *you* didn't break into the zoo?"

"No."

"Pamela can't fire you for something your sister did. She's not even your boss anymore. You're my volunteer."

"Okay," I said. "So what should I do?" I was shocked that he'd said I shouldn't have been fired.

"I'll talk to Pamela. Can you come in tomorrow or do you have school?"

"It's Christmas break."

"Great," he said. "I'll see you in the AM."

When he hung up, I clutched the phone to my chest. Something good had happened to me. The zoo belonged to me, and Lizzie hadn't ruined it.

At the zoo the next morning, Pamela even

365

apologized for firing me. "I shouldn't blame you for what your sister did. I should know better, growing up with the brother I had." She told me that her brother had burned her parents' house down when he was young.

"Wow," I said, and remembered how Pamela had given me the bucket of butternut squash and told me to be good to my sister. The zoo was taking my sister to juvenile court, but we didn't talk about that. Then Pamela went back to her office, and Dr. Rotherwood showed me how to suture stitches on a zebra, a deep bite wound from someone else in the herd.

"I'm glad you're back," Dr. Rotherwood said. I felt really lucky to know someone like him. Thanks to Dr. Rotherwood, and to the zoo, I was no longer stuck in my sister's shadow. I was my own animal now, the same way a red panda or a flying fox is its own creature. A flying fox is really a fruit bat, not a fox. Some scientists even used to think that flying foxes evolved from primates, because of their monkey-like features and behavior, but they've since found that out to be untrue.

When Dr. Rotherwood dropped me off at home after work, everyone was sitting in the living room with a woman wearing a gray sweater and a chunky gold necklace.

"This is Jana," Dad said. "She's the world record adju— how do you say it?"

"Adjudicator," Jana said. "Lovely to meet you, Elvis." Jana had a British accent and perfect white teeth. She looked like a toothpaste model. "I hear you had a large part in making this world record happen. Your sister said she couldn't have done it without you."

"Well, maybe I could have," Lizzie said, turning red. "Elvis, you have dirt on your face."

"Tough day at work," I said, slowly realizing why Jana from the Guinness World Records office was here. I'd forgotten that Lizzie's certificate was unsigned, and I think everyone else had too. Dad had already framed it.

"Jana was about to sign the certificate," Vanessa said.

They'd all just gotten back from a tour of the walk-in freezer at J&M's Meat Market. Lizzie told me later that Jana hadn't counted each one of the cakes, she just gave the freezer a once-over. She hadn't noticed that the collection was a little short of a thousand, only in the nine hundreds, because of the ones I'd smashed on the ground. The certificate claimed that the rabbit cake collection was one thousand cakes, and that wasn't true anymore.

"There," Jana said, after she'd stamped it. "It's official." She took a photo of Lizzie then, holding her official certificate on her lap. "Guinness is going to love the wheelchair," she said.

"How did you end up working for Guinness?" Dad asked, looking more relaxed now that the certificate was signed.

"I'm actually a world record holder myself," Jana said. "World's largest collection of salt and pepper shakers."

"Wow," Dad said. "That I'd like to see."

Jana said they were in storage, back in London. She had just relocated to Atlanta, where she was now the southern representative for Guinness World Records. "It's an adjustment," she said.

"It's a long drive back to Atlanta," Dad said. "Will you stay for dinner?"

"Sure," she said, and Dad looked delighted. Atlanta was only an hour and a half away.

Vanessa made chicken-fried steak for dinner, which Jana said she had never had before.

"Welcome to the South," Dad said.

Jana took only a few bites of the steak and mostly ate the green beans and the biscuit, but she laughed at all of Dad's jokes, including the several he made about our salt-shaker.

"My mum really deserves most of the credit," Jana said. "She started the collection."

"Our mom deserves credit for the rabbit cakes too," I said. I told her about Mom, how she used to make rabbit cakes to celebrate every new beginning.

"You must really miss her," Jana said.

"We do," Dad said. "She was a wonderful wife and mother."

Jana said it took her a really long time to stop wanting to call her mother every time she bought a new salt and pepper shaker, but finally the collection became her own thing.

"How many months did that take?" I asked.

"Oh I don't know," she said. "Almost two years."

"Eighteen months?"

"Perhaps," she said. "That sounds about right."

Jana left after dinner, and Dad hugged her good-bye. I wondered if we would ever see her again. Mom would have liked her, I thought. Mom didn't like fried food much either, she said the grease gave her a stom-achache.

45.
~~December,~~ January

It was the start of a new year, month nineteen without Mom. Our family was doing okay, but I was glad Ms. Bernstein had given me two bonus months on the grieving chart; I needed some more time to go on missing my mother, even if we were no longer stuck in the quicksand of her death.

Lizzie had promised she'd try to be less impulsive, and a new therapist was working with her on that. She and Vanessa made me a rabbit cake for my twelfth birthday, and no one got sick from it, and the cake didn't flinch when she cut into it.

But Lizzie wasn't perfect either, she never would be. Dad was pretty mad after he caught Lizzie and Vanessa making pot brownies again.

"They're medicinal," Lizzie argued. "My bones are broken."

But Dad wouldn't listen, of course, because he wasn't stupid, and he was a better

371

parent now that he'd had more practice. "Lizzie is an old dog, she has no new tricks," he said.

The old dog who really worried me, that was Boomer. His muzzle was stippled with white hairs. He took forever to climb the front stairs after a pee. Sometimes I'd get frustrated and call for Dad to carry him up and down the front steps, even though I thought it hurt Boomer's pride. He weighed only forty pounds, had lost seven. That was a lot to lose for a dog, I knew.

I called Dr. Rotherwood for advice; Boomer seemed to be getting frailer every day. Dr. Rotherwood said he'd give me some joint supplements and some pain medication, advised me to administer a hot water bottle on Boomer's hips for fifteen minutes twice a day.

"In fact," he said, brightening, "the pygmy hippo's in labor. It's going to take hours, and I could use an extra hand tonight. I know you're not supposed to work off-hours as a volunteer, but then I can give you the meds for your dog. No charge, my gift to Boomer."

Dr. Rotherwood was the kindest man I'd ever known. He always saw the best in people and in animals. Vanessa drove me to the zoo and Dr. Rotherwood let me in through the exotic animal clinic's emergency entrance.

While Cleopatra groaned, Dr. Rotherwood drained the water tank, explaining that sometimes the baby hippos drowned. He built Cleo a nest of straw, although there's no evidence that pygmy hippos nest in the wild.

"When's your sister's court date?" he asked.

"Next week."

"I'm rooting for you. It's not like your sister did any real damage."

"She broke the Big Gulp machine." I told Dr. Rotherwood about the sleepwalking defense, asked if he thought we had a case there.

"Sure," he said. "Maybe. I didn't know your sister had sleepwalking problems."

"She's not sleepwalking now, because her legs are broken, but I'm pretty sure she'll start again once her bones heal. It's genetic."

"That's what I've heard about sleepwalking."

"Do you have anything that could help her? A pill or something?"

He sighed. "No, you'll need a people doctor."

"I thought so."

Dr. Rotherwood said Cleopatra was getting closer to birthing, and we could start the real preparations now. He asked me to put on some music. He said sometimes that helped animals relax. "Classical," he said. "Nothing too exciting or new. Something Cleo's heard before."

I settled on a radio station playing Celine Dion. I knew the station never played anything too loud, nothing with curse words.

There's one more legend about pygmy hippos, my favorite, even if it's another reason why hunters want to kill the endangered animals: the pygmy hippo is said to carry a diamond in her mouth at night. She uses it to light her way in the dark, to keep her from tripping over roots, falling into sinkholes. The diamond shines brightest when the hippo swims underneath the water, and then, just before dawn, she swallows the gemstone whole.

Mom and Dad used to dance around the kitchen to a song called "Diamonds on the Soles of Her Shoes." That would be the perfect song for Cleo, something both upbeat and soothing at the same time. The song was on an album called *Graceland,* but it wasn't Elvis Presley's music, it was Paul Simon's. It didn't come on the radio, so I sang her the words I knew.

The pygmy hippo baby was born at ten thirty at night. Cleopatra collapsed into the pile of straw. Dr. Rotherwood let me hold the baby hippo, and when his back was turned, I slipped my finger into her mouth. I didn't feel a diamond, only soft new gums.

I put the baby hippo onto the ground, and she stood up on wobbly legs. Cleopatra snorted in encouragement. Cleo lay on her side as the baby nursed, the straw sticking to the baby's small wet body.

When Dr. Rotherwood dropped me off at home around midnight, Vanessa and Lizzie were still up working on visualization exercises. It was part of Vanessa's homework; she was taking a winter term child psychology course at the community college. Vanessa wanted to be a guidance counselor, which I thought she'd be really good at, just like Ms. Bernstein. The homework was to interview someone under eighteen who had some sort of emotional or mental difficulty, to try to get them to visualize a better life.

"What do you think about before you go to sleep?" Vanessa asked.

"Well, I usually think about Mom dying," Lizzie said, "and I think about what happened with Boomer, and sometimes I think about what if I drowned in my sleep too."

Vanessa jotted down some notes on her homework worksheet. *Sleep=Death,* she wrote. "Before you go to bed," Vanessa advised, "visualize a place where you feel safe, like a meadow full of poppies."

"A meadow full of puppies?"

"Poppies, it's a flower. It's from *The Wizard of Oz,*" she said. "That movie makes me feel good, and it's such a beautiful scene. Just think of something that makes you happy."

"Okay." Lizzie nodded. "I'll give it a shot."

That night, Lizzie used her wheelchair to sleepwalk into my room. She pushed herself out of the wheelchair and into my bed, where she curled up next to me, her arm draped around my middle.

For the next few nights after that, Lizzie continued to come into my room after she'd fallen asleep. Sometimes she slept in my bed with me, or sometimes on the floor with Boomer. She went back to her own bed before she woke up, but in the morning, she said she was sleeping better than ever, and her face did look more refreshed.

For three weeks after the birth, the zoo had a poll on their website on what to name the baby pygmy hippo. I thought that was a long time to live without a name, but Dr. Rotherwood said it was how the zoo kept the public involved, and invested. The poll finally settled on the name Zola, which means loved.

46.

The day when Lizzie had to go to juvenile court finally came. She wore a knee-length skirt, one Dad had to go out and buy her at the Auburn Mall, because she had never worn anything that conservative. She wore a blazer and a button-down shirt to go with it. Her big pink casts were like hippopotamus feet, but there was nothing we could do about those.

A doctor from St. Cloud's testified. "She's dangerous in her sleep, certainly," the doctor said. "But she doesn't know what she's doing. She is not conscious. She did not have criminal intent, in my professional opinion.

"Sometimes I dream that I'm cheating on my wife," the doctor added. "But that doesn't make me a cheater."

"Objection," the zoo's lawyer said, but I thought I saw the judge nod his head slightly.

After the doctor got off the stand, it was my turn. I had convinced Lizzie's lawyer to let me testify. "You're just a kid," Allan had said, when I'd first asked. But I knew how bad Lizzie's sleepwalking fits could get, how out of control she could be, and then how normal in the morning. He finally agreed it would be a good idea, as long as I didn't go off our script.

"Elvis Babbitt, can you tell the court what kind of behavior you've observed in your sister when she sleepwalks?"

I explained how Lizzie had tried to bake a cake in her sleep, how she had almost burned our house down, about the times she'd peed on the ficus, and how she'd tried to rip out Dad's hair in the hotel room in Charleston.

"And your sister would never hurt you or your father when she was awake?"

"I'm her best friend," I said, and I showed everyone the silver dog-tag necklace Lizzie had given me for Christmas.

I said that no matter what Lizzie had done in her sleep, it was not her fault. She hadn't meant to, she didn't remember. She was not a criminal.

"Were you with your sister the night of the break-in?" Allan asked.

"No," I said. "She must have taken my ID

badge when she was asleep."

"And what were your first words to your sister when you found out that she had broken into the zoo?" Allan asked.

"Were you awake?" I said. "Did you mean to do it?"

"And what did your sister say?"

"She said she was asleep, she didn't mean to, she doesn't even remember what happened that night."

Then I brought out the big guns: I could prove that the lion's cage had never been opened, the way the zoo claimed it had been. *She endangered the zookeepers and the public by leaving the lion's cage door ajar,* the zoo's statement read.

But my ID badge didn't open the lion's door: the zoo volunteers weren't trusted with Seymour ever since he'd killed his lioness; only certified zookeepers had the access code to Seymour's cage. The zoo wasn't telling the truth, at least about that part of the break-in.

I had lied under oath, but it was probably worth it, because Lizzie was acquitted of all charges, free to go. "That worked like gangbusters," Allan said, pumping his fist in the air.

After the courtroom emptied out, we all went for ice cream. We asked Allan to come with us, but he said he had his son's basketball game to go to. The parrot hadn't come to the trial, because who knows what Ernest would blurt out, and Boomer was at home too, so it was just Lizzie, Vanessa, Dad, and me, alone at Suzy Sundaes.

"To being not guilty," we cheered, clinking our ice-cream cones together like wineglasses.

"To Elvis's testimony," Lizzie said, raising up her vanilla cone with rainbow sprinkles.

"To Elvis," Vanessa and Dad echoed.

It was a really happy moment, but I guess that's probably obvious.

47.

There were still parts of life that were terribly, awfully, horribly sad, even at the tail end of the grieving chart. By January 19th, Dolly Parton's birthday, Boomer couldn't walk anymore. I had Dad carry him up and down the stairs so he could go outside, and I gave him sponge baths when he peed on himself. He had stopped eating, wouldn't lick a smear of peanut butter off my finger. I fed him water through a turkey baster when he wouldn't drink from a bowl.

I slept on the floor next to him, with a pillow and blanket. I didn't want him to be alone when he didn't feel well. He was so skinny now, bones and fur. I gave him doggie painkillers wrapped in bacon, but I had to force the pills down his throat. He was getting worse, getting weaker, but when I pet him, he would thump his tail. He looked up at me with the cataract moon in his eye, and I kissed him on the white stripe of his nose.

Boomer had given me so much. He had never been selfish or mean. He'd wake me up with his nose if I overslept. When I'd had a bad day at school, he'd lick my face until I laughed. Boomer was the reason why I'd made it this far in the grieving chart, why I'd never had a problem getting out of bed. That part was simple: Boomer needed a morning walk.

Boomer had been afraid of Lizzie after she scratched him in her sleep, but he had forgiven her. He knew Lizzie didn't mean to be bad. He didn't hold a grudge when she didn't let him out the night Mom drowned. He didn't blame her. Dogs have a lot of things about life figured out; they aren't afraid to let something go. Their hearts are always open to loving more.

I woke up one morning on the floor next to Boomer, and his breath had gone raspy. The rest of the family joined me in a circle by Boomer's doggie bed. Vanessa said she'd call the vet to make an appointment to have Boomer put to sleep, but she didn't reach for the phone.

"He wants to know if we'll be okay without him," Lizzie said. "He says, 'Who will take care of you now?' He knows how messed up this family is."

"He loves us," Dad sniffed. We were all crying. I guess we had turned into a family of criers. "Boomer loves us exactly the way we are."

Lizzie wheeled herself into the kitchen and came back with the child-safe scissors, the ones that didn't have to be locked up with the knives. She leaned down and took a clipping of Boomer's fur. "In case we want to clone him later," she said, and everyone nodded, picturing a house full of very good dogs.

"It's okay, Boom," I said, rubbing my favorite ear, the slightly crooked one. "We're doing fine now. You don't have to stay." I wanted him to stay forever, but I didn't want my best friend to be in pain.

"You don't have to feel guilty about leaving us," Dad said to Boomer. "We'll be okay. Go take care of Eva now."

Dad always said he didn't believe in heaven, but I guess he'd changed his mind. It was too hard to think that the ones you loved were gone forever.

"Go see Mom," I said. "Tell her we love her."

"Go Boomer, go," Lizzie urged in a whisper.

Boomer was a good dog. He listened.

■ ■ ■ ■

I didn't have to go to school; Dad called the Three Rivers front office, explained that there had been a death in the family. Jackie brought me my homework, but I didn't have the energy to do it. Vanessa made me grilled cheese sandwiches, but I couldn't eat them. Lizzie got her casts off, and she showed me how strange her shriveled white feet looked, but I couldn't laugh.

"You okay?" Dad asked, opening my door every morning.

For three days, I said no, and Dad closed the door behind him, leaving me alone. I clutched my pillow as I cried and cried. My snot dried all over the pillowcase, leaving a crust.

On the fourth day, I got out of bed and took my first shower, changed my clothes. I called Ms. Bernstein at her house, and asked if I should start a new grieving chart.

"Your grief can feel as heavy when you lose a pet as if you lost a human family member," Ms. Bernstein said. "But you're better practiced at loss now. Let your grief run its course and it will resolve itself, in time."

"Excellent advice," Vanessa agreed.

Vanessa had gotten an A on her test in child psychology, but she was a long way from treating patients, so that's why I'd asked Ms. Bernstein first.

After a week off from school, I felt well enough to go on Monday. I had to take only one break during the day to cry in the bathroom, after Jackie gave me a drawing she'd done of Boomer, a perfect likeness, only she didn't draw the clouds in his eyes. Cataracts must be hard to do with colored pencils.

Boomer was the first one of us to die of old age. My nana had been pretty old, but maybe if she hadn't smoked cigarettes she would've lived longer. Boomer died because he was an old dog, no other reason. We didn't know how old exactly, because we got him as a full-grown dog from the shelter, but we'd had him for almost eleven years. It was always strange to me that we couldn't ever know Boomer's birthday, didn't know which day we should give him an extra scrap of people food.

Dad wanted to go right out and get another puppy from the shelter to cheer us all up.

"No replacements," I said. "It's healthy to be depressed after someone you love dies."

"I think that does sound healthy," Lizzie agreed.

Boomer died of old age, but I'd figured out by now that death never makes sense, no matter how someone dies: murder, accident, old age, cancer, suicide, you're never ready to lose someone you love. I decided death will always feel unexplained; we will never be ready for it, and you just have to do the best you can with what you have left. That was what I'd finally pieced together, and I felt like I had solved a major mystery. I said something to Lizzie about it.

"No shit, Sherlock," she said. Lizzie could still be awful sometimes, but you can't expect someone to change completely.

I had wanted to bury Boomer in the cemetery, but it wasn't allowed in our town, and the nearest pet cemetery was in Mississippi, so I'd let Dad send Boomer to the pet crematorium. When we got Boomer's ashes back, the plastic baggie was identical to the one we'd once received holding Mom's ashes.

I remembered Dad's friend's funeral, the one where there was a bagpipe recording of "Amazing Grace." I thought there was something nice about that, something that felt right about a funeral. I researched funerals online to find the style that I liked, and then I made up invitations for everyone in the family.

The morning of the funeral, I baked a rabbit cake, the first ever I'd made myself, since I wanted the day to be a celebration of Boomer's life. I made it from a Funfetti mix, speckled with multicolored confetti; I didn't want the cake to look realistic.

We all dressed in black and Dad drove us down to the river. The cake was squashed in the Tupperware by the time we got there, but I put it out on the picnic table anyway. I'd used vanilla frosting because everyone knows chocolate is toxic to dogs. I placed the baggie of ashes next to the cake, and also Boomer's red collar and one of his squeaky toys.

Vanessa gave the sermon, since she knew the most about how to do it. I'd found a prayer online that I wanted her to say, from Prayersforpets.com. I made her change a few of the words, because I knew Dad would think it was too religious, but I thought the message was good.

"Oh heavenly God," Vanessa said, and we all bowed our heads. "We feel that it is with understanding that you look down on a scene like this today, when one who was so loved is gone. As Boomer was unto his caretakers, ever loyal, ever faithful, may we, as we leave this river, this place of solitude, resolve to find strength to be more loyal and faithful to one another. Thank you for entrusting us with a devoted dog. Thank you for letting him teach us unselfish love."

"I'm sorry," Ernest said, after everyone else said "Amen." I wondered if the parrot really was sorry for all the times he'd called Boomer a bad dog. But it was easy to forgive the parrot for that, because I was sure that Boomer knew he was a good boy, the rest of us told him that all the time.

"Now we will lay our loved one to rest," Vanessa said.

I put a spoon of Boomer's ashes in the water, and passed the baggie down to everyone else. It felt good to mix Boomer into the river, knowing that Mom and her beloved dog were together now. I guess that's why people are buried in family plots, so there's something about the end that feels like coming home.

Like Mom, Boomer had loved to swim, even though border collies aren't a real water breed. There was one time, a few years ago, when Boomer wouldn't get out of the river after the rest of us had already toweled off.

"Boomer boy, time to go," Mom had

yelled from the bank. Boomer had slapped his paw against the water, making a splash. He'd barked, urging us to come back in.

Dad had said, "Let's leave him here. He'll follow us home."

Mom had thrown her towel on the bank and dove straight back in. "You can leave us both here," she'd said, when her head reemerged, her smile wide as an alligator's. "We'll be fine."

48.
~~JANUARY,~~ FEBRUARY

Lizzie's *Cosmopolitan* magazine was wrong when it said the only way to get over someone is to get under someone new. I've learned that waiting it out is the only way to get over anyone. We're not going to get a new dog to replace Boomer, not for a long time anyway, and we're not much closer to having a stepmother, even if Dad has said there are a surprising number of single women in this part of Alabama.

Lizzie wouldn't poison a second girlfriend, either on purpose or accidentally. She's not angry anymore, or guilty. She's sleeping a lot better too, which probably helps. Dad has decided that Lizzie will be sent to a private school in Georgia, since public school wasn't working for her. She'll be starting during their spring term. It's called the Pine Mountain Culinary Academy; Dad found it online. The program doesn't have regular grade levels, so Lizzie won't have to repeat sophomore year. She's been cooking up a storm to get ready, both dinners and desserts.

We came into some money; that's why the spot at Pine Mountain isn't going to be a financial problem. Dad also started a college fund for me.

It happened after Dr. Lillian responded to the email I'd sent last summer, when I'd asked if she knew where I could get a grant for research to help finish my mom's book. She wrote that she missed Eva dearly, that she was so sorry to hear about her death. Dr. Lillian said the manuscript was impressive, and she suggested selling it to the Animal Network since no one really reads books anymore. In fact, she'd already taken the liberty to forward it on to the television execs. She hoped I didn't mind.

I didn't mind, and neither did Dad, not once the Animal Network came knocking with its elephant-sized checks. They've already started filming *The Sleeping Lives of Animals* and Larry, the sleepwalking beagle in Wyoming, will get a starring role and Dr. Lillian is narrating. Mom's name will be mentioned several times in the credits, and mine will be listed twice.

When a naked mole rat becomes a queen,

her spine lengthens, the vertebrae separating during her pregnancies. Her length makes it easy to distinguish the queen naked mole rat from the rest of the colony, before you even observe their social behavior. She is much larger than all the other mole rats in the colony, larger than the warrior class, the worker class, even the breeder males.

During my last checkup, the Three Rivers Junior High nurse said my spine looked totally normal.

"It's possible that you were just slouching in your exams before," she said. "I can never really tell unless we get an X-ray."

"I don't have scoliosis anymore?"

She took the plastic brace from me and threw it on top of a pile of back braces in the closet. "You're cured. It's a miracle."

Cured is a funny word: sometimes you're better completely, and sometimes you think you're better and the disease comes back.

Lizzie isn't cured of sleepwalking, but she's not tortured by it either. She hasn't eaten anything in her sleep in months, and her doctor said she probably just grew out of it; he said that's what happens with the majority of eating disorders. We thought it was strange that it was called an eating disorder, and not a sleep disorder, but now we don't have to worry that Lizzie will be poisoned. And she says she doesn't feel guilty about Mom's death anymore, so I don't think she'll climb up onto the roof again. That's good enough, at least for now.

I think we are mostly cured of the sadness following Mom's death. Even if we aren't a completely normal family, and our mom wasn't just anyone, I don't think our grief has turned abnormal. We have more rabbit cakes than ever before and have still found things to celebrate, like the new jungle gym Dad bought for the rats. Dr. Rotherwood did our spaying and neutering of the rats for free, after Dad said we didn't need to start an inbred rat farm. Dr. Rotherwood didn't ask where we'd gotten the rats.

Most things are pretty good, other than that I don't have a dog to sleep on my bed or welcome me home from school. At Three Rivers, everyone stopped talking about Jackie Friskey's STD, and she could have gone back to Stephanie's lunch table, but she's still my friend. My sixth-grade English teacher recommended that I start taking some eighth-grade-level classes. I added Latin and switched to eighth-grade English, and school is more interesting. When I come home, Vanessa helps me with my math homework, and Lizzie is always there with a plate of fancy French cookies. She says the recipe still needs tweaking, so she's making a slightly different batch every day.

Of course, there will always be things I wish Mom was around for, like when I got an A-plus on my first Latin test. Dad says Latin is a dead language and he wasn't really impressed, he wants me to take Spanish instead. Languages become dead after people stop using them. I still use Mom, the things I learned from her. I imagine all the time what she would say if she were still around. I use her scribbled notes on pages of *The Compiled Studies of the Naked Mole Rat;* I'm studying more about the animal's resistance to cancer. Lizzie and Dad still use Mom's clothes; Dad says her bathrobe is so comfortable he'll never go back to men's pajamas. And the parrot still uses Mom's voice, even though we found out he can also imitate Dad.

"Come on, be a team player," Ernest said the other night, in Dad's exact voice. Then Ernest let out Mom's big chuckle while the rest of us choked on our dinner.

So Mom doesn't really feel gone, but she's no longer here either. I've thought about it a lot, for almost two years, and I don't believe in reincarnation, in one spirit fitting perfectly into a brand-new body. It's a nice hypothesis, but it makes death too simple when it's not neat and tidy that way.

Still, every time I hold Brigitte Bardot the rat, Beebee for short, I can't help but wonder if there is a scrap of Mom's spirit inside her. It isn't even the rat's gapped teeth, it's more about a feeling I get. Mom would have remembered the time I asked her about being a lab rat in her next life, and how she said she wouldn't be a lab rat forever. She would have thought it was a pretty good joke to show up as a rat, especially a rat that Lizzie would save.

When I pick Beebee up now, she looks at me, her whiskers twitching, and she licks my hand like a kiss. Our *How to Raise Your Rat* guidebook says that licking is a sign of acceptance and love.

I stroke her belly with my pointer finger and she leans back in my palm, her tail wrapped around my wrist for balance. She blinks very slowly, her body relaxing. She closes her eyes for longer and longer moments, her eyelids pausing shut as if she is about to fall asleep right there within my grasp.

ACKNOWLEDGMENTS

I am extraordinarily lucky to have many people to whom I owe a great deal of thanks, and here they are in no particular order (just kidding, I spent hours on this):

A humongous thank-you to Katie Grimm, who is the world's best agent, who loves Elvis as much as I do, who deserves so much credit for this book — I promise I'll never go out of the country again without telling you first. I also owe a major thank you to the team at Don Congdon Associates: Annie Nichol, Kayla Ichikawa, and Cara Bellucci — your hard work and attention to detail are so much appreciated.

An equally humongous thank-you to my amazing editor, Masie Cochran, for having a vision for the book, for making Elvis shine, and for your enthusiasm and kindness through it all. Thank you also to all the other wonderful people at Tin House: Nanci McCloskey, Sabrina Wise, Diane Chonette,

Jakob Vala, and Meg Storey.

To my teachers: Christopher Kennedy, Jonathan Strong, David Huddle, Kevin McIlvoy, Christopher Castellani, James Scott, Wendy Rawlings, Bebe Barefoot, Michael Martone, and Kellie Wells. This book would not exist without your guidance. Thank you also to Katheryn Doran, because before I was a fiction writer, I was a philosophy major. You will always be my role model and your leadership in college changed my life.

Thank you to the Associates of the Boston Public Library for the crucial early support for the book and for giving me a home to write for a year. And to my friends at the bookstore: Mary Cotton, Jaime Clarke, Deb Handy, Jacqui Teruya, and Matt Denis — you are my people.

Thank you to Tasha Graff, for reading every single draft. How lucky I am to know you, my brilliant friend. Also thanks to Jessica Schneidman, Lauren Foley, Winter Burhoe, Mackie Mescon, Marika Plater, Dave Goldstein, Ellen O'Connell, Caroline de Lacvivier, Jordan Wade, Susan Pienta, Lauren Fletcher, and Kenny Kruse. Most of you haven't read the book yet, but I trust you'll buy many copies if I put your names here.

To Nancy Criscitiello (Mrs. Cris), my next-door neighbor growing up, thank you for giving me my very first short story assignment. Your guidance and friendship have meant so much to me.

Thank you to my parents, Liane and Paul Hartnett, for your unwavering support, love, and faith in me. Thanks to my brothers, Jake and Michael, for your love and friendship. And thank you to the extended Hartnett and Callahan families — I know only one of you has gotten a *Rabbit Cake* tattoo, but I'm sure more of you are soon to follow. Also to Leslie and Peter Linsley, Jeremy Linsley and Ariel Brumbaugh, my West Coast family, thank you for welcoming me into the fold.

I tried not to thank my dog — really I did. Harvey, I know you can't read, but I love you so much. Thank you for being the inspiration for Boomer, and for taking the job of Good Dog so seriously.

Lastly, thank you to my husband, Drew. Thank you for always believing in me, and for your patience, kindness, brilliance, partnership, and love. You're my tuna fish.

ABOUT THE AUTHOR

Annie Hartnett was the 2013–14 winner of the Writer in Residence Fellowship for the Associates of the Boston Public Library and has received awards and honors from the Bread Loaf School of English, *McSweeney's,* and *Indiana Review.* Hartnett received her MFA in fiction from the University of Alabama and an MA from Middlebury College's Bread Loaf School of English. She currently teaches at Grub Street, an independent writing center in Boston. Hartnett lives with her husband and their beloved border collie in Providence, Rhode Island.